URGENT

LAUNCH

ENJOY THE
JOURNEY!

Larry Pratt

Also by Larry Pratt

Fiction
> *Urgent State*

Non-fiction
> *Fuelish Pleasureboats*

ACKNOWLEDGMENT

The science presented in this book would not have been made public without an army of fact checkers. Before the author presented this work, a number of writing checkers was needed. Thank you to them all.

To gain confidence in the presentations herein, an informal poll was taken, which helped define the size and style of type, the chapter layouts, even the presence (or lack) of the Glossary. Thank you to all who had the patience to assist.

The pages you are about to wade through are the results of input from our governmental, scientific, writing, and residential communities. Please participate in, and learn from, what follows.

URGENT LAUNCH

••• ——— •••

Continuing to Save our Species

Larry Pratt

SMP Press   Lacey, WA. 98509

Publisher's Cataloging-in-Publication Data

Names: Pratt, Larry L., 1946- author.
Title: Urgent Launch: continuing to save our species / Larry Pratt
Description: Lacey, WA: SMP Press, 2021
   | Series: Urgent series; book 2 | Summary: continues the
   storyline of Urgent State, presenting a near future look at ways
   to mitigate climate change and save our species, with an
   emphasis on reforestation efforts.
Identifiers: LCCN 2020906833 | ISBN 9780996385565 (pbk.)
                     | ISBN 9780996385572 (ebook)
Subjects: LCSH: Climate change mitigation -- Fiction.
   | Economics -- Fiction. | Education -- Fiction. | Reforestation --
   Fiction. | Technology -- Fiction. | Tongass National Forest
   (Alaska) -- Fiction. | Wind River Indian Reservation (Wyo.) --
   Fiction. | BISAC: FICTION/Nature & the Environment |
   | FICTION / Science Fiction / General.
Classification: LCC PS3616.R38 U74 (print)
                     | LCC PS3616.R38 (ebook) | DDC 813--dc23
LC record available at https://lccn.loc.gov/2020906833

Printed by Bookmasters :   www.bookmasters.com

Questions regarding the content, or ordering of this book
         should be addressed to:

SMP Press   or:
PO Box 3852   *urgentbooknotes@gmail.com*
Lacey, WA 98509-3852

ABOUT THE AUTHOR

Although in the midst of a pandemic, Larry Pratt adheres to the thinking that our most serious problem is the existential threat to our planet. The result of that focus is the book in your hands: *Urgent Launch.*

He began his speculative fiction tale by rounding up years of research on the climate change subject and outlining a "what if" story. The author's imagination and experiences took over. The obvious need to develop the characters, and further explain the story line, caused the simple book to become two volumes. This is no surprise to those that know him: Larry's projects always seem to be more complicated than originally conceived – even when pursuing his woodworking hobby.

The first title, *Urgent State*, has given birth to a recent request for book talks. Not wanting to give away the ending, Pratt has delivered the story behind the story at these gatherings. The printing of *Urgent Launch* now allows the readers and the curious to enjoy the conclusion. He wrote of a fictional series of events and the author encourages the public to dream of other, more favorable outcomes.

However, please adhere to a Larry Pratt hard-and-fast rule that might explain the rose-colored glasses he wears – it must have a happy ending.

INTRODUCTION

The band of cooperative and hard-working citizens has formed a unique community in the Wind River Indian Reservation. Urgent is now a village large enough to support a busy steel mill complex and massive energy production sites. The public can see the towering wind turbines and acres of solar panels. However, the invisible research facilities below ground are equally large.

This is the real work of the most spacious town in Wyoming: research of all kinds. Scientists in fields ranging from agriculture to wind energy are housed and working in a vibrant, ever-changing setting. A long row of subterranean laboratories is serviced by a public transportation system. The lack of routine makes the daily interruption by a rocket launch a non-event. The bus stops moving across the canyon for a few minutes and traffic at the airport also pauses.

The public was aware of the long-range plans behind their civic existence and accepted those goals whole-heartedly. Outside business, on the other hand, is striving to learn and share in the scientific advancements credited to the underground facilities. Should that be allowed?

The more important question, though, is:
Do we have time?

CAST OF IMPORTANT CHARACTERS

Native Americans
Chief Joseph White: first generation in our story
Edward White (Jr.): Joseph's son and young look-alike
Pope: Edward's son and astronaut
Marina Whitehorse: assistant to Steven (phil.)

Philanthropists (phil.)
Eduardo
Henry
Lucille
Steven

First generation (founders)
Sean Crockett: President of the United States
Bo Elliott: recruiter and construction consultant
Emmet Fitzpatrick: former FBI, now security chief
Jeff and Ellie Foster: retired firefighters, primary
    recruiters
Brian Knight: financier and liaison to philanthropists
Harold Knight: chief scientist/recruiter and Brian's
    brother
Tom Lacey: intelligence and electronics expert
Brittany Odom: Brian's assistant, initially
Anne and Vern Osborn: former lobbyist, now education
    leaders

Diversion team (dissolved in Book 1)
Courtney: quickly finds Bo and a better mission
Looser: charter member of team
Rosita: flyer in Albuquerque mission
Ruth: matures into mentor and wife and mother
Sara: flyer in ABQ, moves on to reforestation projects
Stretch: joins Looser in life

Community leaders

Leah Elliot: daughter of Bo and Courtney, educator
Willard Graham: ex-FBI, on Fitz's team
FJ Guindo: reforestation project, astronaut
Lizzy Guindo: sister to FJ, educator
Dennis and MaryAnn Hall: reforestation and
    eduction projects
Myrlene: assistant to Brian Knight, replacing Brittany
Sandy Watson: agricultural researcher, son of Senator

Other team members

Captain Dan: boat skipper for Alaska reforestation
Randall James: worker in Lacey's security shop
Ethan Linn: visitor from Int'l. Inst. of Tropical
    Forestry
Mark Madison: aide to Sean Crockett
Javier Rodriguez: aide to Eduardo (phil.)
Harry Stone: river pilot, helper in Marina's lab

ONE

•— •—• —•—• •— — •—

"It's not enough - nor fast enough. Did you see the front-page story about the 6-foot flood tide that put St. Mark's square in Venice under water? The *Piazza* for God's sake, and water inside the basilica. Those high waters are supposed to be the crest of a 100-year high-tide, not rise every nine years. Are we too late? Can we do this?" Steven was overwhelmed. Gradually his emotions calmed as he looked out at the white mountain peaks that seemed to blend with the clouds.

The village of Davos is located high in the Swiss Alps, almost a mile high. This year-round destination resort is home to approximately 11,000 people and visited by tens of thousands more. No longer exclusively a winter skiing destination, Davos' alpine location also provides summer recreation. And, once a year, the community lures the world's richest and most powerful into its luxurious convention center to discuss earthly problems.

The World Economic Forum normally fills a week in the calendar of these influential people. There is a formal schedule with a choice of 400 seminars and speeches. The panel format is a popular method of discussion. With topics of a global nature it is not unusual to witness a head of state exchange ideas with a foreign tycoon.

At one such panel presentation Marina Whitehorse was closely watching the businessman from Mexico debate an economic issue with the Chinese delegate. She was taken with what she saw, and she remembered what Steven had ranted earlier: "... out of time."

She was scheduled to have dinner with Steven – her boss, later that evening. Actually, she had more than a platonic relationship with the widowed philanthropist, but this was not common knowledge. The public only saw her as an employee, albeit an important one, of his foundation, and the second-in-command, next in line below Steven.

Even before the salad, Marina began to share.

"I can't tell you how much I was impressed with his thinking. He was too logical and fast with his response to be making any of it up. I truly believe he has thought through our earthly climate conundrum. We need to talk with him, Steven."

Her dinner companion nodded his head. He was enjoying the wine and her company. Although he knew that until they mutually agreed on the conclusion of this conversation, she would be a one-topic date. Her tenacity was one of the traits that appealed to him, but in these surroundings they needed to exercise caution. His security team had examined the hotel suite for listening devices, but the restaurant was not secure.

"Marina, why don't you find the guy, or call him, and ask him up to the room for breakfast, or coffee and sweets sometime tomorrow. Nothing on the program for the morning would be more important than devoting a half hour to talking with Eduardo."

She broke into that disarming smile that he loved so much and attacked her green salad. Now it was his turn to think. Having agreed to meet with a potential partner, he was down to the wire on formulating a plan and organizing an agenda. The broad talking points had been discussed on the flight two days ago. Steven, Marina, and Henry, who was also invited to speak at Davos, had begun discussing the success of Urgent.

They then turned their attention to the other high-priority items on the to-do list. Assuming the growth of their first project continued, climate change and income inequality could remain off the list. What other man-made disasters should they attend to? Deforestation and water issues won. Henry suggested this was actually only a single large topic. Was one sufficient? The yes answer was unanimous.

As the primary employee of the foundation, Marina had always taken on the job of learning a little about a lot of things. When the deforestation issue came up, she realized she needed a better understanding of this issue if she was to explain the importance of forests to the two men.

Their two-bedroom suite in the destination resort was not ideal. It overlooked the village, while the snow-capped Matterhorn was in full view from the other side of the building. When their security team insisted that the curtains remain closed the view became insignificant. A quick peek between the heavy drapes was all that was allowed.

When the visitor arrived the next morning, he noticed the closed curtains first thing.

"They make you turn the lights on also I see. Growing up as a young man in Guatemala I only dreamed of visiting this place. It existed in the movies. Now that I'm here I am kept inside."

Marina began the introductions. Although she made formal introductions, including full names, she had not needed them. Each philanthropist was so well-known that surnames were rarely used when referring to these ultra-wealthy individuals. She directed them towards the living room area. Steven began the conversation by confirming that his security team had swept the room. What they were about to discuss was something that they would like kept in confidence.

"There are projects that are easier to accomplish if the general public does not know of their existence. Even folks with good intentions can just get in the way."

Marina had been in enough meetings with Steven to know he was about to dive right into the main reason for the meeting. Her perception of the visitor's alert senses caused her to interrupt.

"I know you are aware of big business in the United States, and how tax is avoided on sizeable amounts of earnings when a businessperson sets up a foundation. These foundations are actually funded by the owner-executive, not the business itself. While the tax system has some hard and fast rules as to how much money those foundations can keep, the founders have some leeway as to where those funds are spent. We need to be clear that in this room is a gathering of foundation directors, NOT business owners. Both Henry and Steven are each the taxpayer/businessman responsible for the sizeable foundations you have undoubtedly heard of."

Eduardo shifted in his seat and leaned forward. She knew he needed to hear that what Steven was about to share was not a normal investment, or profit driven. Her guest would need to listen carefully and learn.

"If memory serves," Henry offered, "ten years ago this group first met with the President of the United States. The purpose of that initial meeting was to advise him that we wanted to take the lead in saving the planet. The earth as a whole had not had a cooler than average month since December 1984. That trend bothered us." Eduardo leaned farther forward.

"We allocated money and personnel from both our foundations and began a long-term project. Our motive is simple: if we don't spend the money necessary to save our species, what good is money? A decade later, the idea still holds. In fact, it is more urgent than it was then. The first item of business was to address climate change through energy production and conservation. We are nearing the date we can turn on the largest energy production facility in the United States. We are furiously researching materials that will allow us to distribute that energy more efficiently."

"What type of power?" Eduardo asked.

He understood the answer as solar and wind and even fusion dreams were mentioned. The scale of the Wind River project impressed him the most. That much territory in the middle of the US should have come to his attention. The fact that he knew nothing of it could only mean this group was serious about security. He was willing to get serious also.

Steven continued, "Allow me to confirm that security is still a concern for us. Our intention is to share an idea with you and ask you to keep this conversation between us. There are no expectations and we harbor no ill will should you pretend this meeting never took place. The original project is successful and will continue. In fact, we are about to begin a revenue stream – but that's not important.

"What is important is that we have decided to expand our efforts and are inviting you to join us. To date we have executives from three large foundations dedicated to acting on behalf of mankind. We are now in agreement that at least one more mind and one more sphere of influence is needed to attack our areas of concern. The new target is deforestation."

"I assume you are talking about the Amazon," Eduardo observed.

"That rain forest is a large part of it, yes," replied Marina. "However, there are other massive forests on the planet that are being mismanaged, to use the term loosely. Many of the leaders in whose territory these trees grow know nothing and care less about the health of local forests. In our opinion, and based on science, this short-term approach cannot continue. What is disturbing is the fact that there is little difference between forest abuse by third-world countries and greedy logging in the modern world.

"The rain forest and its position as the heart of the planet is of upmost importance, the loss of encroaching desert - not so much. The tendency of man to rearrange the landscape has been creating havoc for centuries. Lately, though, it is worse for the land because there is just more of man.

"Concentrating on forests makes sense because of the effect of trees on the atmosphere. Plus, trees are a renewable resource. Sufficient energy and money spent wisely will show results more quickly than some alternative projects. We ask ourselves, how do we reforest the planet, and what about water?

"Prior to today's meeting, I opted to do a bit of research on how widespread this problem is. The facts are mind-boggling. We have destroyed twenty percent of the Amazon rain forest in pursuit of land to graze livestock and plant crops. In Indonesia and Malaysia, we see massive deforestation in order to plant oil palms. The main concerns here are twofold.

"Naturally, the oil palm seedlings take years to achieve the size where they produce as much oxygen as their predecessors. But they will never catch up. These trees are themselves harvested when they get too tall for humans to easily harvest the fruit.

Equally as disturbing is the creation of fragmented forest which endangers wildlife. In Borneo, that's orangutans. Today, deforestation and poaching kill about ten thousand per year. That, too, is not sustainable."

"Pardon me for interrupting," said Eduardo, "but you need to know that I really don't care about a bunch of monkeys."

"Miss Whitehorse's focus may not align with yours," interjected Steven, "but the message is still important. We can arrange the facts in any order we see fit, but the money will need to be the same. We must fund the planting of billions of trees in hundreds of locations by thousands of paid workers.

"The logistics of the project will be complicated. We currently have access to highly intelligent people with a network of like-minded locals. What you would be asked to contribute, besides money, is multi-lingual personnel to help organize and recruit on behalf of these international efforts. We have found that the more indigenous peoples that participate, the better our suggestions are received. But rest assured, there is no formal format or gameplan for these unique endeavors. We need to be responsive, flexible, and creative.

"This creativity may come into play when finding the manpower or money for some projects. It may be easier to get help from an entity interested in saving the wildlife in Borneo than just searching for tree huggers. I would imagine it to be a simple sale to get trees planted in a wildlife-friendly country if the governing agency knew how important the large, green canopy is to the health and welfare of the animals.

"We know of a similar problem in Uganda as it relates to chimpanzees. Success in one country may result in a smooth transition and relocation to another country. Just move the entire crew, ship all equipment, and start all over again. It has been our experience that these nonprofit outfits operate in a small world. Have some success with a couple of projects and you improve your chances when you address other agencies and have other needs."

The guest rose and commenced pacing around the suite. He was responsible for tens of thousands of workers and billions of dollars in assets. Not long ago he realized the future of his empire was in jeopardy because of the shift in weather patterns. Within the last year, his closest advisor had called his attention to a new article warning society that they, the public, were the reason for change in weather.

Scientists had determined that these new weather systems were not present as part of some long-range cycle of good, then bad, then good weather again. No. Today's systems were the new norm. Man had caused the climate to change. This was a fact.

Being a bit of a risk taker, the gambler side of him had wanted to know the odds that this fact was real. He knew his name was on a portion of a science facility at the university in Santiago, Chile. He also knew how to contact one highly placed scientist.

Their brief conversation of last year began to educate him on the field of attribution science – a new discipline. These scientists study the likelihood that climate change was responsible for extreme weather events. During two of the previous three years they had been able to explain the actions of mankind that precipitated the altering of weather patterns.

It took a bit more time to help him connect the heat wave on the Tasman Sea with the drought in the U.S. high plains and then with the floods in Bangladesh. When Eduardo had hung up, he knew he did not like those odds.

The first reaction to the climate change news had been an analysis of his business future. Once that knee-jerk thought process was completed, he directed his concerns to his workers who were the real reason he was a success. The majority of Eduardo's business entities were in Latin America. His labor pool was under-paid and living in third-world conditions. Their homes had no air-conditioning to help them as the planet warmed.

The older used cars were all his average worker could afford. With alternative energy replacing fossil fuels, the price of gas was creeping up and wages were not keeping pace. He knew that food prices were impacted by the warmer, dryer weather, because he had investments in the food industry. How would the workers continue, and likewise be part of his dynasty, when his people had to fight that many battles at once?

"Please tell me about the power facility in the United States."

Marina took the conversation and proceeded to detail the most recent history of the changes at the Wind River Indian Reservation and the building of a village named *Urgent*. She elected not to share the information surrounding the continued involvement of the President of the United States. Also, she withheld the details of her associate's masterful efforts in helping declare emergencies in five states. Ten years of history would make this too long a meeting. A quicker synopsis is what she chose to deliver at this, the first of what she hoped would be many chats.

It was Steven who noticed the time and suggested that they leave the suite and get back to the conference. The executives compared schedules and agreed to meet again the morning after the closing gala banquet. Marina followed them out of the suite and closed the door behind the two men. Almost invisibly, she reached forward and lightly grabbed Steven's coat tail. He turned and winked.

At the end of a week of high-powered meetings and detailed socializing, many of the powerful people that attended the World Economic Summit were anxious to get home. The squadron of executive jets left the airport in a long and uneventful parade. Two of these exclusive aircraft scheduled a rendezvous over the Atlantic and approached the Unites States in tandem. The flight plans had been filed for both to touch down and refuel in Denver. Only one plane went aloft after topping off the tanks, the other was pulled into a hangar by the small airport tug.

Steven and Marina had asked Eduardo to occupy the seat of honor, in order to see the passing sights. He had expressed a need to visit Urgent before committing to the proposed venture.

URGENT LAUNCH

They thought the grand tour would be in order.

It was unworthy of the location to do a high-speed fly-by in a jet aircraft. Instead, they approached the area from the north and entered Urgent's flight pattern above Yellowstone National Park. Their route took them parallel to the jagged summits of the Rocky Mountains for 100 scenic miles. While absorbing the sweeping view of the expanse of the Great Plains, they began to reduce altitude and landed at the high-plateau airport.

Leaving the guest's aircraft in Denver seemed like the polite course of action. In reality it could not land at their destination. The jet being used was outfitted with a STOL package: short take-off and landing. The pilot expertly put the plane on the ground and taxied directly into the hangar. Chief Joseph and his son Edward welcomed the group as they deplaned. Two white vans awaited them.

Before they began the tour of Urgent the Chief asked if the visitors felt well-rested. He and the two Edwards got in one of the vans. The remnants of the party jumped in the other vehicle and headed for the research facility. They wanted some facetime with the lead scientist housed at the complex – Harold Knight.

While Eduardo had not seen much detail from the air, the ground tour of greater Urgent gave him all the specifics he needed. The river and dams, solar panels and wind turbines, village and industrial site, even the invisible pipe routes, all made sense to him. In his mind's eye he saw the community quite accurately. Given the choice of dinner or visiting the underground facilities, he chose the latter.

He was told that the mill and adjacent buildings were above the research labs. This gave him a simple understanding of the subterranean caverns. Once inside he realized the full scope of what had been built.

Steven and Marina joined them for a late dinner. The dining area was centrally located, beneath the similar above ground cafeteria. Throughout their meal, people with a colorful array of outfits approached Harold and shared snippets of information.

"This man," Eduardo thought to himself, "must be more than a scientist." The sight of an outsider seemed not to discourage these exchanges. It was obvious to Eduardo that Harold's presence at this table was his security pass. Acting more like members of a family than employees, these gringos had built something special. But were they out of place? How did the Native American connection work? What's with the multi-racial concentration?

He decided to go forward with some reforestation help. He also decided to find out more about the origins of this village. "Will you please tell me a little more about the how and why of this place."

Harold spoke: "A large part of the how, and our rapid growth, is because we are not in the United States as we sit here. Officially we are in the Wind River Indian Reservation: a sovereign nation of indigenous peoples. When it comes to grand plans and governance, our Nation is much more hospitable than the United States. Out of respect, the US knows what we are doing, but has no say over most of our activities.

"The why should have been explained to you. We are fast-tracking efforts to mitigate climate change.

URGENT LAUNCH

The complex construction project you saw on the surface is a steel mill. We anticipate experimenting with numerous elements in the making of unique alloys. One of our goals is to develop a better conductor of electricity, and then generate that power with the help of water, wind, and sun. You saw evidence of that on the surface. No fossil fuels are used in the production of any electricity. What we do not use we can sell back to the power utility in this part of Wyoming.

"We have dedicated ourselves to cutting edge research. Adjacent to this dining area, along an underground tunnel located just beyond that wall, is a series of laboratories. Our materials science, temperature, and chemistry research is being done by a group of inquisitive, young scientists. You undoubtedly picked up on some of that shop talk during the interruptions that took place at dinner. Down here, research and sharing or questioning never stops.

"It may be of interest to know that our agriculture lab is conducting experiments on crop growth, changes of growth-rate if we supply less light, or considerably more. The next project in agriculture is to add the study of big trees. Hopefully, that's where you come in.

"Not in the research naturally, but in the understanding of the options we have in what we use to replant in a forest. We might not have time to use the same species the forest has spent centuries growing. To some it will be messy and sacrilegious, but man may have no choice but to use trees that grow faster and have a larger leaf."

Eduardo noticed a young woman in a white smock approach the table. She whispered into Harold's ear and he excused himself.

"Duty calls." He said.

The South American felt he had a duty too.

TWO

•— — •— •••— • •—•• •— —• —••

Javier Rodriguez was used to wide open spaces. Although he had been born and raised in a small wooded village outside of Temuco, Chile, he had seen some savanna grasslands in Uganda and other plains in South America. His travels on behalf of Eduardo, his benefactor, had been extensive.

Nothing though, had prepared him for the expanse and cleanliness of the high country in Montana. He could see forever and feel his lungs filling with pure air. His only similar experience was a flight over the South America Atacama Desert, the highest and driest place on earth. While nothing visible was growing on that high plain, today there was abundant growth within his sight at Flathead Lake.

Brian Knight, his companion and Montana fishing guide, had ordered this excursion as a respite from their research.

"A recreational side trip is what we need after flying around the Rocky Mountains in a helicopter looking at forests."

The two men spoke little while their lines were in the water. The stillness allowed Javier again to thank the gods, his lucky stars, or whoever for the relationship he had with one of the world's richest men. Eduardo had bribed Javier away from his former profession, if criminal hacking can be considered a career. The teen-ager had been on his way to court in Mexico for cybertheft of scientific secrets from federal agencies whose very existence was also a secret.

One of the judges scheduled to hear the case had contacted the billionaire. The judge feared that a brilliant mind was about to be numbed. Eduardo flew into Mexico City for a brief evaluation of the precocious youngster and flew back to Guadalajara with a new employee. The kid was sharp, and he knew most of the languages needed to travel seamlessly around South America. A brief criminal history did not bother Eduardo, who himself occasionally stepped outside the law.

The meeting of their minds had not been a particularly smooth one. The elder man had a tendency to want to involve Javier in more than the agreed upon duties. It was almost as if Eduardo wanted to groom a successor, or even a son. On more than one occasion he issued loud and strong rebukes and reminders of the deal involving reforestation responsibilities and nothing more. It took three years before they found common ground.

Brian shattered the silence: "I'm disappointed that they're not biting today. Do you suppose it has to do with the time or the bright sunshine?"

"I'll tell you my friend, it just doesn't matter. Look at this lake, those mountains, look into the distance. For a few days we have been talking trees and out there we see millions of them. I'm anxious to soak this all in and then get on our way deeper into Canada. Will we find good fishing farther north?"

"Let's go find out," said Brian and he reeled his line in. They took the thirty-minute walk to the rented four-by-four. After driving an hour to Kalispell, they decided that seeing more of Glacier National Park was worth spending the night. However, it would be a short night. The next morning they filed a flight plan for Juneau and left Glacier Airport before dawn.

They sat next to each other in the private plane and began discussing the forests in Southeast Alaska. They knew the ancient forests in the western part of the continent had one particularly destructive invader: the Spruce Bark Beetle. Over the years thousands, if not tens of thousands, of acres had been killed by this small insect. They agreed that re-forestation begins with stopping the de-forestation wherever possible. Was it possible here?

Brian wanted to see the devastation and talk science with the natives. He then planned on sharing that information, along with eye-witness accounts, with his brother Harold. Brian knew there was an agricultural research lab at Urgent under his brother's supervision.

As the sun began to illuminate the ground beneath

the aircraft the damage was all too obvious; it was also widespread. Large swaths of trees that should have been green appeared either rusty or dark and ashen. From the Canadian Rockies to the shores of the Pacific there was rarely a view totally filled with green trees. Javier's limited knowledge of the beetle's life included knowing that the warmer the temperatures, the more it multiplied. Obviously, efforts directed at slowing the beetle down would be uphill all the way.

As he began the descent the pilot advised that a local bush pilot was standing by to give them a lower, slower tour. Once aloft in the smaller craft they had to yell to be heard, but the close-up view of what used to be healthy forest required little conversation. The small plane proceeded south toward the Tongass National Forest, an area they thought worthy of investigation. They could have landed at any number of places but the weary passengers saw no reason for a closer view. The scale of the problem as seen from above was impressive enough. They returned to Juneau to spend the night.

For two nights in a row, Brian and Javier failed to get a full night's sleep. Their pilot had phoned at dawn to report that an incoming weather front threatened to ground all air traffic for two days. He suggested they take off ASAP.

They met in the hotel lobby 15 minutes later and took a cab to the airport. The jet was immediately cleared for takeoff. The sky along the coast of Southeast Alaska was cloudless. Brian asked that they fly over the area just south of Mt. Denali – McKinley on some maps. The pilot checked on the weather up north and gave Brian the thumbs-up.

Scientific reports mentioned a large beetle infestation in that border area between Alaska and Canada's Yukon Territory. The real time view was disheartening. Even though the incoming clouds partially obstructed their view, the destruction was obvious.

Javier only stared out the window. Brian Knight asked the pilot if they had sufficient fuel to reach Urgent.

"No problem, and will do sir."

Brian turned to his companion. "The reason I thought we should visit Alaska has to do with the possibility of teaming up with universities, governments, and indigenous peoples to attack this epidemic. We've got a little time. Let me explain.

"Our earlier slow-speed fly-over of yesterday covered an area called the Tongass National Forest. A United States national forest is protected by an agency of our government. This particular forest is also sacred to and historically a land of two Native American nations: the Tlingit and the Haida.

"With few exceptions our natives do not trust the US government, and for good reason. There is a history of making and then breaking treaties. To atone for this bad-faith undercurrent, many agencies within the government emphasize their resolve to favor any project involving Native Americans.

"The system that has evolved from a simple request of the government is now referred to as a written grant application. We don't want a loan. We want money to do research to help mankind. When it comes to grant writing, the best institutions on the planet are universities. As luck would have it, University of Alaska Southeast (UAS) has campuses that flank the Tongass National Forest; to the north is Juneau and to the south, Ketchikan."

Brian retreated to his laptop for a few minutes.

"UAS has programs involving students interested in some of our areas of interest. It is not uncommon to write grants with objectives that require manpower. The university has that labor pool in the form of students studying forest management, natural resources, environmental studies, biological sciences, earth science, tribal management, even chemistry. Can you see how these interconnect?" he asked.

"I am visualizing your web of studies and applying it to my country," Javier replied.

"The grant process may be different south of here but your scheme of involving indigenous people and the governments still applies. While the forests consist of different trees, the solution may translate."

Javier was quietly thinking as the jet continued on the heading toward Urgent.

As is often the case, more pressing matters resulted in a delay in returning to the issue of trees and the planting thereof. The more he learned the more he realized the importance of bringing a major labor force to this endeavor. More than any other solution, vegetation helps the earth reduce the carbon dioxide content in the atmosphere. In wanting to address these matters, and to investigate the topic of forests, he decided to postpone retuning to Urgent. He flew home to Guadalajara.

URGENT LAUNCH

Javier knew the industrialized countries could not continue to contaminate the planet. For as long as he could remember, the target date of 2050 had been talked about in scientific circles. He found that the scientists were now moving that date up. Plus, they were moving the targets up and publishing new data:
-- Alternative energy needs to comprise 70% of our energy output by 2030.
-- We now experience millions of toxic-air related deaths in China and India.
-- Warming soil is releasing carbon dioxide faster than ever before.

His research had identified an organization of possible use in their project: the International Institute of Tropical Forestry. In cooperation with the University of Puerto Rico, this experimental station had morphed into a formal organization bringing together the research about tropical forests and grasslands. After discovering they had experience in reforestation, Javier knew he would need a face to face visit - soon.

From the air, chunks of the island of Puerto Rico still looked like a war zone. A few years ago, this part of the Caribbean had been devastated by a hurricane. It took a year to get electricity back to most of the inhabitants; longer than that to provide running water. In fact, some of the villages were just abandoned. Javier was hoping that San Juan was in better shape.

The Institute offices were in San Juan. He had an appointment today and wanted their blessing and some information. After time in the tutelage of Brian Knight last year, Javier had an idea of how to approach the deforestation issue at the edges of the Amazon rain forest.

The public face on such an immense project needed to be politically neutral. The university leadership should be local and the indigenous people partners. Unlike Southeast Alaska, though, where nature destroyed the forest, in the Amazon one is dealing with farmers. Man is the culprit.

The Puerto Ricans were all too ready to help. As a tropical forest, the Amazon basin would be similar to other forests in South America with which the Institute had experience. Everyone Javier spoke to was concerned about the recent increase in the rate of abuse of this massive rain forest. The government of Brazil, which houses most of this rain forest, had recently expressed an interest in building a few dams and miles of roads, inside the fragile ecosystem.

These projects would not necessarily change the area of the rain forest significantly. The primary problem was the potential to disrupt the complex environment of the rain forest ecology. The jungle, the rain, the clouds, and the balance of it all was at risk.

The Amazon basin pumps 20 billion tons of water vapor into the atmosphere per day through leaf transpiration. The clouds formed by this vapor affect the entire Western Hemisphere – they travel a continent away. The cloud cover appears to be a nationwide thick layer of moisture-heavy air. In reality the layers are thin but many, and the cover is not one blanket but many patches. Prevailing winds gradually move this collective across the land. Scientists worry that large gaps in the forest created by logging might result in large gaps in the clouds above.

Such an interruption would cause the warm sunlight to adversely affect the moisture content of the independent clouds from the top, and around the edges, more quickly. If it were no longer one impenetrable cover, the closed formation could disperse sending the loose clouds in their own direction – possibly to evaporate.

Atmospheric moisture had been reported as being more stationary and more concentrated in north Brazil than it used to be. Recently Sao Paulo, the country's largest city - and to the south - experienced a severe drought that some say was attributable to the change in the flow of the clouds. If logging continued, might a permanent drought be the result?

Much to Javier's delight, the administrator at the Puerto Rican Institute wanted to hear more about the reforestation plans in which Eduardo's foundation was a participant. The American involvement in reforestation had been slow in coming, but still welcomed. Javier knew thoughtful world leaders would more quickly agree to help with a multi-country effort. Well-publicized international cooperation would help bring more manpower to the saving of the planet.

He intended to fly Institute management to Urgent.

THREE

•— •——• — ——— •••

The tugboat captain kept his eyes focused on the spit of land five miles off his starboard bow. Radar displayed clear waters and the GPS coordinates confirmed the destination. He needed to begin the process of snugging up the barges – but slowly. Many a tug has been taken to the bottom by a misbehaving tow. Barges were particularly nasty, and he was pulling two rows of two.

The weight was evenly distributed when initially loaded and the balance allowed the skipper to tow without major concern. However, rough seas could bounce the load around and redistribute that weight. When a barge became bow-heavy and encountered more rough seas, waves breaking over the front could force the tow beneath the surface. If it sank it usually meant an inexperienced captain was at the helm. They tended to keep the power on and continue forward momentum forcing the barge deeper. Seasoned skippers know to kill the power. Release the tow if necessary and let the barge sink, thereby saving the tug.

Today, the seas were cooperating and Cape Fanshaw was a welcome sight. The tug was headed east into the shallow end of Farragut Bay. The tow now needed to be tight. The job called for anchoring at a likely spot around the corner, into the North Arm where more protection is provided by the land and forest.

A small fleet of tender vessels was tied to floating docks in that harbor. Captain Dan was not expecting such a reception. He had seen the floatplane give him a wave yesterday and only anticipated being welcomed by the pilot and maybe a passenger or two. Who thought 20 college-aged kids would be the official welcoming committee?

As he cut power, two twenty-something foot dory-type craft approached his tug. One driver asked for permission to tie up and come aboard. "Permission granted."

That was the initial contact with a project that would involve Cap'n Dan, as his crew called him, his friends and associates for the rest of their lives. The waters around Southeast Alaska would act as the conduit between his nautical knowledge and the For-CI, Forestry Consortium International.

True to his word, Brian Knight had made the inquiries necessary to initiate the cooperation of the Forest Service, the Native Americans, and some universities. The Alaska region of the US Forest Service had agreed that the partially dead forest on the peninsula near Cape Fanshaw could be used as a research location. The University of Alaska Southeast (UAS) then developed a project involving three different departments and introduced this complicated research program to a limited number of students.

The acceptance rate was nearly 100% and the Office of Academic Affairs and Research at UAS had to enlarge the program, even before the first class left for the field. The fact that full-ride scholarships were attached to the program may have helped with enrollment.

Each cohort would be committed to a yearlong effort with as much of that year as possible spent in the forest. Only when weather decided otherwise would the students, faculty, and other workers be ferried into Juneau to continue processing research results in a warm campus laboratory. As the student population matriculated through ForCI, the cohorts also grew.

During the first year, Cap'n Dan became the shuttle driver and ran personnel between the North Arm, the research site closer to the point, and to the Juneau docks. The larger, heavier equipment needed in the field was transferred to smaller vessels at those city docks. The smaller craft could get closer to shore and offload more easily. The captain's connections in the marine community invariably enabled him to get the perfect vessel when needed.

The first phase of this forest research was to get rid of a swath of dead trees and clear land to make room for buildings and possibly planting. Cap'n Dan understood; the students could not be expected to do the logging or drive the log trucks to mill.

In fact, there were no trucks and there was no mill.

The ForCI leaders had consulted with the Tlingit Nation regarding the entire project. The Nation was happy to recruit paid volunteers with logging experience and the appropriate tools. A few old-timers around the Juneau waterfront knew who was likely to have retired trucks. Cap'n Dan would find and haul the equipment to the site on a barge. He also would haul in a portable sawmill and the trucks. He had already brought in the crane, some prefab buildings, loaded fuel tanks, small 4-wheelers, large tool chests, containers of kitchen equipment, furniture, and much more, as cargo in his initial tow from the South.

The first goal was to determine the location of the area to be studied and build their encampment nearby. Permanent shelter and a cookhouse were tops on the priority list. The dorm modules were hauled in once the planning was completed. Then they brought the dual-purpose classroom/lab.

University staff and forest service personnel were coordinating the timing of the extensive list of tasks that needed to happen simultaneously:
   -- Logging roads to be carved out of the forest.
   -- Better docks should be anchored at the bay.
   -- Dig and build two outhouses.
   -- The portable sawmill to be built.

The loggers needed to process the trees which had been harvested to make room for their small campsite. Large piles of downed fir trees occupy too much space. The first load of lumber Cap'n Dan hauled into Juneau would have been well received by the lumber market; however it was already spoken for.

The agreement between the ForCI parties stipulated that marketable lumber would be traded to logging concerns that had signed contracts with the Forest Service. The deal was a trade for the release of the acres of trees about to be cut as per the terms of those contracts: leave the subject trees standing and get paid in ready-for-market lumber. At the end of year one, this amounted to only fifty acres worth of trees.

During that first year, the hired laborers were busy making a research site: logging, trucking logs to the mill in the meadow, hauling the tree bark to the makeshift pier on the shore, cutting and pulling the stumps out of the ground, and grading that ground. The students spent their time erecting more shelters and buildings to use as classrooms and research facilities. The Native Americans had invested time too.

Before breaking ground, the project, land, and other aspects of the endeavor required a blessing. The Nation's holy man performed the ceremony after which the Tlingit and Haida had sent advisors to make sure no unintended damage was done to the water and their fishing grounds. No more than one month into the season, the Tlingit leaders expressed an interest in having their young people join the team.

The ForCI administrators agreed that it was a good idea, and that a better idea would be to waive all fees and tuition. Native American participation was a gift, and the youth were registered as part-time students at UAS. The USFS Office of Tribal Relations willingly funded what normally would be room and board.

URGENT LAUNCH

University of Alaska Southeast enrolled and credited these young researchers in the Forest Management and Tribal Management programs. It would be possible for a student to work through three years of this program without adding to the student's debt.

Although many of these members could go home on weekends, the majority of them continued to help alongside their peers with the seemingly never ending work. When not exerting enormous energy in the forest, the students attended classes in the small, fresh class-rooms. University faculty had planned every hour of every day. These students had signed on for this rigorous routine and soon bonded over their ability to undergo this torture.

The Forest Service (USFS) had wanted research done on how to eradicate the beetle larvae that were born inside the trees. As part of the second year of research, the students thought they could now activate that grant by going into action. Prior to the exploratory logging they ventured deep into the healthy forest.

One team had been assigned the study of the wooded area and the tagging of diseased trees. They selected a sample of trees in varying stages of dying, had them taken down, and hauled them to the mill. Considering that the beetle larvae lived just under the tree bark, the researchers agreed to run the freshly cut trees through the sawmill and isolate the first cut that was attached to the bark. The remaining wood was good marketable lumber. But what about the outer layer?

After a few false starts, the researchers proposed that submerging this bark in sea water for a few months might kill the larvae. They looked at the map, sent up a drone, and chose a suitable cove on the other side of the peninsula.

The Sandborn Canal was narrow well protected river mouth. Rather than load the bark on a barge and take a lengthy voyage around the point, they cobbled together a road to the northern shore. Trucks would haul the bark overland to the water's edge, dump their load, and small tenders would assemble rafts of bark and push them into the canal. The drivers of these small craft were students. They had learned to pilot the boats as part of an orientation to the water and woods.

The second year of the project proved more popular than the first. Growth in participation came mostly from city folks from the Lower 48. Word of the program had reached campuses all across the country, but the ForCI staff needed to control growth. They elected to add one university to the consortium: Oregon State in Corvallis, Oregon.

OSU was the largest and closest land grant university, well known to administrators at the other campuses for having one of the top forestry schools in the country. The similarity in administration, schedules, curriculum, and environment made Oregon State the logical choice. Also, the forests in Oregon contained many large trees similar to those found in Southeast Alaska.

Out of the hundreds of different species of bark beetles, those being studied at OSU would probably not be the same insect as those attacking the trees in Alaska. The life cycle and impact on the forests, though, would be similar. These coniferous forests have coexisted with beetles for centuries. Evolution has caused many beetle species to live only in dead or dying hosts. A deterioration in forest health often precipitates a more severe attack than usual.

The most recent environmental changes in average temperature, snowpack, and rainfall placed stress on millions of acres of forest in North America. The beetles had responded by causing extensive tree mortality which had adverse economic and social implications. To improve cooperation and stream-line research, three western Forest Service research stations had agreed to form the Western Bark Beetle Research Group: WBBRG.

Investigations into insect development, landscape dynamics, and chemical ecology, all led to the need to study the consequences of any treatment. Oregon State faculty had a place at the table during the meet-ings of the WBBRG. They brought that connection to ForCI.

Late in October, Cap'n Dan had one eye on the weather and the other on the load of lumber he was taking up to Juneau. This was the last load of the season. The heavy rain that had just started would not damage the exposed wood, but that dark storm front to the west could surely do some damage to any boat caught out here. His small freighter was not too speedy.

On board was the usual crew of two plus two col-lege kids that had elected to lock up the site for the winter. Cap'n Dan was realizing he would not make Juneau before the seas turned violent.

He called all the youngsters to the bridge.

"You two are seasoned enough to know what storm clouds look like. Take a gander at those."

As the student's gaze followed the direction he was pointing, the ever-alert captain was slightly altering course.

"Now take a peek at the charts on the table here. There's Juneau, here's us, there's the storm. At our current speed and the track of those clouds, I doubt we get to land before it gets rough as hell out here. We gotta lotta logs on board that are causing us to sit low in the water. What do you think?"

During the course of each season, everyone had a turn at the helm. In fact, every student was briefed in all aspects of seamanship. The large logging equipment was too complicated for a novice to operate but riding shotgun in the cab was always encouraged. The company Cap'n Dan had in the wheelhouse was familiar with his vessel and his musings.

The students examined the charts closer and noticed a familiar harbor nearby. It was unanimous; head for the protected waters of Sandborn Canal. The tide was in and the freighter could safely get into the channel. Juneau could wait, as could its warm research lab.

It took over an hour to round the peninsula. All the while the crew was double checking the lashing of the lumber and the hatches on deck. The students went below decks to the galley to lash and latch whatever they could find. The vintage Pacific Coast freighter was seaworthy, but her 175-foot length meant she bobbed about in rough water, even when loaded.

URGENT LAUNCH

The entrance to the canal was in sight when one of the crew remarked at the population of bald eagles above the treetops. When closer to the entrance they could see the birds swooping down to the surface and plucking nice fish from the waters.

"I wonder," mused Cap'n Dan, and he switched on the dormant fish finder. He hadn't needed that device because it was too late in the season for any good fishing.

The electronics took a minute to warm up, then displayed a swarm of activity. He looked curiously at his crew, they just shrugged. One of the students asked an innocent question: "When did you bring in the last load of bark?"

It had been over a month since the logging had ceased, and the mill had quieted down. These past few weeks had been devoted to clearing the forest floor and planning the following spring's activities. No one had visited the bark burial site.

The student continued, "Could these fish be eating dead larvae, or exoskeletons, or what? If the release of the larvae, whether through their own attempt to escape, or the effect of the water on the bark, has changed the migration and feeding patterns of this species of fish we need to study this discovery.

"Depending on the tide, the canal has fresh water meeting salt water at different depths and in various concentrations. This needs to be factored into our work next season. We are already scheduled to monitor water quality. It's apparent we need to add fish activity to our to-do list.

"At the very least we know where to catch dinner."

FOUR

—•— • —•—— •—— • ••• —

The enthusiasm and efforts of the young students in Alaska were the only visible results of ForCI in the early years. Coordinating the faculties and administrators of universities with help from a federal agency and Native Americans proved to be an exhausting exercise. While the papers were being pushed, the student-workers went to class in the forest.

The size of classes grew and resulted in the need for more faculty and/or chaperones. Not that college kids needed baby sitters, but the setting could be romantic at times, and all gatherings under such conditions required careful planning.

There was an ongoing call for mature, experienced faculty to work in Alaska. This job offer was known throughout the offices of the ForCI participating groups, and also circulated within the labs and offices at Urgent. The students may have been oblivious to funding channels, but the philanthropists behind the formation of Urgent were the same folks making ForCI a reality; therefore Urgent was in the loop.

One senior researcher in the Ag Lab (agriculture) mentioned this opportunity to FJ Guindo. FJ had been in that under ground lab for over a year and immediately decided the wilds of Alaska needed his help. Hard work never bothered the young man. He was physically fit and anxious to visit a part of the world he had not experienced. His introduction to his new jobsite had been a student conducted orientation. The short lecture and tour were incomplete and left FJ with a notebook full of questions.

The primitive faculty housing at Cape Fanshaw included a small private room equipped with a mini-refrigerator and two-burner propane stove - that was sufficient. However, he was lacking clarification of many issues covered only briefly in the lecture. Rather than bother the head honcho, he searched out another incoming faculty member and compared notes.

"Sara," she said, responding to his self-introduction. "Actually, it's my second year here. I just like to attend this orientation to get to know the newcomers."

"I can guarantee that I'm a newcomer," FJ replied. "And in need of some answers. Can I pick your brain over some *gourmet* coffee?" he asked, pointing to the air-pot on the counter.

Their sessions of questions continued well into the first semester of class. The reforestation of the large swath of dead or dying evergreen trees was a complicated process. The faculty was expected to be familiar with all aspects of the activity. Certain trees were marked to be felled, others were to remain standing. Paths and roads were cleared and cleaned up so vehicles would find traveling easier.

Water transportation was also available. Both power boats and human-powered vessels were to be mastered and used. Maps and charts illustrated the lay of the land. Battery-powered drones provided a birds-eye view of all terrain and real time analysis of a variety of situations. Small drones had even been used to herd wildlife that required redirecting – for example a black bear too close to a survey team.

The class schedule called for field exercises to wrap up before the weather in Southeast Alaska turned ugly. Cold, windy, and dark was the normal forecast through the late fall and winter months. It was customary to lock down all structures before Thanksgiving, and return the students to the safety of the university buildings in Juneau. FJ and Sara were assigned the task of conducting one final sweep of the shore to find a missing canoe.

University protocol required that at least two qualified people be aboard the small runabout the class used for scooting through the local waterways. The two friends decided to follow the north wind and see if the two-person canoe was being propelled south by Mother Nature.

Fifteen minutes into the search Sara spotted the aluminum hull bouncing down the shoreline, from rock to rock. They knew to overshoot their target and approach the canoe from the south, letting the wind bring the little boat to them. Making a wide gentle turn to come around and meet the canoe nose-to-nose, they found themselves far enough into open water that they could see down a seldom visited inlet. At the far end Sara noticed a white hull. She tugged on FJ's sleeve and pointed, giving him an inquisitive look.

"Let's get the canoe first, then we will check it out," she offered.

They plucked the runaway canoe out of the water and lashed it to one side of the runabout.

"Sara," he said. "You drive this thing while I try to figure out what's happening. Stay close to shore and just putt along. These binoculars bounce enough without also having to do battle with big waves." He put the field glasses to his eyes.

"I wish we had our large drone. I don't feel comfortable getting any closer, or even being seen. There are at least four men in that boat, and they are tied up to an old piling about thirty yards offshore. It looks like there are more pilings nearby, as if some dock was abandoned and either rotted away or was taken apart.

"One of the men is on the large boat, examining and picking away at the top of the piling. A few feet away they have a small dinghy tied to another piling and a guy is also picking at the top of that log. Let's quietly turn around and head for the camp."

As soon as they were completely out of sight of the other boat, or even the water behind it for that matter, they increased speed and began to speculate.

"The shore around that cove was full of healthy

trees, growing all the way down to the beach," FJ shouted above the scream of the motors. "If those men were going to do anything on land, they would first have one serious logging operation to perform. The way I see it, that's their plan."

Sara wondered aloud, "Do you think they were testing the strength of the pilings? If they are planning on getting timber out of there, they will need to anchor a barge or boat as close to shore as possible. We have seen those ocean-going barges in Juneau. One of those with a crane on board could pluck logs out of the water and carry tons of good wood to market."

"Don't you have to get a permit to log?" FJ asked.

"If that is still in the national forest, can you even get a permit?" she said.

"We need to ask a few questions, but not here and not now. Our radio could be on the same frequency as theirs and we don't want those guys to know we saw them. We can use the secure cell phone when we get back to camp. I know just who to call."

Tom Lacey took the incoming call from Alaska. He knew of the reforestation efforts and of Urgent's involvement in helping with personnel and equipment. He also knew FJ Guindo. After a few minutes of listening, Lacey spoke.

"I have a tendency to agree with you. This does sound like a preparation for a logging job. Most likely an illegal one at that. I have a map of the Tongass up on my screen, and the inlet you describe is within the boundary of the forest. Hang on just a sec," he said.

"OK, FJ. That number you gave me belongs to a boat owned by an Alaska corporation. They are registered as importers but that can be a ruse. Let me look up the officers."

After a few more seconds of silence he said, "Right - we have a member of the board of directors that is listed as president of a logging company. Oh - and I see that company also sells lumber through a mill of the same name. You're looking at pirates all right."

"Is there anything we can do from this end?" inquired FJ.

"Not right now," was the response. "Keep up your schedule and normal routine. We will do more investigating and will be asking for help soon enough. Thanks for keeping your eyes open. Good work."

Tom Lacey had more research to do and his supercomputer at the Urgent underground center was definitely capable.

The final outpost exercise of the school year was to double check all the locks on all buildings, then meet a small freighter at the dock. The ship would have a load of logs on deck destined for Juneau, but would save room for the runabout to be put aboard. The on-deck davit would set the little boat down but leave the lifting cable attached.

This precaution allowed the small crane to lift the runabout quickly and drop it over the side if there was an emergency. Also, upon the conclusion of an uneventful trip, the runabout would be the first thing dropped over the side – she would motor to the marina for winterizing.

FJ and Sara spent three days on the closing routine and were finally *en route* to civilization. Traveling on the bridge of the freighter with Cap'n Dan, FJ casually asked about the activity in the inlet at the south of Cape Fanshaw.

"Earlier this week we happened to notice activity in the South Arm of the bay on the other side of Read Island. Have you picked up any scuttlebutt around the waterfront about that particular part of Farragut Bay?"

"Nothing recent," Cap'n Dan replied. "I seem to recall a few years back when some lumber outfit from down south was trying to negotiate a deal with the Forest Service to log a stand of diseased trees. The parties almost ended up in court because an inspection showed the trees in question not to be diseased at all."

"Do you remember who the lumber guys were?" asked Sara.

"Sorry. But I do know that the state decided not to spend the money chasing them down after they disappeared. I guess they went into bankruptcy," he added.

The two young people exchanged looks, indicating to each other to drop the subject.

The old freighter was slowly motoring north in Stevens Passage with Juneau as the next stop. The day was calm, and the rhythm of the big diesel engine was hypnotic. In such instances Cap'n Dan had a practice of using teaching as a cure for drowsiness. All occupants of the wheelhouse were studying, and talking about the nautical charts of the area when FJ excused himself and went out on deck to take a call. It was Emmet Fitzpatrick in Urgent.

"Tom Lacey asked me to give you a progress report

on that suspicious activity you two discussed a few days ago. We have been playing with scenarios since that first alert and can find no reason to let these pirate loggers jeopardize the project we legitimately organized in that area. Our job now is to think through various possibilities that result in these folks packing it in. But first we need to talk manpower. What do you have as qualified help that can quietly and secretly set up an operation?"

Young Guindo knew he could recruit from the Lower 48, but had to think about his connections in Alaska. "Let me call you back." He started to disconnect but then blurted into the phone, "Emmet, please give me a scouting report on Captain Dan and his Alaska outfit. I'm on one of his boats now and suspect I can at least organize some transportation through him."

Upon returning to the bridge, FJ apologized, "Sorry - that was my folks calling from the Lower 48."

The first job when they arrived at the Juneau waterfront was to lower the tired runabout over the side. When asked, Sara agreed that she would take one last ride for the season. They began to glide towards the local marina and boatyard; along the way, dodging the crabbers.

"All right, FJ," Sara started, "What's the deal. I have practically lived with you for over six months and never heard you talk about your parents, and now they call . . ." his phone interrupted her.

He held up his hand, palm facing her, asking for silence.

"Yes Emmet."

After a few minutes of listening, he thanked the caller

and ended the conversation - placing the phone in the cupholder next to the helm. He looked her directly in the eyes and began.

"Sara, that explanation was for the benefit of the skipper. As you know, I have been in contact with a security team about our pirates. Not knowing how trustworthy the Captain is, I needed a quick, plausible excuse. You are right, obviously. I do not get calls from my parents in the Lower 48.

"Please bear with me. Right now, we need to get this boat in to be winterized. The next item on our agenda is to get our appetites looked after. Allow me to buy you dinner at a local dive. We can talk openly there, believe it or not."

They found a remote table in a rough looking dining room and quickly ordered. The food was not galley food from a cook in the woods and thus was noteworthy. FJ began his story.

"That last call was the information on Cap'n Dan. I needed to know if he could be trusted to work with me on discouraging our illegal loggers. I have been told I can trust him implicitly, and even go along with whoever he recommends join me on the team. We have options to explore, depending on the size of the crew. By the time you return next year, and I really hope you do, I would guess that even without involving the law, our unlawful threat will be gone."

"Oh, FJ. I don't leave Alaska during the winter break. Didn't I tell you?"

"That's great news. I'm sorry. That's selfish, but still great news. Everyone should be able to go home for the holidays, but a few of those that can't might be able to help each other. I won't be leaving either."

"Can you use an extra pair of hands on your pirate project?" she asked.

"Always, if they are your hands," he said. "I would put my life in those hands."

At that, she balked. He noticed the immediate change in her demeanor. This was not like her, he thought to himself.

"OK - out with it. What did I say or do? You just switched off and I don't know why."

"I'm sorry. I want you to trust me and need you to understand. I won't go south because I am in a self-imposed exile. Kinda like my own witness protection program."

"Why?" he asked.

"I killed somebody."

It took all his willpower to avoid looking as astonished as he felt. Trusting a reasonable explanation was about to follow, FJ signaled to the bartender to bring two more, then returned his attention to her eyes. He did not speak.

"There are only a handful of people that know this story," she started, "and I trust you to keep it confidential. Those in the know are all living in a town called Urgent, but I doubt you can get any corroboration of this accident without my being with you; this is the nature of our friendships.

"The young village police force built an under-the-radar team of early citizens that specialized in adversary control, getting in the way of those that would interrupt the growth in Urgent. I was a member of that team until four years ago when we disbanded." At this she signed the air-quotes signal.

"Sara," he whispered, "I know Urgent. In fact that last call I got was from the new security chief in Urgent, a former FBI lifer. Recruiting him was the hot rumor on the grapevine just before I came to Alaska."

She smiled, then continued, admitting to her rewarding involvement with that team until the accidental death of a helicopter pilot and his passenger – a US congressman. She did not share any information about the other operations her team had performed. The incident was not one he had heard of, but FJ was beginning to realize that her involvement in that tragedy resulted in both a physical and psychological prison for her.

"An accident is an accident," he told himself, and set about to confirm his position on this matter.

"Sara, you are not the only one at this table that cannot return to the lower forty-eight for the winter. Although I'm not wanted in the eyes of the law, I too am hiding from my past. More accurately, my family."

He proceeded to tell the story of his ultra-controlling father and the drop-outta-sight solution he had chosen via Urgent. When he paused to take a deep breath, she reached out and took his hand. For a few moments neither of them spoke.

Finally, she broke the silence: "So, tell me about our plan for the illegal loggers."

FIVE

• — • • — — — — — — • — • •

The cathedral was spectacular. There it was across the plaza, the Cologne Cathedral standing tall and ornate. It was hard to imagine that it was virtually destroyed during WWII. What a testament to the resilience and traditions of the German people. However, Brian Knight was not there to look at the sights.

Although they had first touched down in Switzerland, Brian wasn't one of the speakers in Davos this year. He was a world-wide liaison for a trio of well-known foundations but intended to remain unheralded. He had parted company with the other Americans and flown on to Germany.

His brother Harold had made an electronic introduction and arranged for Brian to meet with a well-respected German scientist. Their schedules were such that Cologne University offered a secure, neutral place to have the first conversation. The resident scientist had agreed to meet Brian at a campus library.

The Max Planck Institute for Plasma Physics had been studying the feasibility of a specific fusion device for power generation. Of the projects taking place around the planet, the Wendelstein 7-X program was researching the safest option – relatively speaking. Brian wanted to learn how 7-X was progressing, what the future looked like, and what it might cost.

Fusion thermonuclear *fire* does not ignite until the vacuum chamber is 100 million degrees. There is a lot of science behind the microwave heating process that brings the temperature up to such an extreme. It then is necessary to maintain that heat level if the objective is continuous power production. How much energy does that heating process require? Actually, how safe is it?

The feasibility of this concept was proving out. Initially, the scientists got the temperatures they needed to start the reaction. When this temperature was attained, fuel would be added, and immense power generated. However, getting to temperature took a lot of power. Four megawatts of microwave heating power was producing a one-second plasma pulse. The Institute recently upgraded the equipment and eight megawatts of power rewarded them with a ten-second pulse.

The goal of the $1.7 billion project was to determine the feasibility of this type of magnetic-confinement fusion system in power plants. This was one of the safer options being considered. The environmental and climate impact was minimal. Brian speculated there was a worldwide need for this device. Thermonuclear reactors can use seawater as fuel. One kilogram of fuel for a reactor is the equivalent of burning 10 million kilograms of coal.

Glancing up he noticed a figure reflected in a brass plaque hung on the nearby library wall. Brian realized that he saw someone that was actually on the other side of a short wall, out of sight but within hearing range. He quickly wrote a note to his associate, asking if he knew the party in question.

"No - !"

As a matter of security, he suggested they leave by different doors and meet at Brian's hotel in one hour. They cleaned up the visual aids and left the university library.

The American turned right at the first two opportunities and then quickly ducked into a doorway. The sidewalks of Cologne had little pedestrian traffic and Brian was able to watch all activity along the entire block. He saw no one familiar. No one even paid attention to him. He returned to his hotel. The scientist from the 7-X project soon joined him and they agreed on lunch in the hotel dining room.

He received a crash course in thermonuclear power over a delicious meal. During a post-strudel bottle of sherry, they quietly discussed issues of safety, cooling, emissions, power requirements during production, costs, and personnel. Having his radar activated earlier, Brian watched everyone in the room; as they ate and as they came and went.

He noticed nothing unusual. The last topic of conversation was an invitation to fly to Greifswald the next day to see the machinery. The 7-X site was on the edge of the Baltic Sea, a two-hour airplane ride away. They agreed to meet for breakfast and share a taxi.

The whirlwind tour of the project was impressive, and tiring. Brian wished that his brother were with him. The language of science was not that familiar. Brother Hal was the one with the PhD and an insatiable curiosity. Brian was the hands-on sibling. He was certain that his naivete resulted in the shortening of discussions about certain complex aspects of fusion.

Nevertheless, he was continuously impressed. So much so that he contacted Davos and asked that Henry join him in Germany. At least Henry was on this continent and could add a set of eyes and ears to the research. The American philanthropist had been scheduled for a round-table discussion early in the week. That event was over. Within three hours the executive jet was briefly on the ground, depositing Henry at Greifswald.

For one more day and night, Brian and Henry talked nuclear fusion. The personnel at Max Planck were more than pleasant. The Americans received an in-depth tour with unfettered access to the equipment. They were able to inspect and touch almost anything. Yet they continued to feel that they were intruding. As an aside at lunch, they talked about letting these good people get back to work.

During dinner that evening, Brian quietly told their host that they needed to continue their homeward journey the next morning. He explained that their private ride home had already left Switzerland, but arrangements would be made to catch commercial flights. The departure was friendly enough and the Americans felt as if they had done the right thing. Do not overstay a welcome at this stage of business.

The flight the next morning, however, was not on to the US, but rather to Marseille, France. Some planning and plotting the night before had enabled the travelers to be received at ITER, the world's largest fusion project, in Aix-en-Provence.

Harold, again, had set this up. Now that Brian and Henry had a small, working knowledge of future power possibilities, he asked that they visit this operation.

"And pay close attention! You will be smack in the middle of one of the few international science projects. Over thirty countries have gotten together and contributed science and money."

The International Thermonuclear Experimental Reactor (ITER) was practically a tourist attraction. They began to notice road signs directing them to their destination as soon as they left the Marseille airport in their rental car. The complex was massive. Construction was obvious at different locations, with a large dome being the focal point. They later learned that this critical component, called the tokamak (a Russian acronym) is part of the most complex experiment ever designed.

The ITER Agreement was signed by China, the E.U., India, Japan, Korea, Russia, and the US. These countries funded it, but not always with money. The ingenious agreement called for most of the contributions to be in the form of completed components. This approach meant that each country was vested in the project and shared in the intellectual property generated by the project. In addition, the scientific and industrial communities of each member were prepared for what came after ITER – the actual prototype fusion reactor that would create electricity on a grand-scale.

The next two days disappeared into the guided tour that was just as detailed as their previous tour at Greifswald. This location had a much larger staff. Brian felt comfortable with the scope and speed of their comprehensive observations. As they said their formal good-byes, Brian asked one more question of their guide

"You did say that this project will cost upwards of twenty billion dollars, yet this machine won't produce electricity?"

"That's right," came the answer. "All we are doing is proving it can be done. We want to bring the vacuum chamber up to 150 million to 300 million degrees and energize the atomic particles, encouraging them to release huge amounts of energy."

Yes, Brian thought, he had heard that part right. He also thought that the gathering of scientists at Urgent could sort through the problems much more quickly. Then the materials group would be able to build a working reactor by taking the test platform and constructing a prototype that made electricity. So what if it looks a little unrefined?

The construction model used at the ITER project was quite creative. Various countries built and had proprietary control over a piece of the large puzzle. Without total cooperation the structure would be just that, a skeleton structure. When they did cooperate and bring the dream to reality, each country could build its own version, with the help of the other countries that would build the component they owned.

On the trans-Atlantic flight from Marseille to Montreal, Canada, Henry and Brian compared notes on their understanding of the events of the past week. Not just the technology but the testing process and obedience to scientific rigor both projects practiced. The minutia was a luxury the Urgent long-range plans may not enjoy. They knew Harold Knight felt, as they did, that there was no time for luxuries.

During dinner at the Montreal airport Brian's secure phone silently vibrated. He checked the caller ID on his wrist device, then answered. Speaking with Tom Lacey in Urgent's research office was not unusual. Having the call initiated by Lacey was.

"Yes, Tom."

Since he heard only one side of the dialog Henry did not try to interpret but proceeded to finish the meal. He knew Brian would fill in the details.

To everyone involved in this project, Tom Lacey was known as the ultimate security *officer,* although this was not an official title. He had built and coordinated a system that managed to monitor the physical and electronic workings of all-things Urgent. The Wind River Indian Reservation (which was now a much larger nation than 10 years ago) was entirely Lacey's responsibility.

He took communication security seriously.

"Tom Lacey just told me that my name popped up on a Europol inquiry, started in Germany," said Brian. "His computers red-flagged a message from an operative in Germany to a person in France that then followed us to ITER and back to Marseille. Now, we have a shadow here in Montreal and some curiosity about the executive jet on the tarmac that has come to pick us up.

"Lacey wants to know if we care to talk with these guys now or wait until they board the plane."

"Europol?" queried Henry.

"I don't get it either. Let's fix this now. It's still light, we just ate, and we can sleep on the jet."

Finding the location for airport security was not hard. Locating the right person to talk with was. Suspects just do not jump the gun and walk into the security office before they are even spotted at an airport. The security officers that had the descriptions and photographs were all on alert and spread throughout the facility.

It took a while to get all parties in the same room, after which the serious questions revolved around how the suspects knew they were being monitored. Canadian law enforcement had no reason to be familiar with Urgent, its sophisticated electronic systems, nor the personnel. This education took a few convincing phone calls and a lot of talking.

Tom Lacey was at his desk in Urgent when the demonstration started. At the Canadians' insistence, Tom and the head of Montreal airport security were deeply involved in a show and tell contest for over a half hour. As a test, Tom (in the US) was asked to provide the exact gate of each aircraft on the ground in Montreal at that moment – he did. He added the little-known facts of which aircraft had a mechanical problem that would lead to a departure delay. This was not convincing.

Brian Knight interrupted the security chief: "Tom, I am being interviewed by M I C H…" and he carefully spelled the officer's full name as it appeared on a plaque on the wall. Seconds after the spelling was completed, Lacey's team pinpointed the security chief's home, car license plate number, and mother's parents' address. There was no more doubt in the accuracy and capability of their resources. Then it was Brian's turn to inquire as to why they were flagged in the first place.

The Canadians proceeded to electronically back track through France, into Germany (where everyone was now asleep), and finally to the Davos airport. The inquiry was begun when registered passenger Brian Knight did not deplane in Davos. His passport was tagged when he entered Germany, and they immediately located and followed this suspect that had suspiciously entered the country. Due to the importance of the attendees at the World Economic Forum, security was on high alert and all private plane traffic was monitored as closely as the scheduled airlines.

"Problem solved?" asked Henry, looking at the security chief.

"Sorry about the intrusion," he replied. "I have cleared your flight out with customs."

Henry was anxious to get out of Montreal.

SIX

— • • — • • • • • • • — • • —

The atmosphere around his world was not the same. Brian Knight was missing his assistant, Brittany. It was only natural that she wanted to work near her lover. The fact that the lover was Brian's brother was not the issue; it was the down-to-earth help she had provided while he flew around the continent.

Although tough to admit, he had been fooling himself. He had almost convinced himself he could handle this alone, until last month's trip to Urgent to brainstorm about the nuclear reactor. Almost! He told himself he had better find a replacement.

There was no easy way to advertise for help with a venture that was top-secret. He placed a phone call to Marina Whitehorse on the chance that she might have an idea. After all, she recruited other bigwigs.

Her advice was exactly what he needed. He sent a text to his former employer and asked for a short meeting. He wondered why he hadn't thought of that.

Brian and Steven agreed to leave the Northwest since neither wanted to be interrupted or have the reason for a meeting misinterpreted. They had chosen a two-day mini-vacation at a hot springs hideaway in Montana. The resort had a runway, for small aircraft only. Each took his own jet to Bozeman, where a prearranged rental car met them. Brian drove them to the resort.

Early morning hours were spent on business that could not wait. All other time was devoted to catching up. Brian had long wanted to update his former boss, Steven. The philanthropist wanted to hear first-hand of the successes and failures of the fusion reactor project.

"Politically, it has been quite interesting," said Brian. "The Nuclear Regulatory Commission gets into the act with all projects that involve nuclear reactors, we needed to clear this with them. As you know, our contacts in Washington, DC are such that many of our requests are rubber-stamped. It was not that simple this time around.

"There is a small cadre of young politicos that are convinced the Native American growth at the Wind River Reservation is some sort of conspiracy. No one can pin down what they are conspiring to do, but obstruction is the name of the game. We ran into one of those at our last committee meeting. Thankfully, Tom Lacey had his eyes on this guy and was able to smooth the way by tactfully getting him to resign in order to serve on a more prestigious committee in Congress."

"I must compliment your resourcefulness," said Steven, "The escapade in Alabama, if I can call it that, was pure genius. You set that in motion four years ago and only recently did I get confirmation that those greedy businessmen you punished have actually been hiring entry level workers at a better wage, and three union shops have negotiated better benefits. Heretofore there had been no successful negotiations for over a decade."

"Thanks," said Brian. "We have some creative and enthusiastic young talent that spent long hours designing and performing that operation. They get the credit, and I will pass along your appreciation. As you know, our involvement in that is not common knowledge. Most of the public believes Alabama had the perfect storm of traffic, and that thinking is to our advantage.

"Speaking of young people, I wanted to get your input on a different situation. You will recall my young associate, Brittany. You may also know that she recently relocated to Wyoming. I need a replacement."

The conversation over coffee and dessert was a review of the duties performed by Brian's previous assistant. They discussed the extreme security needs and the flexibility required to keep up with Brian's ever-changing travels and schedule.

Steven agreed that they couldn't just advertise this position. "What if you talked with my sister?"

"Excuse me?"

"We spoke just the other day about her future at

the foundation. Not career wise, she is set for life, but she needs a challenge. She has fine-tuned the administrative systems in the foundation to the point where they are self-operational. Now what does she do? I know she is a little older than Brittany, but she's also carrying a maximum-security clearance and no need for a heavy salary.

"You know she's a widow. Her family consists of just the two children, only one of whom is still at home. He is enrolled in college and is fully capable of doing his own laundry when he does fly home between quarters. What if I get you two together to chat about it?"

Brian just nodded. He had met Myrlene years ago at a company picnic. She was rumored to be caring for her ill husband, yet even with those responsibilities she was pleasing, vibrant, and energetic. The pride she shared in her brother's successful computer company was contagious. She admitted she did not know what the company did, but knew her brother had worked long and hard to get where he was. The generation before him was not wealthy. Her older brother was.

"She must be 45 or so by now," Brian remarked after performing some mental gymnastics.

"Actually, more like 48, but she can still work rings around all her peers. If you think you can keep up, I will ask her to contact you."

"Sure," was Brian's last word before adjourning to the fireplace and cigars.

Breakfast at the rustic retreat was still a formal event. The white tablecloths were in place, and half the tables were occupied at the time Brian Knight awoke. He wanted coffee but not in his room. When he arrived at the dining room he found Steven and Myrlene seated at a table near the far wall.

She rose to meet him. "After Steven called, I couldn't wait." She was still beautiful. Taller than average and with a business-like short hair style; even in jeans and a plaid shirt she was pleasant to his eye.

"I'm glad you didn't," he murmured. They both sat down. She poured him coffee.

Having a working knowledge of the foundation as a common bond, Brian brought her up to speed by mid-morning. They had adjourned to the lounge near the fireplace to continue his story, and returned to the dining room for lunch. When Steven later joined them, he picked up on the spark in the conversation and had to smile. It was obvious he was missing one full time member of his foundation staff.

During lunch the three discussed the various aspects of Urgent's growth. They settled each topic when the progress and name of an overseer of each was briefly summarized. Fusion energy was mentioned as one looming and important element in future plans.

"It might be a good idea to swing by Urgent and pick my brother's brain," observed Brian. He made a quick phone call and told her they were all set for the next day. It was time to relax. Myrlene asked the concierge to round up three horses. "Make it two," Steven interjected, "I have work to do."

The resort was nestled in the wide valley of the Yellowstone River, north of the park itself. Behind the cabins, and away from the river, the land rose to meet a ridgeline that ran along the back of the resort's property. Actually, this was open range with no fencing and miles of equestrian trails. While they slowly rode the crest of the ridge, the conversation turned to Urgent. Not just the future of the fusion reactor, but the agricultural experiments and the complex reforestation via ForCI.

That Institute seemed of particular interest to Myrlene. Brian asked her why.

"You talk about the need for foreign students to change places with American university pupils. I seem to recall a friend of ours mentioning a national program that encourages that very type of exchange. I can get more information if you wish."

"Sure," replied Brian. She expertly brought her mount to a halt and took out her satellite phone.

Brian made a mental note about the speed with which this woman acted on decisions or agreements. Myrlene ended her conversation and advised, "It's called COST, for Consortium for Overseas Student Teaching.

"While the exchange arrangement revolves around student teaching, what interests me is the oversight on each end. The receiving university lines up a home stay for the incoming student. They are registered in classes, get credits and all other college perks.

"The exchange students also attend English speaking events and spend a lot of time in the public schools that partner with the local university. Call it a full immersion type of exchange. My friend feels the success of this program would encourage any participating institution to experiment with a larger, longer program such as the ForCI project we were talking about.

"This international exchange does not take place in all countries, but does have a presence on almost all continents. At this level, the education world is not that large. I would imagine we might investigate any community we deem desirable and the good folks at COST could open some doors for us."

They continued riding in silence, enjoying the wide view of the Yellowstone River Valley. It was then Brian's turn to stop his horse.

"Tell me about your interest in education," he said as he turned toward her.

"It is not so much the education," she responded, "as it is the exchange concept. I feel quite strongly about young people having some type of international experience. Being on the receiving end of a student exchange counts. But doing the traveling to a different country is the best. We need young people to be well educated and part of that learning needs to be of a different culture.

"They don't need to enjoy the food or the weather, but they should have some photos from, and a pen-pal in, a foreign land. The forestry consortium must fulfill that dream for quite a few students. I can imagine that graduates of the program that sent them overseas are looking to replicate that enjoyable time for others. Do we know how many returned to teach in the same program?"

Brian indicated he did not know the answer to her question, but would find out tomorrow.

They rode slowly back to the lodge in silence.

The following morning, Brian and Myrlene took his aircraft to Urgent. A waiting shuttle retrieved their luggage and transported them to the far side of the canyon, and the stairwell closest to the underground guest quarters.

"My brother Harold will join us for lunch. First let's get you comfortable in your room and acquainted with the area."

Brian escorted her to the guest quarters. Then they peeked into the adjacent underground scientists dining room. He explained that this large, comfortable room was the nearest neutral, semi-private space within which meet – plus the coffee pot was handy. They returned to the guest suite, whereupon he excused himself.

"I'll see you at that table in one hour."

The food in the belowground dining room did not disappoint. The conversation was equally as engaging. Once Hal understood he had an intelligent audience, he got more detailed in his description of the facility and elaborated on its accomplishments. He was obviously proud, and had reason to be.

When the topic changed to energy production, Hal offered to lead the tour of the complex. His personal electric cart was in a tunnel adjacent to the dining area. Not wanting to waste time going to the surface, he ushered the group to one of many wall-mounted closed-circuit monitors.

He was able to access the feed from any of the surface cameras. They were told of the power produced by the solar system and the wind driven turbines, as the surface cameras panned to those features.

They returned to the cart and drove to the control room of one hydroelectric dam, stopping at a glassed-in viewing area to see the turbines. Hal chose not to get any closer due to the noise made by the machines. Then they were off to visit the nuclear reactor.

"We have been working on nuclear energy for a short time now. Our progress is rapid, thanks to some connections I have and a field trip my brother took last year into Europe and the depths of Europol."

Brian laughed, Hal grinned and Myrlene just shrugged. The escapade with the Canadian airport officials was briefly explained to her.

"Our reactor is medium sized," he continued, "but can be scaled either up or down. As of yet we do not have foolproof evidence of that statement, but my calculations are usually right. The spherical object you see behind that glass will soon be producing enough power to launch our space vehicles. Beyond that, we have plans to lease reactors to other countries."

Myrlene raised a quick eyebrow in Brian's direction, then turned to address her guide. "What - are you planning to drive to the capital of Uzbekistan and ask the prince if he wants to rent a reactor?"

"I know it sounds a little fishy, but our long-range plans call for helping undeveloped nations solve their poverty, deforestation, and education problems by bringing them electricity. We will encourage them to stop burning coal and wood and switch to alternate sources of energy. When solar and wind won't deliver reliable power and dams cannot be built, fusion may be the only option.

"Obviously, there is a labor component in such projects. These nations can use the work. Also, we can use the same living modules provided to the laborers as classrooms for their children. You know we place major emphasis on the education of the next generation. We must never lose sight of that fact.

"It may be a hard sell to convince a corrupt, selfish dictator to sign on to saving the planet, but we will attack those issues on a case-by-case basis. We have technology, peer pressure, international networking, and unique gadgets on our side, plus a psychological edge.

"We don't want the credit or headlines: just the deal."

SEVEN

— •— —— •——• •—

While in a geology class in Madison, the young man overheard a group of three classmates talking about a formation out in Wyoming. Not a rock formation, as normally discussed in the class, but the formation of a community. The college students were coordinating their schedules. They were planning to attend a lecture given by a hot young scientist, rumored to be an underground recruiter for a village on the Wind River Indian Reservation.

Sandy Watson was not taking geology class because of an interest in the subject. He needed to get a couple of quick credits in order to graduate from the University of Wisconsin. With excellent grades he wanted to be a valuable commodity upon graduation. In fact, his advisor recommended that he stay and attend grad school. "Not an option," Sandy had said.

URGENT LAUNCH

As a good faith gesture, the advisor had allowed him to load this last term with lightweight classes. His next stop would then be anywhere out of state. This Wyoming location would be perfect.

His plans for the following evening were now refocused. A scientific endeavor, or even science-related education, was worth considering. All the better if the village was not well known.

The young man had grown up in Wisconsin, and had traveled throughout the state. Any native could not help but be impressed with the forests. Sandy had been enthralled. An active Boy Scout for years, he had learned about the outdoors. He knew tree types by sight, which plants were edible, which branches made the softest bedding. Forestry classes at UW-Madison had been a welcome extension of his scouting education.

A little digging provided the information for tomorrow's lecture: Harold Knight was speaking in the Materials Science Center. Sandy arrived early for the lecture. The talk was unforgettable, although less about trees than science in general. The brief conversation he initiated after most of the audience had left was life changing. Hal had been his usual engaging and entertaining self. Sandy had found his destination and his destiny.

With only a few months remaining in Madison, he decided to slowly liquidate his assets. The off-campus apartment he shared with a roommate did not contain many belongings. College students did not equip their rental units with anything of value. He did have some money in the bank and an emergency fund his parents rarely checked on. The limit on that credit card would provide him with running money at the last minute.

After he sold the car, he tended to stay closer to home than usual. He told his roommate, and anyone else who got curious, that his heavy class schedule required heavy studying. No one was to know his activities, or his destination. He remained vague when questioned about post-graduation plans. The possibility of attending grad school was always the perfect answer.

With one week of classes left the partying schedule on campus became frenetic. Sandy's entire social circle was locked in a celebration routine that resembled a traveling circus. He made arrangements to take some final exams early, packed one suitcase and just slipped out of sight. He did not walk to get the hard-earned diploma. He did not say good-bye to anyone. He vanished.

Working at her computer, Brittany Odom heard the office door open. The figure of a man entering the room reflected on the monitor screen. She turned around to see a young, handsome, and tired looking man.

"I'm trying to find Harold Knight," he said.

It was a rocky introduction. Sandy did not know what he really wanted, and Brittany did not yet feel comfortable with her new job in Urgent. She had only recently agreed to leave her office in Washington State and work closer to her Harold. So far, every day was filled with new interruptions, and they all seemed dramatically important.

Sandy's days were filled with hope and resolve. He would remain invisible, and he would get away from Wisconsin.

"I met him at a lecture in Wisconsin," he continued, "and he told me to look him up if I ever got to this town. Didn't he say something about an old-fashioned pager – or paging system?"

Brittany was more at ease after that last question. Very few knew that the earth and underground structure blocked most radio signals, and part of local communication was an elaborate P.A. system. She agreed to find Harold Knight.

Security and protocol dictated that Hal maintain a small, above-ground office. Having Brittany there made it seem like a real business location. It was convenient, but only a gesture to the expectations of outsiders. The real work was done at other workstations in various labs scattered throughout a labyrinth of subterranean facilities. Hal made his way to the surface.

He immediately recognized the bright young man from the aura of determination and the shock of white in one of Sandy's eyebrows. After the usual pleasantries, they retired to the adjacent office and closed the door.

Admitting that he had no idea why he felt so drawn to Urgent, Sandy became embarrassed and began stumbling for words. Harold took the lead and spent the next half hour explaining the basics of Urgent and the groundwork that built this scientific community. When he touched on reforestation, he noticed the change in posture and attention of his guest.

This is worth pursuing he thought.

Slowly, Sandy's story unfolded, revealing a bright and dedicated mind on a collision course with his powerful, political father. After demanding confidentiality, he began to explain how he was certain that the group of far-right politicians in his home state, and including his dad, had been bought.

"Ever since I was ten years old, I have tried to understand the stance my dad and his cronies have taken on all big issues. Occasionally they would vote to improve life a bit for the average voter or to protect some insignificant area or animal. The larger issues, though, have always been driven the wrong way in my estimate. And I think my estimate is in line with the majority of voters.

"At first, I would ask about these votes at the dinner table. My curiosity seemed to make my father uneasy. He always changed the topic and confusing conversation ensued. As I got older, I would pin Dad down in the car and receive a raised voice reply that left no room for dialog, or even a simple explanation. For a while I would throw tantrums and only receive punishment in response but no real political answers. It was a typical father/teen-age son dialog.

"The ultimate offense came two years ago when the state governor lost an election to the other party. It seemed to me that the state might get back on track. That optimistic view was shattered when the outgoing politicians from the ousted party passed a piece of legislation that stripped the incoming party of its ability to govern. My father and friends had quickly, quietly, and substantially weakened the incoming politicians. That was it," the young man said.

Regardless of legality, it was pure, rotten sportsmanship, and politics, in Sandy's eyes, was not sport. The majority of voters sent a message that they did not appreciate the governing style of the folks in power and had voted for new leaders, not new rules. They wanted new leaders playing by the same rules.

It was at that moment that Sandy had decided he would never speak to or even visit his father again. He would vanish and live a worthwhile life. Sure, he felt sorry for his older sister, but she was married and now carried her husband's name. As for his mom – who knew. That was two years ago. Now that he had graduated, he could fulfill his dream.

As far as he knew, no one knew where he was. Obviously, his father had access to investigators, but Sandy had traveled using only cash and had not activated a single piece of electronics. He had even taken the chip and battery out of his phone.

"I know it's unusual, and I might sound a bit unstable, but with all sincerity I can tell you I am not going back. In our earlier conversation you mentioned reforestation. I am a student of trees and forests, with a degree to prove it. Is there any chance we can combine my interests and your issues?"

"Do you have any place to stay?" asked Harold.

After a few seconds of macho "I can sleep in an alley," Hal led the young man downstairs and along a wide hall. The guest room, as he called it, was more like a suite. A kitchen was the only thing missing but moments later the two men ventured into the scientists dining room.

"Order from the menu and eat what you want. No money changes hands down here, and there are no hours. Most of these folks in white coats are scientists. I'll meet you in the guest room in two hours, after you eat and shower. Then we'll see what we will see." He left Sandy standing alone at the table.

Returning to his office, Harold asked Brittany if she had heard most of that conversation. She had because the office and anteroom were wired for audio.

"Give Tom Lacey a call, get him that rough image we got from the closed circuit in the guest room, and find out what you can about a Wisconsin politician that's likely to be extremely conservative and have a young son."

Back in the guest room, the two began by talking about trees. The recent graduate carried most of the conversation when Hal led him into discussion about the Tongass National Forest, the beetles, and the efforts to save that land. His knowledge of the conifers was an asset to Hal's understanding of what they were facing.

When sharing the names of the parties involved in this project, Sandy winced at the mention of academia. Not lost on Harold, he glossed over the importance of the university.

The Tongass forest was owned by the United States and managed with the blessing of the Native Americans. In exhibiting typical curiosity, Hal wanted locations and content of other wooded portions of the planet that needed similar help. Sandy was able to name the surviving species in the jungles, rain forests, equatorial areas, and savannas. It was impressive to follow the mental check list of the young expert as he moved from continent to continent. He knew the species to be found in the various regions but had no knowledge of how much had been deforested. Harold Knight decided he could use this guy's help.

"OK, Sandy, I've got two projects that would benefit from your talents. The one that is the best fit is actually in the planning stages. We are not organized at this time and don't need another body adding to the confusion. More about that later.

"The research that is currently underway, and does have room for new eyes and hands, is just down this hall. Would you like to check out the agriculture laboratory?"

Just down the hall was closer to half mile, but when they entered the Ag Lab Sandy knew it was worth the walk. He marveled at the expansive, clean, well-lit space, and well-defined agricultural experiments. Hal introduced him to the lead technician and then stepped back.

Harold always enjoyed watching a scientist explain the chemistry and concerns about the project at hand. The newcomer was obviously asking the right questions, to the point that they both turned away from Hal. He overheard their conversation about the world not being prepared to protect vulnerable communities from food shortages.

The Intergovernmental Panel on Climate Change (IPCC) had emphasized that human activity was to blame, ergo only human activity could fix it. There was further talk about research confirming a reduction in nutrition from rice if grown in an atmosphere of excessive CO_2. Such rice contains significantly lower levels of protein, thiamine and riboflavin. In addition, infants and pregnant women were at risk when levels of zinc and selenium fell, as they were expected to.

They thanked the staff member for her time and returned to the guest room. It would be useless to talk further about Sandy's interest in that type of work, obviously, the new arrival was totally enthralled. Just as obvious was the housing dilemma. Hal explained that Sandy could stay in this guest room for a while longer but needed to try to solve this problem. The staff bulletin board was just down the hall, and the electronic classifieds offered options as well.

"Please meet me in the office upstairs in the morning. I'll get there around nine. Brittany will have some papers for you to go over, and don't worry, we can work around your need for anonymity."

It had only been two or three years since another young man had arrived requesting anonymity. Hal had received no negative feedback about those arrangements. He trusted that Lacey and Fitz could hide this kid as well. At the moment he had other issues that seemed to dampen his enthusiasm for the newcomer.

Five or six of the senior members of the community had just been involved in a last-minute diversion operation in New York state. Their mission was to confuse and interrupt communication between a former associate of Fitzpatrick's at the bureau and his client. They were successful but the Lake Chautauqua detail had not been fully debriefed. Not that out-of-area shenanigans were Hal's area of responsibility, but the philanthropists and decision makers were scheduled for a serious meeting soon, and he had a spot on the agenda.

Harold Knight did not want any surprises when he met with that group, which included the former President of the United States.

EIGHT

--- --.. . -. - --- -.

Captain Dan was finishing a beer in the Red Dog Saloon in Juneau. Perhaps the alcohol affected his thinking, but he kinda' liked the kid's plan. FJ and Sara had cornered the seasoned skipper at his favorite watering hole and wanted to talk privately.

"We are concerned about the likelihood that those guys we spotted yesterday near Read Island are about to do some logging," said Sara. "FJ and I watched them scope out the lay of the land and the soundness of some pilings that march right up to the shore. FJ has been in contact with the researchers he knows and was told that the boat they used yesterday belongs to some shady characters."

Signaling the need for another round, Cap'n Dan asked,

"Why do you care?"

FJ burst out, "Are you kidding? We have put together an elaborate partnership with the Alaska University, an Oregon university and two Native American tribes in an attempt to save trees and the planet. Why do we care?

"We're trying to stop a billion bugs from eating all those trees you see, and you wonder why we want to stop some guys with chainsaws. Come on !!"

Sara noticed the twinkle in Cap'n Dan's eye, "FJ - I think you've just been played."

The skipper smiled, Sara did too, FJ paused then released a sheepish grin.

"Tell me more about your plan," said Dan.

The idea was to return to that waterway and block access to the pilings with a partially sunken barge. Sink the barge at an angle that prevented the pilings and the surface of the barge from being used. The big question was the availability of a scrap barge that could still float. Dan said there was one "a bit up the channel, towards Skagway."

The old salt that owned it had been hurt a few years back and was lying around his cabin waiting to die. Giving him some money and something to do might benefit all concerned. They agreed it was worth a try. The group decided to spend that night on the skipper's freighter and motor up Lynn Canal the next day.

The young folks could have taking the project's runabout out of winter storage. Instead they opted to contact the local boat yard and rent a comfortable cruiser for the day. Two cold hours north on the frigid canal, near Lena Cove, they spotted the barge tied up to a short pier. They tied up on the other side.

Since the small group was unannounced, Cap'n Dan sounded the ship's horn a few times and they climbed up the ladder to the pier. A rundown house sat at the far end, up on a narrow knoll.

Old Man Newman was well known by the "water rats" on the Juneau docks. His coffee was not much but his interest in getting away for any reason was making the trip worthwhile. He was up for anything.

"Sure, you can use the barge. You can have it if ya' want it," although he offered a word of caution in that it was a spud barge.

This defined it as having tall poles in the corners that could be lowered to stabilize the platform. The spuds, when lowered to contact the bottom, stopped any rocking and simplified loading. Cap'n Dan thought spuds would also make it easier to partially sink the vessel and raise it later. The spuds presented no problem to this mission.

Newman and Dan consulted the tide charts to decide when they might hook up the tug and allow the current to work to their advantage. Since timing was the big unknown, they agreed that tomorrow morning's tidal swing would be perfect.

"Go back to Juneau, get the tug and be back here by four in the morning," Newman ordered.

As they approached the pier early the next morning, Cap'n Dan switched on his powerful emergency flashlight. Old Man Newman was sitting on the dock next to a duffel bag. The skipper began barking orders to FJ and Sara while helping Newman on board. They were underway in less than ten minutes.

By noon, the group was close enough to Farragut

Bay to send up a drone. The old barge owner had never watched such aerial cameras at work and was fascinated by the maneuverability, speed and clarity of the picture. The drone flew over the collection of pilings that was their destination and revealed the all clear long before the tug entered the mouth of the bay.

The tug powered back near the pilings. FJ dropped a kayak over the side and asked Sara to toss him "that forward line." The crew had earlier prepared large ropes (lines) they would use to secure the barge to the pilings. FJ paddled off towards one specific piling, so Sara dropped another kayak over the side and set off to explore the shore. Cap'n Dan prepared to lower both spuds on the outboard corners, and open two valves to allow water into the barge.

Newman motioned to FJ to return to the barge and grab a second line to tie off on a second piling. He wanted two points of attachment to control the gradual sinking of the barge in case one of the spuds slipped on the bottom. FJ boarded the rusty barge to survey the piling arrangement from a more advantageous height.

Sara found an opening through which she could drag her boat out of the water and, in the process, noticed a tree with a white dot on it. Obviously applied by spray paint, the eye-level mark was on other trees as well. Her curiosity kicked in now and she looked for a pattern and wondered why these particular trees were marked: height maybe, or ease of felling?

Her gaze settled on the rugged forest floor as she

searched the openings between trees to determine where one might land these large firs. A shaft of sunlight created a small reflection off something shiny. Sara reached down to retrieve the object - then realized, too late, that it was the trigger for a trap. Her reflexes were quick, but not quick enough. The trap closed on her hand, just above the fingers. She let out a truly blood-curdling scream.

With little thought for his own safety, FJ ran to the wheelhouse and pulled the rifle off the bulkhead. With the other hand he yanked the fire ax from its mount and slipped the lanyard of the walkie-talkie over his head. He jumped into his kayak and headed for the shriek.

"Keep up the noise," he yelled. "Sara, keep screaming."

Five minutes of furious paddling brought him around a slight bend in the shoreline and within fifty yards of her. With rifle at the ready, he jumped into the cold water and ran to shore, pulling the little boat as if it weighed nothing. He threw the kayak near a massive tree and was at her side almost instantly.

A quick survey of the situation and he grabbed the walkie-talkie while helping Sara lean against his knee. "Dan, Dan, come in Dan."

"Yea kid."

"Do not open the valves. Repeat, do not open the valves. We need a place for a rescue chopper to land. Also, can you reach the Coast Guard on the ship's radio or should I use my satellite phone?" asked FJ.

"I'll let ya know."

FJ dropped the radio and asked Sara to hold his coat. He ripped both sleeves off his shirt, helped her put the thick coat collar in her mouth, and picked up the fire ax.

"Sara, this ax will pry the trap open enough for you to get your hand out. As soon as we can, we will use those cloth pieces as wraps for your wounds and then sit down for a minute.

"We want to calm you down and survey the situation. If I do anything that hurts, bite down hard."

She was wide-eyed and probably going into shock, but she nodded.

Once freed, FJ examined it and determined that her mangled hand was useless. Three of her four fingers had no structure. The trap had broken the skin in two places. Blood loss was not major, but looked life threatening as it always did. He covered it all with the cloth pieces and reached for the radio in response to a call.

"FJ - come in FJ."

"I'm here."

"I got through to the Coast Guard and they can send a helicopter. We have been reminded that only life-threatening situations are free," Cap'n Dan squawked.

"Get 'em in the air damn it, and I need some way to get two people back on board. A one-person kayak is all we have."

"Got ya' covered," Dan replied. "I've already got the life raft standing by. It holds four. I'll meet you where you went ashore."

"Oh, and Dan," he added, "figure out a way to lower those two spuds on the front so the chopper can land. Cut the towers if you need to."

"OK kid."

FJ had Sara wrapped in his jacket and gently set her on the ground, with her head in his lap. Her breathing had become regular. When the bright orange rubber raft came into view, he asked her to join him for another boat ride; that brought a small smile.

Her evacuation went smoothly. The first aid kit on board supplied enough antiseptic and gauze to cleanse the wound. FJ made radio contact with the local hospital, and he contacted Urgent to better her chances of expert, and hurried, medical care.

After the Coast guard helicopter lifted off, the men set about to scuttle the old barge. FJ sent the drone aloft and again found that there was no boat traffic in the area. Cap'n Dan closed the valves when the edge of the barge started to get wet. The idea was not to completely submerge it. He wanted to be able to refloat the massive steel vessel by driving the spuds deeper and pumping air into the flooded chambers.

They left the area, but not before posting the No Trespassing signs they had prepared for this occasion. FJ stapled them to the pilings on either side of the barge and taped them to all sides of the barge itself.

Two days later a large ocean-going tug began a two-barge tow from the Petersburg area to the south. An experienced eye would notice the decks littered with logging apparatus, and see too much tugboat for these inland waters. The boat was big enough to sleep and feed eight. It would take the large tug a day to reach its destination, during which the northward progress of the flotilla was monitored by numerous aircraft.

Cap'n Dan had spread word throughout his network of old-timers that some pirate logging was being suspected in the Farragut Bay area. All local bush pilots were part of this informal rural network. Naturally, they were known to the pilots of the scheduled airlines. Hundreds of eyes had focused on that particular portion of Frederick Sound and the Tongass National Forest.

When the tug rounded the point marking the entrance to Farragut Bay, the barges in tow were pulled in tight in anticipation of a quick tie-up. It was immediately obvious that no piling or dock was available. In fact, it would be treacherous to try to secure this tow to that lopsided, half-sunken wreck of a barge. There were too many sharp edges and no level decks.

The captain dispatched a raft to get a closer look and determine if beaching the barges was an option. The deckhands soon returned and pulled their small raft back on deck.

"Skipper. We'd better forget it and turn this load around. Those big No Trespassing signs have been posted by the Drug Enforcement Agency. We don't want anyone around here even thinking we have a part in running drugs. Let's get back to Petersburg."

A bush pilot at 10,000 feet watched as the huge tug tried to make a U-turn inside the South Arm of Farragut Bay. He sent a radio message to Cap'n Dan at the Red Dog Saloon in Juneau. Only a select few knew why the old skipper was laughing out loud.

On board the retreating south-bound tug there was a brief conversation about retrieving the chain of animal traps they had set down a few days back. Since the traps were not traceable, the crew felt it better to concentrate on putting distance between themselves and that part of Alaska.

They would never know what animal they had already caught.

NINE

•— •—•• •— —— • —•• •—

Brian had told Hal they were expecting a visitor to land within the hour. Harold Knight did not normally leave the subterranean lab when working, but Brian told him about Javier, and he was looking forward to this meeting. Hal spoke a quick "OK" into the wall-mounted speaker/mic and headed to the surface.

The airport at Urgent had been enlarged to receive jet aircraft. It could not handle the large commercial jets, but the smaller executive planes that required less runway. Hal and Brian were chatting over a cup of coffee when the wheels touched down and the hangar opened.

As the two men descended the stairs, Javier saw Brian and brightened up. The four climbed into the 4-wheel drive car after introductions were made, and drove to the mill compound. Ethan Linn had never been in Wyoming. Today was hot and dry but it was a different heat than he experienced in Puerto Rico.

Brian suggested they cool down around a beer in the company cafeteria. They walked down a brightly lit hallway into the cavernous room. Although the room was large, the acoustics were such that noise was at a minimum. They sat at a corner table, removed from other workers. No one had an agenda, but Javier wanted to allow Ethan to discover what ForCI-Tongass was all about. Brian would carry that topic.

Even though in different hemispheres, the similarities in needs were becoming evident. The Forestry Consortium International partnership and the Tongass operation could be replicated in the tropics and around the Amazon. In fact, they needed to be.

"Popular wisdom is," said Ethan, "that it will be necessary to employ many strategies if man is serious about saving the planet. There is so much involved in climate change and we know the rate of that change is increasing. We also know that we do not know it all."

He was asked about the process of reforestation the International Institute of Tropical Forestry had success with. Ethan was also questioned about the research that went into replanting and the variety of species used. His curiosity about those items resulted in the need for a tour of some of the in-house facilities.

"Please let me make arrangements for a reception for us," Hal asked, and picked up a house phone on the wall. The conversation was short, and he escorted the group back to the car. It was a three-minute drive to a large, roll-up garage door which opened when he input a code on his smartphone. Once inside the building, they followed their guide to the elevator, descended, and walked to a brightly lit laboratory.

Bright green plants of different species and heights surrounded the central work platform. Standing next to the lab entrance was Sandy Watson, introduced only as Sandy.

"Mister Linn," said Sandy, "I am so pleased to meet you. I have researched the work of the Institute and admire the dedication of you and your staff. Our work here should be of interest to you. Our experiments even have application in the tropics. May I give you a short tour?"

"By all means," said Ethan.

"I trust this will be of interest to the Knight brothers as well since some of this is breaking news."

"During the past year there have been astonishing developments in the botanical community. One has to do with growth rate of plants, another with how much light they can use or need. What you see here are early results of some genetic engineering designed to improve the efficiency of photosynthesis.

"We all know that farmers and scientists have been working for years to improve plant yield. Fertilizers, crop rotations, and better watering have all been advances towards better results. Lately science has added gene manipulation to its arsenal.

"Many plants, such as that section of tobacco, those potatoes, soybeans, and corn you see, are the same age. Those obviously smaller plants are not altered while the others, growing alongside, have been genetically tweaked to modify photorespiration. That is the breathing of the plant which cleans out many of the toxins it does not need when converting CO_2 into sugars.

"We are testing these species because they waste cellular energy in the production and removal of one particular enzyme. When we genetically eliminate that long-chain chemical reaction that affects photo-respiration, the plant grows larger. You are looking at a 30% to 40% improvement in biomass – a better return than only adding light.

"During the final descent to our airport, you may have noticed the field of solar cells and array of mir-rors that are similar in size. What is harder to see is that they are built about six feet above ground.

"We have always been experimenting with plants of various types beneath those panels. Some block out all sunlight while others allow small shafts of light to reach the ground in a pre-determined pattern. This research is ongoing and complex," said Sandy.

"It may be too hot to visit our test field at this hour but suffice it to say we have growth comparison data that has encourages us to try more species. However, we have yet to experiment with trees. I expect that to be the topic of conversation during this visit. What might we do to help you in your reforestation efforts?

"Needless to say, we will compare the growth rate of trees versus plants and the rate of photosynthe-sis in the two species and how much oxygen each re-leases into the atmosphere. Into this mix we then will compare deciduous trees against evergreens. When the leaves fall from hardwood trees, they suspend photosynthesis for the season. Evergreens may go a bit dormant, but some O_2 action continues. We want to know much and how important it is?

"Finally, we should discuss where future experiments should take place. We know it is possible to build quality greenhouses that keep the weather out. Should we experiment in such an *otherworld* environment, or should we research tropical flora in the tropics and cold tolerant species farther north?"

Ethan was the first to speak, "Did you say 30% to 40% improvement? On a broad leaf plant, given the growth rate of an annual compared to that of a hardwood tree, I'd take the plant for a few years. However, the big question is altering the reproductive structure of future generations. When one tree can drop 1,000 seeds per season, how does that stack up against the plant's reproductive capacity? Any ideas?"

The over-emphasized shrug delivered by Sandy said it all. More research would be needed, particularly research on conifers. Those large evergreen forests had evolved for a good reason. Introducing a significant population of deciduous trees, regardless of how fast they grew, was not the ultimate answer. A return to lush, healthy coniferous grandeur was the goal.

Brian broke the silence with an offer to tour more of the complex. Once cocooned in the comfy, air-conditioned vehicle he drove the guests across the field of solar panels. Javier remarked on his observation that the panels did have a lot of room beneath them.

The group got closer to some experimental crop locations to get a better view, but the party stayed inside the cool 4-wheel drive. As they ventured back towards the steel mill, Brian explained the process of receiving military arms, melting them down, and fabricating world-class transmission towers. "That huge mill complex is all about repurposing military materials."

When asked about the power needed to operate such a factory, Harold explained the full complexity of power generation: reflector array, solar cells, wind turbines (in rows next to the solar panels) and hydro-electric dams.

The tour took them across the canyon. The group stopped at the Tribal Facilities building where they gathered around an area map. Harold used a laser pointer to direct their attention to areas of interest. He outlined the actual size of the underground research labs. He attempted to give scale to the labyrinth of cooling pipes that wound around the land, beneath the acres of solar array. Described as an experiment in warming the soil beneath the experimental crops they had seen earlier, he divulged nothing of Urgent's long-range plans.

They rearranged the furniture to face inwards and the four sat in rugged, well-worn chairs to discuss how to help each other. As an international organization, ForCI would welcome partners from another country. The Institute, as a spin-off of the Forest Service, was already an ad hoc member.

"In its stages of infancy," Brian explained, "we house the consortium at Oregon State University. The College of Forestry provides us a street address. That's about it. With conference calls, electronic visits, and computer managed finance means we don't need a full-time staff yet; that may change as we grow.

"Come to think of it, that will definitely change as we ramp up our grant writing. The federal agencies within this country have large budgets. The public is entitled to some of that in the interest of research. We have a handshake agreement with University of Alaska, a wink-and-a-nod with our participating Native American nations, and a letter of agreement with the US Forest Service. Many more players and we had better get some of this in writing."

Javier expressed concern about finding similar organizations to join the project in South America. He suggested an Amazon border area involving two governments would be a good starting point, and said he could find the names and numbers of neighboring landowners. Creating motivation for the indigenous people would be more of a challenge.

"The new administration in Brazil is still finding its way. We see a lot of uncertainty in their attempt to justify being in power. Proposals for new roads, dams, and infra-structure projects make for big headlines – but what's real? It may take some time to find a hidden entree into that dynamic and to earn respect.

"We have started on a small scale by hiring off-duty police as guards and setting up the university students with labs and living facilities. The students believe in climate change and are enrolled in programs that encourage environmental field work. Our intent is to grow this effort exponentially, but not without the government and other universities as willing participants. We are exploring all avenues and will keep ForCI informed."

Harold had been purposefully silent. He intended for his brother and Sandy to handle this tour and not only deliver information, but generate curiosity in Ethan and Javier. It wasn't going well. He decided to guide the conversation.

"The work that has begun in the Amazon is only the first phase. We have discovered that when you want to engage the big players, you need to bring some irresistible offer to the table. For the University, that might be an exchange program with a prestigious US institution.

"Take a look at the American colleges that offer great forestry programs and start thinking student swaps," Hal suggested. "In the sunbelt we have Florida, Georgia, and Auburn. We even have a California school, Cal Poly, that has a great reputation.

"What would it take for any or all of these schools to participate in an international forestry work-study exchange? Get some of the kids from the Tongass program to travel as advocates. They would love it.

"As for the government, that may take a different carrot. The fact that we are talking about cleaning up the air may not be a salient point. A better approach may be through economics. We know that the large-scale projects bring large-scale investments. We could prepare a report selling the financial impact on these smaller regions of the country. If the government is a bit third world, the report needs to be more focused on what's in it for the administration. Tweaking those figures would not be that difficult.

"Also, we should enter into agreements with respect to proprietary rights and profit from new innovations created in the host country. If we file patents, trademarks, or copyrights, we will share revenue.

"In these smaller countries we may be able to sell the networking story. What other countries might be sending students into the project? What other countries will be getting better acquainted with the host nation? New working relationships are often meaningful to smaller, poorer nations.

"Finally, please remember to investigate the feasibility of increased tourism as a result of better forest and wildlife management. All countries have the potential to promote their safeguarding of the environment. Within the ecosystem they are protecting is often a unique animal or two that the public wants to see. This type of tourism is clean and profitable. Do not lose sight of the fact that some of the target nations may already think that way."

Hal continued, "The Convention on International Trade in Endangered Species (CITES) is a United Nations collective. This Secretariat researches and consults on biodiversity – specifically wild flora and fauna. Every so often representatives of various nations gather at the Conference of the Parties (CoP) to revise their procedures and understandings of the Aichi Biodiversity Targets and the United Nation's sustainable development goals.

"The US had a presence at CoP21 in Paris when the trend to roll back coal-fired power plants was on the agenda. Most of countries agreed to act accordingly. We did not attend the next few meetings when these Paris goals were slowly eroded by our President and other world-wide dictators. However, all conservation efforts appeal to these member nations. Do your homework.

"Would it help if I lined up an advisor for you that is well known and respected in these circles?"

Ethan and Sandy both nodded. Although he sounded seasoned, Sandy was a new arrival at Urgent. Ethan was there as a guest and had no idea who could advise on international issues.

Harold used his secure, satellite phone to call the President.

TEN

— • — •　• — •　•　• • •　— • — •　•　— •　—

The agreement with the government was that the nation at Wind River would buy entire vehicles and items of military surplus. It was not the responsibility of the armed forces to ready these items for transport. Surplus was, by its definition, disarmed and available for scrap. The buyer had the responsibility of stripping the former items of war. Urgent had the manpower to do that.

When carloads of product had worked their way this deep into the mill, the individual components had been isolated. All glass was removed and placed in one warehouse, steel was in another, aluminum in a third. The materials scientists that worked in the research facilities beneath the mill knew the inventory and knew what they needed for their experiments. Harold Knight in his underground compound would place a call and obtain any materials the scientists could not find upstairs.

As the alloy engineers in the basement announced that they needed some old aircraft other workers would react. Computer organized supply lines commonly changed material sources and personnel could follow the revised delivery on their monitors. E-diagrams of the position of the train cars carrying various loads showed the route the discontinued product should take – push those cars up railroad spurs into warehouse X and bring the aircraft down different tracks from warehouse Y.

The computer organized it all, but people still did the driving of the small switching engines. People also had been disassembling the vehicles.

Four years before, when they first fired up the steel mill, the workers melted tanks and ship parts. This process yielded steel basic enough to build the first turbine towers. Urgent's first financial milestone was the nonrenewal of the contract with the outside steel supplier.

Recently they had been developing steel with which to build the improved wind turbine towers, a product they hoped to sell to commercially. They had been instructed to find a lighter material. Today's alloys on the test bench had too much weight for the size of the structure. They wanted to try a mixture with a bit more aluminum and a smattering of nickel. The latter would help the orientations of the minute grains and deter small cracks from becoming larger ones.

URGENT LAUNCH

The lab working on the transmission towers was in touch with other facilities farther to the east along the underground corridor. When a specific material was called for, each project sent an announcement to all others that an order was being placed. They all joined forces and combined orders to make the mill inventory control and production more efficient. Any lab could chime-in on the any order.

The tower team put out an inquiry about the supply of titanium at various locations. There was a chance they would try this material in the alloy structure being designed. A few hundred pounds had been found at the Cryo Lab experimenting on a superconductive material, that was plenty.

Design parameters for this scientific group called for minimizing magnetic losses along a typical railroad rail. Standard steel would rust, a reaction expressly forbidden in a project which required maximum conductivity and no corrosion or oxidation. These scientists knew the fusion reactor used ultra-magnetism to hold the plasma fuel in place. There was speculation that the rail project assigned to this lab was part of the vacuum chamber support system for the reactor, they were wrong.

Regardless, the scientists had been exploring the literature supporting their hypothesis of alloys with a rare earth concentration. The workers in these labs had years of education in gaining an understanding of where atoms needed to be in order to produce a material with very specific properties, and then figuring out how to get those atoms where they wanted them. One crew might be working on energy conservation, while energy transfer was another's goal; each requiring a different atomic arrangement within the materials being made.

The basic properties of the element lanthanum were the place to begin when massaging magnetism. Copper and lanthanum melt at nearly the same temperature, making the alloy production less complicated; in addition they occur naturally in abundance. Both aluminum and magnesium are often added to fine-tune strength and conductivity. The scientists working with the transmission tower team were not overly concerned about the alloy's melting point. Those researching the nuclear reactor were predominately worried about reaction to heat. Obviously conflicting studies were taking place in Urgent's labs.

One pressing question requiring an early answer for all experiments dealt with the ultimate use of the information. Does the research merely produce an answer to a scientist's question, or will the results be the basis to build a product? Harold Knight's researchers wanted an answer to that very question, in short, they wanted a bit more guidance.

The scientists sent word to Harold Knight that they needed to meet. Hal's wife Brittany was his research assistant, and coordinated his complicated schedule via his public office near the mill. For this gathering he invited them down to his office one floor below theirs. Hal's *compound,* as it was affectionately referred to, was an underground lab/office unique to the planet.

The inquisitive scientist had spent years watching, learning, and replicating, in all fields. Resulting projects and experiments, both successes and failures, haphazardly littered numerous work benches. Photographs and charts lined the walls. Yellow notes peppered all large illustrations. Gizmos hung from the high ceiling, some by visible means. The one clean area in the lecture hall sized room was the conference table in front of the large monitor.

At Hal's invitation, they all took seats at the table. After the team voiced concerns, Hal instructed the computer to secure the room and open the window. All glass except the screen went dark; he was about to unveil his vision.

"Anybody that can't keep a secret is invited to leave this room. I repeat, this is not to be shared."

The perpetually active visitors from the level above glanced at each other – nobody moved or spoke.

"This project will undoubtedly be announced within two years, but you need to know now. We are building a launch facility. Elsewhere in this scientific complex we have peers that are laboring over plans for the rockets. Others are contemplating the cargo and the payload. Your job is to get this endeavor, literally, off the ground."

As he paused the entire room was silent, as though the scientists were breathless.

"The spacecraft will be built and assembled one level below this one. You will have access to this cavern in the near future. Our people are fitting pieces together as we speak. The completed vehicles will be transported to the launch site by large platforms which will roll on rails, not unlike the ones you are planning, although this first journey along horizontal rails will have nothing to do with magnetism. Gravity will help us here. At the end of this short trip, though, the true test of your abilities comes into play.

"The package will transition to a vertical attitude and into launch position. Guided by three rails equally spaced around the vehicle that are in close contact with three steel grooves on the ship, our super-powerful magnets will be activated and pull the craft upward until it clears the top of the towers. We anticipate the towers will be at least one-thousand feet tall and that the magnets will have drawn the spacecraft through an ever-increasing rate of acceleration

"To allow this craft to escape earth's gravity, it will need an acceleration rate of almost fifteen times the pull of the earth. We would like an escape velocity of one-thousand feet per second and will try to program an acceleration rate that results in the vessel leaving the top of the towers at a speed of nearly eight-hundred miles per hour.

"Seconds after the rocket clears the towers and begins to decelerate, the compressed gas boosters will activate. Three double chamber tanks equally spaced around the rocket will simultaneously provide momentary boost forcing the projectile to increase speed. A few thousand feet later, the second chamber will deliver more thrust and we will be at sufficient altitude to achieve orbit.

"You are all visualizing the problems now, and I appreciate that.

-- We have the magnetism issue and the need for the strength to handle one thousand feet of compressed material.

-- Those rails must be arrow-straight.
-- How hot can they get when carrying that much signal?
-- How fast will an electric impulse travel through your rails?
-- What is the material inside the rocket that the magnets will react to?
-- How many lines of code will we need to accurately time these events?

"These are your concerns. I can only tell you that we have the brightest minds in the world down here and the best testing equipment we can find. I scour the planet searching for new science and the latest in materials. Rest assured, there is no facility that surpasses yours.

"Together, we can make this happen."

ELEVEN

— •• —•— •• •• •••

He felt the ground tremble. Sitting in his rolling desk chair, which had rubber casters, and on top of a soft plastic, non-skid mat, he had experienced the shudder. Bo Elliott stopped work and looked out the window. Everything looked normal – but he knew there would soon be a new normal.

Harold Knight had forewarned him of the test that morning. Most likely, all of Urgent knew since it was still a close-knit village. The nuclear chamber was beneath and east of him only a half mile, so his experience was different from those on the other side of the river. Bo thought that this first, one-second burn was not as earthshaking as he expected. The real thing might not be so bad.

The construction of the steel mill and research facilities on the edge of this canyon had not been going well ten years ago. Bo's subsequent involvement was quite accidental, yet ultimately fortuitous.

Throughout the years, Tom Lacey had occasion to visit numerous construction sites. He recognized a unique trait early in their relationship, that Bo had an inherent ability to coordinate materials and inventory. Bo could see the plans and understand the project. Lacey knew that the primary factor behind the steel mill's on-time completion was Bo Elliot. Once he turned the construction over to Bo, Lacey never looked back.

The steel mill along the canyon rim had been under construction for years. Large buildings had been erected to house the ovens and the nearby areas needed to pour steel and shape products. Beneath these buildings were pipes leading to the river, pipes coming from a dam on the river and pipes carrying water away from the river toward the massive temperature retention tank, the temptank. Above this tank the solar array and wind farm represented two huge examples of clean energy.

The solar array consisted of acres of conventional solar panels and thousands of mirrors. All these reflectors were simultaneously adjusted by a computer to *reflect* sunlight onto a specific tall tower, while the darker solar panels were constantly moved to face the sun as it traveled across the sky and *receive* the sunlight. Superheated liquid sodium was circulated through the tall towers, picking up heat produced by the reflected sunlight and later depositing that heat in the temptank.

When needed, normally at night, that heat would

boil water to create pressure to turn turbines to produce electricity. By design, the solar panels made electricity during the day. The wind turbines made electricity when they rotated, just like the hydroelectric dam always made electricity when water was passing through its turbines. Urgent was a massive, multifaceted power plant producing electricity for the steel mill and the village.

Following the canyon rim to the North of the steel mill was a complex of large, one story warehouse-type buildings. Personnel offices, locker rooms, maintenance facilities were all here. Also stored here was the heavy equipment needed to maintain the village and industrial section. A few of these structures housed the raw products, usually military surplus about to be melted. Other buildings were empty in anticipation of future needs.

Beneath these rectangular structures lay the research facility. Few residents knew the exact size of this subterranean portion of Urgent. The power needed to operate the labs for with various projects, was always available. By making electricity on-site, Urgent was off the grid. Without knowing the true nature of what was beneath the surface, one could not determine, or even guess at, how much research was being done in the various fields.

Lately, though, the new construction was a challenge even for Bo's talent and visualization. The newest fusion reactor was being built on the grounds. Halfway between the mill and the solar fields, the new machine would harness the energy created by nuclear fusion and create electricity. The strange fact was that it took more energy to make it than was produced in this new type of device. Bo didn't quite understand, even though it had been explained. It was not an even exchange.

When this aspect of Urgent's energy portfolio had been first brought to light, Brian Knight, his new assistant Myrlene, Harold Knight, and Marina Whitehorse had invaded Bo's secret office. Bo was responsible for the basic project grounds, Hal was the scientist, his brother Brian had investigated foreign locations, the two women were the right-hand *men* of two philanthropists. The confidential meeting had been scheduled for three days, which was a long time to keep these high-powered people cooped up.

Bo Elliott had erected a soundproof barrier at the interface where the noisy mill met a storage facility. It was actually a windowless cavity that extended from the roof down into three layers of basement. He had supervised the installation of plumbing, stairs, ventilation, and partitioning within that space. That was his destination this morning. He had retrieved his guests from the airport and driven nonstop across the canyon.

It was difficult to maintain security for influential people for three days. With Tom Lacey's help, Bo had quietly scheduled Brian Knight and Marina Whitehorse to join Harold Knight in Bo's secret office.

Bo drove the off-road vehicle into the building through a wide roll up door and parked in the back, behind a partition covered with vertical pipes. The SUV could not be seen until a visitor reached the far, back corner.

Bo walked the group through a tall, open door.

This area, next to the mill, housed meeting rooms and bathrooms. A map of the *business* side of Urgent covered one wall of the meeting room. Another map displayed the surface with color coded outlines of the structures, roads and alleys. An adjacent map illustrated the first underground layer, highlighting all features. One more layer – one more map. There were four maps in total, covering two adjoining walls. Bo asked his guests to be seated and proceeded to explain the layout of his lair.

Beneath them were guest rooms with beds and facilities. The central lobby area opened to the hall leading to the dining room. Coffee and pastries would be delivered in the morning. They could eat in the dining room or have meals delivered to this room. The monitor was encrypted and connected via satellite to whatever they wanted. No other computers were to be used. In fact, none could be used because of the composition of the surrounding structure.

"Your personal phone systems won't work either," he advised. "You can connect to the outside with this computer," he motioned to the large monitor, "but, of course, your call won't be very private. If privacy is required, we can get you out of this building to make a call."

Before he excused himself to return to work, Bo called attention to the phone unit hanging on the wall. He explained how it was unusual in that the device would track him down as soon as his name was spoken into it. He left.

The next days were packed with discussion and

resolutions:

A. The team knew it took four megawatts of electricity to produce a one-second burn in the reactor. Did they have that much power at their disposal?

> Answer: Such a burn needed about 60 acres of solar mirrors, which they had.

B. It was common knowledge that the signatories to the ITER project in France were expected to build, then bring, completed portions of the machine to the site. Could they be persuaded to build another, smaller one?

> Answer: affirmative – for a price.

C. The fuel used in nuclear fusion can be extracted from seawater. If we bring in a container of water from the ocean, will the week-old product be too stale for use?

> Answer: no.

D. Investigate all possible scenarios of meltdowns, power losses, waste containment compromises.

> Answer: no catastrophic results found, but in limited amount of data.

E. What is the estimated size of the finished chamber?

> Answer: The basic chamber needs a 25-foot diameter; ancillary systems probably three times that.

F. The 50 superconducting magnetic coils form a ring around the chamber. Will we be able to divert that energy for 15-minute bursts of magnetic energy?

> Answer: unknown.

Referring to the maps hung on the walls, the team

was able to locate the chamber, route the cooling and power systems, and hypothesize human traffic patterns and needs. The thoughtful layout and supporting infrastructure routing looked ideal.

At dinnertime on night three, the Knight brothers and Marina decided on a catered event. They invited Bo Elliott and asked Lacey and Emmet Fitzpatrick to join them.

"We can tell you this right now," Harold began, "and ask that you keep it to yourselves. We have just received approval to build a fusion reactor on this site. While it does not sound impressive, this type of nuclear electricity generation is huge. It's the safest and most cutting-edge source of power we know of.

"The addition of this to our arsenal of power generation weapons will put Urgent at the forefront of clean energy production on the planet. *We* anticipate scientists from all over the world will want to learn from us. *They* anticipate they can take our technology to their countries and decommission all coal and oil-fired power plants.

"You need to know that construction will involve minimal disruption to our active research projects. There will be excavation and building taking place along the north side of the temptank. You can all imagine the amount of work needed to marry our existing systems with the new technology. In fact, you may have seen the tentative plans as outlined on maps in your meeting room. I can confirm that we will be building out new space beneath the surface and filling it with computers and more scientists.

"We will be writing millions of lines of code and

moving billions of molecules of materials around. Fusion reaction involves playing with electrons, ionized gas, and superheated plasma. Superheated meaning millions of degrees – no, hundreds of millions of degrees."

As Hal paused for a breath, Fitz expressed his concern over the additional number of visitors he visualized. "If you are planning on converting part of this complex into a tourist destination, we need to have some conversations about security and traffic."

Harold looked at his security chief. "Your concerns are duly noted. You and I can discuss these matters at a later date. For the moment let us continue our celebration with our guests before they depart in the morning."

Hal added: "This is exciting." And it had been.

Bo Elliott had just felt the ground tremble. The ten years of construction and interruptions was about to pay off. He was certain that what he felt was not the vacuum chamber vibrating. Nuclear fusion would not produce that physical effect as he understood it. No – it was probably the thrust bearings on the turbines reacting to the pulse of the reactor.

That atomic *fire* took place in a billionth of a second, and generated one serious burst of energy. If steam was superheated rapidly, the pressure on the turbine would be a quick thrust. He would have to check with Harold Knight to confirm his understanding of what had happened in the unfamiliar realm where mechanical engineering meets quantum physics.

The Chief would also need to be involved in this

new project. Bo knew that Harold would address all things scientific, but any above ground decisions get into Edward's area of responsibility. For example, where would they store the excess parts if there were plans to make more than one of these reactors? He felt the answer would be, on the surface.

Bo was aware that the structures which deal with various projects have different support systems. Heavy items might require a crane and gantry inside warehouse buildings. Large components are only moved off premises on rails. Occasionally, internal temperature needed to be controlled. This was all in Edward's stable – the man responsible for all structure and infrastructure, the man who was the acting Chief of all Wind River nations.

Edward's concern extended to the impact this breakthrough would have on the planet, specifically the water supply. Bo and Edward had discussed water issues many times over the years. Bo was from the Deep South where fresh water was plentiful. He usually took water for granted, unless there was too much of it.

As a Native American, Edward had come to know the importance of water – not just the flowing rivers and deep blue lakes, but also the invisible aquifers. He knew that other parts of the earth used underground water sources to maintain life. He also knew that two-thirds of the planet's largest groundwater basins are drawn down. Mankind systematically withdraws more water than Mother Nature deposits.

Groundwater was used by over two-billion people for drinking and irrigation. If the aquifers were depleted, another source would be needed to sustain life. A nearby source of electricity with enough power to operate a salt-water desalination plant could save millions of lives in heavily populated areas. Imagining even a partial solution to one nation's water problem brought Edward joy.

He had seen the maps of the aquifers. He knew of the Arabian Aquifer, the Murzuk-Djado Basin, and the Indus Basin – all being drawn down. He knew water shortages alone result in hundreds of thousands of deaths every year.

He also knew his destiny was to help these people.

TWELVE

•• •—•• •—— •— —•—• ———

Dennis Hall was gazing out his office window toward the Mendenhall Glacier. University of Alaska Southeast has buildings situated within sight of the lakes created by melting glaciers. He practically worshipped this view as part of his daily, morning routine. Reality set in when his secretary knocked, and briskly entered his office.

"I'm sorry to be so abrupt, the President is calling."

"Which one?"

"Former United States President, Sean Crockett."

Doctor Hall swiveled around to face the desk, straightened up, and answered the call. He motioned for his aide to be seated while he engaged this powerful politician. The phone conversation was mostly one sided – the President had done the talking.

In response to her raised eyebrows, Dennis explained that he had just received a job offer.

"Word gets around this campus fast so I'm asking you to keep this quiet for a couple of days. Besides, it may be too good an offer to refuse and I'll soon announce.

"As you know, I retired from government service to return to my home state. When President Crockett left office eight years ago, I had to do the same. The position I held in the EPA was significant only because of his influence and reputation. I became one of the casualties you hear about when administrations change in this country. Don't misunderstand – that was all right. Those eight years allowed me to do some great work, just as these past eight years have in this office.

"My position as Director of the Office of Academic Affairs and Research is not really a career job. You have been here longer than I have, and undoubtedly know the history of my predecessors. University presidents have a short tenure, as do college deans and directors such as myself. We all know that and quietly plan for the next job. In my case, I thought that was another retirement. Now I'm not so sure.

"You will recall that when we agreed to participate in that reforestation plan with the Native Americans in the Tongass National Forest, we formed an alliance called ForCI. That Forestry Consortium International has indeed become a border-crosser. Sean just filled me in on the efforts taking place in the Amazon and the involvement of our International Institute of

Tropical Forestry. At this level the ForCI participants can accomplish their goals. Things have changed, and he needs my help.

"A scientist named Harold Knight is part of a large experiment that has been going on for twenty-two years according to Sean. A quick description of his effort is saving mankind. Recently his labs have been researching the genetic tweaking of plants and have made progress. They now want to play with trees – on a worldwide basis. Sean wants me to lead them. It looks like another massive project with unimaginable implications.

"During our conversation, he rattled off locations where forestry is an issue, including Brazil, Malaysia, Haiti, Congo, Indonesia, Gabon, and our own North American forests. Man is the primary culprit, and we need to get man to start fixing it. Due to climate change, the beetles in our forests are doing more widespread damage than ever before. However, in other areas we cut trees down to make room for herds of animals, to make room to build, or to plant other types of trees. This trend needs to be reversed.

"President Crockett wants me to retire, build and staff a headquarters for the ForCI group, and take the solutions to this problem to the world. How's that for a morning phone call?"

It had taken exactly three hours for Dennis Hall to discuss the offer with his wife and decide to move. His secretary was the first to know, the university president was informed next. Then, it was off to Wyoming to meet with Harold Knight. Their short, initial meeting had one agenda item – where to locate ForCI.

The answer to this question would determine Dennis's new address – it would no longer be in Juneau, Alaska.

The need for a large airport, lots of daylight, and proximity to equatorial countries all led to the choice of the San Diego area. Dennis and his wife, MaryAnn, were both educators and familiar with the universities in the city and some of the personnel at those institutions. Those connections would be invaluable in speeding up the process of finding a house and establishing the office.

Dennis and MaryAnn knew that the ForCI group would need a well-planned college curriculum to sell to the foreign countries if work-study and exchange programs were to be an integral part of the reforestation effort. The student's work would be done in the field and possibly in a foreign country, making this program of studies unique. Furthermore, the Halls wanted there to be a few hours of evening education, after a hard day's work in the forest was concluded. In other words: this captive audience would be continuously learning.

When word of this intention reached Edward White at Urgent, he immediately contacted Anne Osburn and asked for her help in this planning. He knew of her involvement in the teaching of all young recruits that arrived in Urgent a generation ago. Edward was also the person who had asked Anne to design a program of study to educate the family members that followed along later. It had been referred to as the *grand relocation*. Ultimately the program had proven to be well designed.

Back then, the early laborers at the young, small

settlement were civic orphans recruited from the Deep South and Appalachia. Before the two groups met each other, they worked to help build a school in Southern Ohio, near the Ohio River. This recruiting scheme was intended not only to get some construction completed, but to expose the different ethnicities to each other and force cooperation among the races, classes, and genders. Many were weeded out, many more adapted, learned a significant amount in a short period of time, and moved on to the building of Urgent.

When the community reached an optimum size, the family members left behind were invited to move to Urgent and participate. Those who elected to do so required a similar, but more thorough, adult-oriented education. Anne Osburn designed that curriculum, moved to the Ohio location for over two years, and taught as well. Edward knew the international, college-aged students could benefit from what Anne had experienced. MaryAnn Hall agreed and flew to Wyoming to meet with her new mentor.

The process of organizing the ForCI project involved more meetings and more introductions. Dennis did most of the traveling. He needed firsthand knowledge of potential sites and needed a feel for the decision makers. One of his most telling excursions took him to Indonesia. There the process of deforestation was the burning of *worthless* trees to make room for the planting of oil palms.

Economically, oil from oil palms is a significant source of revenue. In the ideal world, the government would receive some of the income and make life better for the citizens. However, in the real world riddled with corruption and ruthless business, the poor stay poor.

It is not necessary to burn a forest to plant other types of trees. Who makes those decisions? Once that is known it becomes evident who to talk with in order to begin a reforestation project. More accurately, one knows how to get a project started, or when to stop talking and move on.

Dennis Hall and Harold Knight had talked about the advantages of adding to existing forest as opposed to starting new growth in countries more receptive to the idea. It was not possible to pinpoint when one option was more beneficial than the other because of political persuasion. The forest needing the most help might belong to the government least receptive to getting help.

Fighting with the Congo for ten years to gain access to the forest could be less productive than beginning to plant an area in Australia on day one. While the Congo basin collectively contains 590,000 square kilometers of forest, and Australia only 294,000, the smaller forest would still be sufficient to support enlargement. Besides, Australia was only 20% forested. It could use the increased mass of oxygen-bearing trees to benefit the continent. One final plus was that they speak English down under. Such were the decisions Dennis Hall faced.

While the new Director of ForCI was contemplating the future, his wife was looking at the present head on. She was on-site at Urgent, brainstorming with Anne Osburn. The women took it upon themselves to visit the agricultural experiments both above and below ground. One informative meeting with Sandy in the underground Ag Lab ultimately led to conversation about the reforestation project taking place in Tongass, and the other one in the Amazon. Practically in unison, both women voiced the need to visit the second site in Brazil.

The salient fact that convinced Harold Wright was Sandy's agreement to go along. Secondly, they could be met by Javier and his entourage. With safety becoming a nonissue, the only remaining items to be decided were timing and clearance with husbands. The men knew they'd never change the minds of these women. The trip was a go.

In Sandy's subterranean laboratory research shifted to tropical trees known to grow in Brazil. He wanted to examine the outcome if he pressed Mother Nature a little and brought in some species that were faster growing, but not totally invasive.

This project would involve replacing forest that had been logged to make room for crops or herds. The fact that it used to be forest floor implied that the soil was salvageable and water readily available. He would need to actually get to the Amazon to find out if this was true. He called Javier.

The heart of the tropical jungle would be home to tall, mature tatajuba, freijo, and perhaps some cerejeita trees. These were definitely slow growing hardwoods. Could this area support, say, guanacaste, which grows much faster, or even balsa? Sandy's lab was soon overgrown with small trees destined for the jungle along with others which had been genetically modified to grow faster.

Dennis Hall was involved in this project too because he needed to prepare the government of Brazil for the upcoming projects. He asked his friends in US government to recommend a legal team, and brought them in to prepare the paperwork. The approach to the governing host was simple – the ForCI group would do all the administration, hiring, building and financing, in exchange for clear title to the land. They were not about to invest heavily on foreign soil without some sort of ownership. Considering that the project was to take place on the edge of the rain forest, and at a distance from any population center, there was no disagreement on this issue.

The trip to Brasilia was quick and uneventful. As the Executive Director of the international consortium, Dennis was able to execute the appropriate documents. He departed that nation's capital with the understanding that this agreement would be registered with the worldwide agencies responsible for policing such treaties. Both parties were pleased.

Sandy's visit to the rain forest was considerably more time-consuming. After investigating solutions to problems related to transportation, security, supply lines, and safety, he proposed they ship the buildings and other basics into Sao Luis, a large seaport, and transfer the containers onto trucks, then into the Amazon. There was an area west of Barra do Corda that had been particularly hard hit by fire, the cause of which was unknown. However, filling this hole in the rain forest would be a good start.

While the hardware was being coordinated, the

software, the student curriculum, needed to be designed. An initial brainstorming session was held on the main campus of the University of Sao Paulo. Educators from State University and Federal University were invited as well as staff from smaller local schools. While the larger Brazilian universities had colleges of education, Anne and MaryAnn knew that more than teaching was required for this extensive field exercise. They welcomed participation by the smaller colleges.

They would look for expertise in some subjects, teaching ability, communication skills, and physical ability. The faculty would be working alongside the students, not doing any heavy lifting but definitely hiking into the forest and keeping a close eye on everything. This would be the ultimate in democratic education in that the students would help to decide what they were to learn. All educators would be as much coach and mentor as they were teachers.

Not all teacher applicants would have those skills. Emphasis would be placed on hiring as many local people as possible. The students would hail from villages and cities all across Brazil, but working with local staff would be a definite advantage. The Urgent team concentrated on applicants from communities in the Amazon basin like Braganca, Belem, Castanhal, and Maraba. These were all within an easy day's drive, insuring that medical and other services were also convenient.

The selected section of the Amazon was littered with mining and dotted with areas owned by indigenous people. Neither of these groups normally set fire to the land. However, this portion of the basin had been badly scorched during the past decade. Most had been illegally logged and were owned by the government. That was the place to start.

Edward Knight knew that the mill at Urgent could maintain operation for a few weeks without Bo Elliott at the helm. Sandy and Bo joined forces and acquired the materials. They got the containers to a ship in Houston and later flew to Brazil to meet her. Javier helped translate and shorten the long-distance communication. He succeeded in getting the trucks lined up to meet the ship.

On one eventful day, the ship, trucks, people, and weather all cooperated and converged on Brazil.

ForCI - Amazon was underway.

THIRTEEN

--- - .. ...

It is bad protocol, to say the least, to interrupt cross-country air travel in the United States. The Federal Aviation Administration takes air space seriously. The legal team for Urgent had contacted the Administrator of that agency and introduced themselves. He reluctantly agreed to a meeting because he knew it was his job, but he was averse to making decisions, and meetings usually required one or more. He had been right.

The news that a Native American band in Wyoming was about to launch rockets was downright frightening to the FAA Administrator. He learned of the launches in a phone conversation with former President Sean Crockett. The additional news that these would be regular reoccurring events was worse. Thankfully, his blood pressure had been brought back to normal when told that the landing fields for these craft were already approved for such activity, with the exception of the new strip on Native American land in the same area. Could they do that - allow spacecraft to take off and land in the same neighborhood?

In summation, the FAA Administrator had advised that he needed to discuss this matter with the Secretary of Transportation and together they would make a determination. Normal requests to the FAA might require a hearing, but this was not normal, nor was it a request.

A sovereign foreign nation advised the United States that they would be operating in US airspace. The aircraft were not military and there would be no significant impact on any public airports. This courtesy meeting was to inform the Administrator well in advance of the launches, since the FAA was charged with developing plans for the use of airspace to ensure the safety of aircraft and of citizens. He would need to revise existing plans.

The FAA has published procedures for introducing typical aircraft activity into a new section of sky. They allow for long distances within which to ascend and descend, plus consideration for emergencies and accidents near populated areas. The rules had a narrow area of concern with Urgent's plans because the launch vehicles followed a truly vertical path. Not only would these vehicles go straight up, but Wyoming was the least populated state in the country.

One brilliant organizational step was making this an international operation by negotiating emergency landing fields in California and Saskatchewan. The US Secretary of Transportation would view the thoughtful planning favorably. The two-fold announcement would not add additional burden to the department map makers or others affected. The warning about new restricted and off-limits airspace would be the same, with or without the building of three, one-thousand-foot launch towers.

The ground-breaking for the towers had been without celebration. All citizens of Urgent had been invited to a community meeting earlier in the month. The big news had been the science and progress. The physical structures were just a novelty to be viewed, whenever. Those that were curious saw the three vertical rails protruding from a tarp-covered opening. Each rail was tied to the ground with three steel cables.

Slowly, the rails got taller. Every week each of the rails was raised to allow for a new section to be inserted below ground. The tie-down cables were carefully unwound from large spools, keeping tension on the rails, thereby maintaining true vertical orientation. Continuous testing kept the distance between the rails exactly the same, even as they got taller.

When a height of 300 feet was reached, the strength testing began. Prototypes of the rockets had been built. They had no payload (weight to simulate that of cargo) but did house the metallic alloy needed to test the electromagnetic launch system. The electricity for the magnets was supplied by wind and sun.

Each vehicle launched was gently returned to earth by a parachute carried in the nose of the rocket. Each launch delivered data on the rail efficiency, rocket skin temperature, propulsion force, wind resistance, and speed. Scientists immediately began studying this information, as did the curious.

A viewing area had been cleared on the other side of the canyon, near the upper plateau. The fact that the airport was nearby was of no consequence. Each aircraft landing at the private field was always expected and each departure well monitored. No airport activity would occur when a launch was about to take place. That restriction was brought to the attention of Willard Graham when he made reservations for a charter to get him to Urgent. They had to check the launch schedule.

The fact that he was leaving from New York state meant he would need to hang around his place until lunchtime, so he could jump on the charter jet, gain two time zones, and arrive at his destination - at lunch time What a waste of time. Regardless, he needed to change destinations to land at Casper. There were no rental cars available closer.

He paused to remember the last time he visited the Urgent site. He had been commissioned to spy on the new secret location and determine what the Native Americans were trying to accomplish. He had failed in his mission, and thus failed to get paid. This visit would be different. This job was to monitor the launches and get details and photographs of the enterprise. It was all above board.

He had packed sophisticated photo equipment and the means to edit and transmit the pictures. His laptop had programs for data manipulation so he could relate speed, height and thrust statistics to his employer. He planned to spend at least a week in Wyoming, so he picked up a rental car in Casper and got a room in Riverton. If the nightlife was too boring, he could drive back to Casper for some fun.

The first morning was bright and clear at the overlook. Willard set up his tripod and opened the laptop on the back floor of the rented hatchback. He had backed into the parking space, so his view of the launch was from the comfort of the rear cargo area of the vehicle. He reminded himself to bring pillows from the hotel room tomorrow.

Along the perimeter of the viewing area was a collection of light poles. The public would someday want to see the view at night, and security was a concern. The poles were topped with two large, low-intensity lamps, and security cameras. Security personnel monitoring the site electronically had a view of every square inch. They identified Willard Graham in the first hour. The face recognition software used by the Urgent security team was state-of-the-art.

Emmet Fitzpatrick was a security freak and assured himself that the Urgent system was the best. In his office, as the head of the Nation's Office of Consideration (NOC), he received notice whenever any of his monitors deciphered a familiar face. It was a quiet day, and the alert from the face recognition program caused him to look up from the duty log to examine the subject. He quickly switched his equipment and monitors into sleep mode and got up from the desk.

Willard Graham did not notice the ordinary white SUV approach the parking area. He was listening to the launch countdown and framing the picture about to be taken by his camera. Laptop open and camera standing by, he was seriously pissed when a man approached him and offered, "Buy you a beer?"

At first, he did not recognize Emmet Fitzpatrick. Fitz slowly removed his sunglasses and cowboy hat to reveal his face. Graham just stood still.
"Make it two," Graham said.

"Put your gear in my rig. Your car's safe here.

"We are still not selling alcohol on the reservation, but this private area has been known to provide a no-charge libation or two," Fitz said after they got seated. "We are in the VIP dining room. Usually available to the scientists, academics, and a visitor or two."

Waiting for their drinks to arrive, Fitz took a few minutes to familiarize his guest with the features of that space, and then decided to start the story.

"Before you jump all over me, I will admit that it was my fault you did not get your scoop when you visited this region five years ago. We had not yet decided how much of this should be made public. I am sure you will soon see what a big decision that was. Let me thank you, though, for pushing us into making that decision.

"For an entire generation this community had been growing and getting more and more sophisticated without giving any thought to when they could go public with any of it. Your investigation caused us to have a summit conference and come to grips with the truth. That truth was that we needed to come clean.

"Not a hundred percent because of some ongoing sensitive research, but clean enough as to stop worrying about everyone looking over our shoulder. I don't know who your client is now but let me give you so much information they might double your fee. I owe you that much. Then you might have a decision to make.

"The original idea behind this operation and the driving force even today is an attempt to save the planet. A few really rich folks decided their money was no good if we destroyed the place, so they would try to save it. They got some friends, a few smart people, and momentum: voila! Now we have Urgent. A Native American Nation expanded and populated with a specific class of citizen, all dedicated to that one goal – to save our species.

"At first we needed to build in secrecy and iron out the wrinkles. One of the big ones was the question of who we would allow participate. The answer was that no one can make a profit off our work. That may affect the enthusiasm of whoever you report to, but to this day no profit-making entity does business in Urgent. In fact, with few exceptions, all business is employee owned.

"The citizens have a vested interest in everything. They support each other. The schools, hospital, airport, all public services are just that – public. Even our electric company is a co-operative, like the State of Nebraska electric utility next door.

"Our residents are automatically participants in their own state bank. We couldn't just file it as a Native American institution due to close ties with many businesses outside our borders. But it is led by members of the nation and governed like a credit union

- it is a true state bank.

"The economy of our little community revolves around the steel mill you hear humming in the background. We have a contract to melt surplus military armament and build high-energy transmission towers. At least that was phase one of this plan. You have seen the solar panels, the reflection array, and the wind turbine field that produces the electricity necessary to melt the steel. You may have also noticed the hydroelectric power at our disposal. It takes a lot of electricity to operate that mill and we are self sufficient.

"What you don't see sits below ground. Beyond those walls, and beneath us is a series of sophisticated laboratories within which our staff is doing a massive amount of research. That requires electricity also. To that end we are building a fusion reactor. Still thermonuclear, but it produces clean and safe atomic energy. We have cleared the experiment with the Nuclear Regulatory Commission, even though we are a sovereign nation, and partnered with a few other nations in building our reactor. We may have the first one on the planet that is operational.

"The reactor will not generate continuously, which is what other nations are working on in a big way, but it will be operational enough to give us thirty second blasts. We anticipate that is all we need to launch the rockets."

"Hold it right there," said Graham. "I need to take a breath and get another beer."

"Me too. Let's take a walk first."

Taking Fitzpatrick's cue, he stood up and followed

his host towards a nondescript door. He gasped as the door was opened and revealed a hallway so long that he could not see the end of it. More than a hallway, it was a cavern with small and large pipes along one wall and the ceiling. They entered the area, walked down the hall for five minutes, and turned towards a large door on their left. The door opened into a room that had floor to ceiling windows, through which a large tank was visible.

On the surface to the left was a display with easy-to-read labels and gauges indicating the other side of the window was 100°F, while the material inside the tank was 700°F, and the pressure was within the green zone. The view through the window did not reveal either end of the gray tank – it was huge.

Fitz did not feel comfortable guiding his guest deeper into the underground lab system, or to his private space at NOC headquarters. They quietly retraced their steps, found their same quiet and private seats in the dining room, and sat down in front of cool, full glasses.

"Our laboratories line that long corridor and extend deep into the area south and east of the mill. That large tank behind those big windows was the temperature retention unit which we call the temptank. It holds the superheated liquid sodium that is heated by the sun's energy by the reflection array. What you just saw was a glimpse of a fraction of the space we occupy and equipment we are working with. We are conducting experiments on plants - genetic modification, materials science - rockets and their outer shells, ultra-magnetism - rocket propulsion, and nano-science - space shield material: all at the same time and all big-ticket items.

"Needless to say, when we went public with these efforts our phones never stayed quiet. Virtually every lab and research facility in the nation wants a piece of this, but very few will sign off on the profit potential. We still require partners to be nonprofit or employee-owned: period. Our founders want to work with other like minds that will spend everything to save mankind, or forget it. If anyone wants a seat at the table, it's a serious ante."

"OK Fitz, fill me in on that brief mention of shield material," Graham asked.

"In order to even stand a chance at saving our life form from extinction we feel that man needs to reverse climate change. For years we have known this, yet for years we have been going backwards with respect to CO_2 emissions and environmental damage.

"It is evident that the existing governments will NOT act in time. In fact, many scientists feel we are beyond the tipping point. We cannot possibly remove enough CO_2 and reduce future emissions sufficiently. This place is going to melt, all seas will rise, temperatures will rise, and our extinction is guaranteed. That's their story. We want to write a different ending.

"In the labs below us we are studying materials and the science it takes to change certain properties of those materials. We have a prototype or two that lead us to believe our goal is in sight. Hopefully we will have the shield material designed about the time we have the rocket and launch system designed.

"The intent is to begin daily launches and begin

snapping pieces of a light-weight sun shield together in outer space. It will take years, but we plan to continue to increase its size until we see an improvement in climate down here. Sounds simple doesn't it?"

"All this is happening down here now?" Graham asked.

"It is, and I'm happy to show you, but not right now. I have some work I need to attend to before the day is over, and an in-depth tour would take time. Can we do this in the morning?"

"When you drive me back to my car you can show me where and tell me when," Willard responded.

"If it's all the same, I'll have Randall James drive you back. I'll see you in the morning."

Emmet walked his guest to the door and told him to climb the stairs. His chauffeur was waiting at the car in the warehouse. The two immediately recognized each other from the Ferrari incident a few years ago.

"No hard feelings," said Willard Graham.

Graham opened his computer immediately upon entering the hotel room and began searching the topic *urgent*. The listing was massive. Many of the resources were scientific papers that appeared in recent journals. Fitz had mentioned that a generation had been spent in this place. That could be. They kept it quiet until five years ago, right after he bought the infamous Ferrari.

The scientific topics he saw were as varied as the themes of government regulations that had been refined or introduced in order to accommodate Urgent. What an effort. Lately they had even received the go ahead to land spacecraft on their own property in

Wyoming. He groaned, realizing that he neglected to photograph any of today's test. Then thought twice about any disappointment he momentarily felt. Fitz had said something about telling him more than he had today. This could be great.

At precisely 9:00 the next morning Randall James knocked on Willard Graham's hotel room door. After Graham commented on his punctuality, Randall asked if he thought Mr. Fitzpatrick would allow otherwise.

"No, I guess not," replied the guest. Graham remembered the reputation Fitzpatrick earned for office decorum at their previous employer-in-common, the LA field office of the FBI.

The trip to breakfast was made mostly in silence. Graham tried to engage his driver and get answers to questions he had for years about the incident on Lake Chautauqua. Randall's only reply was that Mr. Fitzpatrick would answer all his questions. Graham was deposited near the stairs leading to the dining room and Randall put the car away.

During breakfast, Graham was amazed at the grace Fitzpatrick exhibited, not only to his guest but also to all those that engaged him – and there were many. Willard thought he remembered his former boss as being business-like and more snooty – not this man.

This man knew the names of all those folks in white lab coats, and the young people sweeping the floor. Apologetically he took the latter half of mealtime explaining the why and how of the operation in New York that prevented Willy from completing his car-buying mission.

"As I mentioned yesterday, we have now gone public. Today we do not maintain the degree of secrecy we did five years ago. You would be allowed to file that report, and still get the Ferrari in its garage on time. I also mentioned that I would get you more information than you bargained for. Ready for a tour?" They rose and left the table.

"Can I bring my camera?"

Walking down the hall and away from the mill building, the never-ending hall baffled Graham. Fitz explained that the north side of their route, and directly below them, was the massive temptank. For that reason, all the labs were on the south side, one after the other, with exception of those that are stacked above others. As an example, he motioned to an ultrawide door, entered the code on a keypad, and escorted his guest into a massive warehouse-type space.

Fitzpatrick began: "The large, solid discs you see are the base of the rockets. The technicians refer to them as *coins*, presumably because they are round and flat and designed to be flipped. We will see many of these components later but let me explain what I know about our launch system; it's magnetism at its finest.

"You have seen the rails protruding from our launch tunnel and heard the relatively quiet rocket as it rises in the air. It's quiet because magnets are pulling the spacecraft skyward. All along the side of the cylindrical center section, the inside of the vehicle has magnets embedded in grooves which are aligned by those vertical rails you see.

"What you can't see is the force of the magnets. Magnetic force lifts and guides the vehicle. However, to get the thing out of the hole we need to overcome inertia. This is also done with magnets, but oriented in the wrong direction.

"Our scientists have determined that it takes too much energy, and time, to let magnets lift the craft from a dead stop and then accelerate through the entire speed spectrum until it hits eight-hundred miles per hour at the top of the guide towers. They felt the launch needed a quick boost to get the craft moving. We now are developing a very powerful set of electromagnets, one to stay on the ground and the other being the built-in coin, which is the bottom of the rocket. The reaction from the repelling force of the magnets will get the craft quickly moving. One second after the initial push the magnetic rails can take over.

"Then the launch process I previously explained continuously accelerates the speed until there is no more magnetic contact with the rails and the vehicle exits at the top of the guide system. One more super-boost comes from another quick jolt of *repulsion* from three magnificent electromagnets at the tip of the towers. They add another boost to exit speed because they react against the magnetism in the coin.

"Our sleek little craft then increases speed with the help of three exterior booster tanks full of compressed gas. It shoots into space, will unload its cargo at the stellar platform, and then load two of the depleted booster tanks. Before taking on the load, the *coin* needs to be reversed so the parachute system is on the outside and any magnetic activity is on the inside. As in all reentry procedures, it takes a 'chute to slow the vehicle down quickly once it's rolling on the landing gear.

"You asked yesterday about the shield. That too is breakthrough science. To build the thinnest, strongest sheet material with tear-resistant properties is the ultimate in job security. I anticipate there will always be at least one person in the materials lab studying a new alloy and combining elements to form new alloys. The material most favored today has some nanotechnology and materials science added to a dash of thermo-chemistry.

"When originally building this facility, our engineers knew that the temperatures of the shell of the temptank may one day be useful. For this reason, they allowed that area above the tank to be completely unsupported. We have since built a flat platform in that space and have a superheated drying rack that is occupied at this instant. The latest shield compound needs temperatures above six-hundred degrees to finish *cooking.*

"Strips of shield material are made in lengths of almost a half mile. The weight of this material will dictate how long the strip is. Successful launch is more important than the size of the shield piece the space vehicle is carrying. We will be continuously sending more material up daily.

"Obviously, the craft's smooth operation is paramount.Let's go back to the dining room. I have something I want to discuss with you."

Before ordering lunch, each asked for a cup of coffee and settled in at their quiet corner table. The wait-staff knew Fitz would signal when the table required attention. Otherwise, stay away but stay aware.

"Your timing," Emmet began, "couldn't be better. To put it bluntly, I need some help."

"Sure Fitz, giving tours or what?"

"Seriously Willy - investigative and security help. Everything I showed you in our brief tour is my area of responsibility - plus stuff you did not see. I don't totally understand the management structure around here yet, but I seem to be part of it, and I'm over-whelmed. Other leaders will interrupt whatever work flow I might have by asking me to attend a meeting. The big problem is that all these meetings are that important.

"Just over five years ago I agreed to take on secu-rity and personnel issues for this project. The rate of growth has been astounding. I have scientists in the underground labs that have not been vetted or given a proper orientation, but they're already on the job.

"We started a program with the University of Alas-ka in the National Forest up there, south of Juneau. University students, natives and our staff are all liv-ing together and trying to save the trees. Who is in charge and what are their qualifications? Is that too much to ask? See my problem - I need manpower. Trustworthy manpower.

"I'm offering you a job."

FOURTEEN

— • • — — • • — • • — — — — —

"What do you mean they have no identification? Surely there are Social Security numbers, tax forms for with-holding, and entries in the Medical Records Bureau."

"Nope," replied Harold Knight.

"Listen. I don't mean to come down too hard, but I have been asked by Fitzpatrick to help him iron out a few nuisance items. Not that any of your secret people are a nuisance, but my experience tells me that an off-the-charts transaction is extremely time consuming and, by definition, a nuisance."

At this, Harold Knight rose from behind his laboratory workbench and worked his way to the other side where his guest was seated. He sat down in a neighboring chair at eye level with the surprised Willard Graham.

"The founders of this community are among the world's richest people. They chose a bunch of misfits and young people to start to save the planet. Intelligence was not the primary trait they looked for; creativity was. Scholastic honors were never even a question when making hiring decisions; compatibility was. We honor nuisance-like behavior.

"Ten years ago, one bright young college student attended one of my lectures. He liked what he heard and was festering over his dislike of the behavior of his ultra-controlling, far-right professional father. That young man found me in this very laboratory four months later without advance notice or waiting to complete a formal application for employment. I'm not in any head hunter's employer listing. How did he find me?

"Your longtime associate, Emmet Fitzpatrick was watching us while all of Urgent was in the middle of what we now call the grand relocation. We had parents moving in from the deep South and construction was never-ending. What was I going to do, turn away a man with initiative just because he did not follow some arbitrary protocol? Never.

"I told him we would work it out. He has become our number-one astronaut. That was a good decision. To my knowledge, he is still untraceable to the outside.

"A second opportunity presented itself three years later when the son of a prominent politician also found me down here. His ultra-right-wing father had lost an election and before leaving office, changed the rules his successor needed to follow. The further tilting of an already unlevel playing field was too much for our recent graduate. He too found Urgent to be a comfortable home and is now the second in command of our agriculture laboratory.

"About that time, Urgent was keeping as quiet as possible while going full speed on our research. I'm sure you have heard about our episode in New Mexico that resulted in the death of a politician at the Albuquerque airport. It was a terrible accident, but we had no way of changing what happened, and talked of making restitution later.

"One action we did take was to recall that diversion team and absorb the team members into the community. They all relocated to the Wind River village except the pilot of the drone that took out the helicopter at ABQ. She stayed in the field, in a variety of locales, until she lost her hand. We could not leave her out there, so we insisted she receive her ongoing medical treatment here.

"To further entice her to live in Wyoming we offered her the "no-identity option" which she immediately agreed to. As of today, her ongoing surgery and robotic trials are taking place in our labs. She is fully welcomed by every Urgent citizen, yet rarely goes up to the surface."

"Tell me more about that helicopter accident," whispered Graham.

"If you have heard the rumors you know most of the story," replied Harold. "The operation was designed to slow down a congressman by crashing a drone into the windshield of his helicopter and keeping the politician delayed because of all the questions he and the pilot would need to answer. At the last minute, the pilot rotated the chopper and the drone took out the tail rotor.

"They dropped a hundred feet like a rock. No one survived. The drone pilot, Sara, was devastated and decided never to show her face around here. A self-exile."

"And the police did not catch up with her in New Mexico?"

"That particular escape," boasted Hal "is a legend among the teams. No one that was there will talk about it. Although, I know that Courtney Elliot, Leah's mom, has most of the story.

"Part of the legend relates to a fire engine I have seen parked in the old vehicle garage out north of the mill. It has no identity, but you can see where the decals used to be. Compare the dusty outline on the doors to those found on the existing Phoenix fire units and you can draw your own conclusions. I say that because the legend ends in Phoenix."

"So, why's she back?" asked Graham.

"Five or six years ago she was working in Alaska with our reforestation team, of which she was a charter member. They spotted an illegal logging operation, and a small group of dedicated members returned to that site to foil the loggers. She got caught in an animal trap and her hand was practically snapped clean off.

"They got her out of the woods and back here. We have been working with her ever since. She is our most prominent volunteer for robotic experiments. Our materials science people are even in the act, trying to replicate skin. Some day we hope to she'll be all patched up. In the meantime, she is totally under the radar."

"We are working on making skin?"

"Sure we are. Naturally it won't grow like real skin," said Hal, "but it will look and feel real. We already have a waterproof version but are fighting with the internal abrasion caused by the mechanics inside the hand.

"Back to the issue at hand, no pun intended, but I need to know more about the three citizens you have collected in your no-identity portfolio."

"Willard," Hal quickly responded, "you are in for a disappointment. Until you come up with a real good reason for needing more information, and I mean - almost earthshattering reason, you have everything you will ever get. If you want to pursue this, I will talk with each of the three and ask if they want to meet with you. That's as far as I can go."

Graham stood and looked down at the scientist.

"Understood." He walked out the door.

To reach Emmet Fitzpatrick's office, Graham needed to take an elevator up one level to the surface and drive a cart almost a mile north behind a row of warehouse type buildings. One of these was the old vehicle garage referred to earlier. He decided not to stop.

Fitz had established the NOC office in a confusing setting at the edge of this complex, within sight of the solar array to the east and the airport plateau to the west. It always seemed easier to drive away from than to approach the headquarters of the Nation's Office of Consideration.

Graham burst into the office, interrupting the peace of the day. He wanted - no HAD, to tell Fitzpatrick the where-abouts of that girl he was looking for.

Ever since their first conversation about the fatal accident in New Mexico, Graham knew that he could make great points with Fitzpatrick if he could find the responsible party. Any unsolved murder was a big deal and this was one of the last investigations Fitzpatrick led. This would still be a burr under Fitz's saddle.

Emmet Fitzpatrick motioned for his associate to take a seat and listened dispassionately as he always had. As Graham concluded his story Fitz asked for clarification:

"This woman is now living in Urgent?"

"Right."

"She is known to the Elliotts and other old-timers?"

"Right."

"Thanks Willy. Let me think about this." Graham left the office.

After only a few seconds, Fitz tapped his desk monitor two times and Tom Lacey's face appeared on the screen.

"You have a few minutes?" Fitz asked.

"I'm in my dungeon." Without signing off, Emmet closed the screen with a final tap and walked to his cart waiting outside.

It took five minutes to drive across the solar panel plain and descend into Lacey's world. During that time Emmet went through a series of emotions. The New Mexico incident had occurred while he was still with the FBI. He had been hounded by a thought that a series of incidents were somehow connected, but did not have any proof or even a plausible culprit, let alone evidence of a crime.

The fatality in that helicopter crash was the first crime he could enter into the files of his newly formed Odd Case Unit. The chase through Navajo country into Phoenix was the first opportunity to corral a suspect in that case. He remembered his adrenalin rush as he followed the van across the state in the bureau helicopter. He remembered the disappointment when we realized that there would be no arrest to mark the end of that complicated pursuit.

Now the chase was on again, but no satisfactory conclusion was in sight. Fitzpatrick no longer needed to close that case file to feather his career. In fact, he wasn't even sure he wanted to talk with Tom Lacey, but he had arrived. Lacey opened his office door and asked: "Do we need visual security for this meeting?"

"No, I just want to run an ID check by you."

"OK. Just a minute. I'll get Randall in here. He's the guru on ID files and identity curiosities."

"Please don't bother," whispered Fitzpatrick. "This is about one of our own and requires total security."

"OK Fitz, tell me what's up."

After listening to the story, Lacey asked, "Where do we go from here?"

"I'm not too sure but I am rapidly convincing myself to let it all drop and get on with life. Not only hers, but mine as well. There is no good reason for me to pursue an accident when all parties have paid dearly – one with his life and another with exile and dismemberment.

"Isn't that enough?" he asked as he looked at his friend.

"For me it would be, but I'm not from the boots-on-the-ground division of national security. You obviously took open case files a lot more seriously than I ever did on the digital side."

"I must admit that just thinking about walking away seems to be lifting my spirits a bit." Fitzpatrick paused, "I think that settles it. If this helps my mental state and makes me a better person, I am convinced dropping it is the right thing to do."

With a decision having been made, Tom Lacey looked his friend in the eye and asked, "Will you be quitting completely and giving up your DC office then?"

Fitzpatrick was speechless. He had joined the community at Urgent two years after the New Mexico incident. That was the only open file he had when retiring from the FBI, so he elected to assume a part time consultant/contractor role. He was not on the payroll but his name was on a desk in a small office at HQ in Washington and was only required to check in periodically. The bureau considered his assignment a type of light undercover work.

He was now working for the group he thought had orchestrated the Albuquerque accident. His only mission was to identify that perpetrator. The officials at headquarters considered his success a long shot – so remote a chance that they had not contacted him, or even asked for an update in three years. If there was no communication, how did Lacey know?

Fitz started, "Listen Tom . . ." Lacey interrupted,

"By now you should know how good I am at my job." Lacey continued. "Research is not only done on subjects out there." And he waved his arm skyward.

"To answer your question, yes. I will send a message to Washington tonight. I know it's the right thing to do. This file will now be closed."

"And the girl?" Lacey asked.

Fitzpatrick straightened his spine and dispassionately looked at his friend.

"I will talk to her myself."

FIFTEEN

— — — • — — • — • • • • •

The list of dignitaries attending the World Economic Forum in Switzerland read like the Who's Who of money on the planet. Not every invited individual was able to attend. Not every attendee was invited. It was a public community after all. Eduardo and Javier met Myrlene and Brian Knight at their suite. Javier and Myrlene decided to go skiing, leaving the men to plot.

The plan was to carefully meet, and then convince, certain representatives from certain countries to attend a seminar at Urgent. Most had never heard of the place half a world away. Most would be suspicious. Brian had pictures, data, and letters of introduction, intended to overcome any objections. The sights at Urgent could be persuasive.

Their spacious suite in the Davos hotel had been carefully chosen for its location. The remote elevator at the end of the hall was used mostly by hotel staff. The elevator doors were around the corner, down a short hall, just past the laundry room.

This luxurious room was on the third floor. One of the busier, large meeting rooms was directly below them on the ground level. To leave a first-floor bathroom, get in the elevator and arrive at their suite would take less than a minute. Theirs was the perfect location. With few exceptions, their efforts were successful. They had a commitment from eight executives, or politicians, to meet them at Urgent next month.

Just over one month after the closing of this year's Davos gathering, the busy leaders began to touch down at Urgent's West plateau. Each aircraft was met by a fleet vehicle from the Wind River nation. The guests were checked into quarters near the lower level dining room beneath the mill complex. However, little time would be spent in the rooms. They had a packed schedule of visits to various laboratories, and joint meetings with the local scientists. The agenda was simple – convince the international guests to convince their peers to reallocate funds.

Urgent was sharing international technology to build a fusion reactor that runs on sea water. If the nations share this energy source in various locations around the planet, they can eliminate a pollution source by shutting down old-fashioned power plants.

Data with the CO_2 count, air quality, and predictions of doom was streaming in constantly. The nation's scientists had determined that over 40% of fossil fuel pollution comes from burning coal. Coal-fired power plants should be a thing of the past. Why were some still active? These were some of the issues to be addressed at this meeting.

Naturally there were murmurs in the room and whispers about costs, timing, and politics. Brian Knight, his brother - Harold, and the computer took over. The overhead lights were dimmed, and without a word, a vivid video of environmental catastrophe filled the white screen on one wall of the conference room. There was no narration for the video, and no moderator at a podium. Ten minutes after the visions of doom began, the screen went completely black. Brian stood up from his seat in the front row and turned to address the guests.

"You all know the facts surrounding climate change. You all know your countries have been impacted in one way or another – the whole planet has. The reason we have asked you to join together in this village is to think our way out of this dilemma.

"Many countries have signed onto at least one agreement indicating a willingness to help. It's not enough. There is one study that calculates how man could keep worldwide temperatures within reason based on a variety of scenarios. They emphasize the results of that model which indicate we would need to shut down all coal-fired power plants and switch to one-hundred percent alternative energy sources.

"We know this is about the carbon dioxide content in our atmosphere and yet are unable to stop making more. Another study suggests we capture the CO_2 and store it someplace, forever. To capture and store the hundreds of billions of tons of this gas would require an infrastructure as large as the oil industry. We would need to start today and invest hundreds of billions of dollars.

"There is a theory that we can extract up to a hundred billion tons of carbon by planting trees. We would need to reforest almost four million square miles of land to help nature along. That's a big forest.

"The truth is, we need to do all of it, and I think each of you can help. By now you know that periodically, not far from here, this community launches a test rocket. We took it upon ourselves years ago to build a shield for the planet. We have been researching, experimenting, developing, and now testing the launch systems and the vehicles to launch. It will be years before we see results, but the Urgent community has taken the first steps. The planet needs help with other steps.

"Part of our success has been learning the secrets behind nuclear fusion. Within a mile of you is the most advanced fusion reactor in the nation. We are close to turning it on. Around the world there are other more powerful and larger models. We have the compact version. What we would like to do is get a team together to build these power plants in any country that expresses interest – more than one in the large countries.

"An adjunct to the fusion reactor is a desalination plant. The reactor can be easily make the energy it takes to turn seawater into potable fresh water. We see our neighbors with water problems, and are excited about addressing them. We will ask these participants to use some of that water on the forest they have agreed to plant, but more about that later.

"Naturally, there are issues to be worked out as to who owns what and who will build what. To keep it simple at first, we can continue talking with the premise that the Wind River nation will own, build and run the power plant. It will even have title to the land the reactor sits on. The host nation will build and own the infrastructure. Transmission towers, lines, pipes, and all the revenue from the utility belong to that country. Now we get down to the question of money.

"A large part of saving the world comes down to whether or not you consider it in danger. Those that do not, will not participate in our venture. The more realistic visionaries will see the urgency in this problem and want to save themselves. Then it's an easy decision. We ask that they rearrange priorities.

"The first country we have entered into talks with is the United States. To prove to you the appeal of our approach we asked that they be present. A NASA representative is here in this room and you can ask her questions later. Using the US as an example, and NASA as the liaison, I'll give you an idea of where the money comes from.

"Some super bright engineers have managed to get a budget of sixty billion dollars to study and build the Space Launch System. This will launch spacecraft from the moon (less gravity) to enable us to get to Mars easier. We have convinced NASA of the more pressing terrestrial issues. They have agreed to back their timing up indefinitely and build ten reactors at six billion each.

"Please don't weep for them, NASA still has plenty of money for innovative space projects. Let's do some quiet addition together – counting in billions of dollars:

"Twenty-two to launch for Mars and then for Jupiter.   Plus,

One for the giant Magellan Telescope is to be built in Chile.   Plus,

One point four for a thirty-meter telescope destined for the top of Mauna Kea.
                    Plus,

Eight point seven for the biggy – the James Webb Space Telescope."

While his brother had spoken, Hal had done the math – $33,100,000,000.

"This is all a massive amount of money spent either looking into space or sending up trial balloons. What if we don't live long enough to even get back to the moon again? Even if we did, how can we colonize an alien world with a handful of people and watch every other member of our species burn?

"Don't misunderstand. Science is spending serious money on trying to solve problems here on earth. More research is going into nuclear power. Massive investment in solar cells and wind turbines is paying off. Businesses will take projects from government and introduce a refined version to the markets as they become feasible. But make no mistake, during the past one hundred years, government had to invest, and invest heavily, in research and development to get many advances to the public.

"The federal government built the system of delivering the Edison/Westinghouse invention of electric power. Eisenhower, as President, championed the idea of an interstate highway system. The Department of Defense invented the internet. The feds took on satellite communication and the GPS technology.

"These were all nightmare development projects, and business does not have the patience for that any longer. The shareholders want a quicker return.

Nothing has changed from that standpoint: the governments must start these efforts.

"I am pleased to receive a cabinet member from the Peoples Republic of China."

The Chinese delegate rose and turned to face the others in the audience. He bowed and sat back down.

"Mister Minister," continued Brian, "Your country is investing heavily in alternative power and is experimenting with fusion. We will need to discuss what can be done to accelerate your research because you also have more coal-burning power plants and pure soot emanating from coal fires than the rest of the northern hemisphere.

"Your country's moon research has begun but possibly some of the funds allocated for the remaining landings can help you in other areas. We appreciate that you are committed to your space program. We can understand how important major infrastructure projects first appear to be. However, a small reallocation of some monies could be used to quickly mitigate the environmental disaster we are facing."

Brian knew there had to be wiggle room in China's $ 30B and $200B budgets for space and infrastructure respectively.

"At this point I should mention, not only to China

but to everyone in this room, that the agreements we hope to have with your nations will not be executed by the United States. The US government does not have a say in our negotiations. The Wind River nation does have a signed contract with the US, but they are not the entity carrying our message to the world. The legal entity of Urgent, Wyoming, by way of its agreements with Wind River, will represent the team building the reactors. Back to business!

"We have leaders in this room who may think beyond spending money on long-term or outer-space risks. It is our hope we might guide these representatives to thinking a little differently. For example, a family member of the King of Malaysia is also here.

"Please understand that no offense is meant, but this planet needs your help. There is money budgeted for a transit system in Malaysia, plus massive funds for two building projects. Iskandar will be a new area, with three ports, near an area that frequently floods. The proposed Kuala Lumpur River City is six-hundred fifty acres on two point five kilometers of river. What happens if sea level rises by five feet only a few years after these communities have been built?"

Brian remembered the numbers: $ 50B and $112B for transit and city, respectively.

"Considering the deforestation problems Malaysia has had for years, could we slow down the ultra-expensive changes, bring in fusion power, build some inland developments in and around a massive reforestation project, and put the citizens to work planting trees and developing a town? We already have had success in such projects and can give a guided tour to anyone at any time. This is the type of thinking we need everyone in this room to get involved in.

"Take a look at the chart Hal has projected on the screen. This is not an illustration intended to disclose any secrets or create neighborly competition. Our intent is to show you how much money we, as a civilization, plan on spending in the near future – without any guarantee of that future."

There was a murmur around the room as the international audience viewed the statistics:

$132B	Develop 62,000 acres on the bay in Kuwait.
60B	Build entirely new Falcons City in UAE
82B	New airport in UAE
15B	Insert man-made islands into UAE
30B	New airport in Saudi Arabia
100B	Build new King Abdullah City in Saudi Arabia
100B	New islands in Caspian Sea
60B	Build New Clark City in Philippines

"There is no question that these countries have thought through these endeavors, but sea level rise might make these projects slums before too long. We suggest various countries meet at the bargaining table and make some short-range plans to mitigate sea level rise. Can't we get some forest started in those lands? Can we study turning sand into soil? Once that is accomplished, they can get back to their modern expansion plans.

The Saudi Arabian prince rose to speak: "I have been told of a large undertaking in Turkey."

"Yes, your highness, that is correct. The Turks estimate four-hundred billion will be spent in the next decade on their urban renewal needs. We will try to get them to the negotiating table but a sprawling, nation-wide project is difficult to deal with. Who makes the decision to bring part of that undertaking to a halt, and allow the other parts to continue?

"A similar problem exists in the European Union. They want to improve their international highway system. This would take five-hundred fifty billion euros worth of design, but where could they stop. In what country could they put the new infrastructure on hold in order to join us in attacking climate change?

"In your neighborhood, your highness, Egypt wants to spend fifty billion dollars to build a new capital city. Israel, even Nigeria, are proposing rapid transit systems with a similar cost. Such well-advertised, desperately needed public projects cannot be interrupted. They would have a rebellion - making the end of the world a moot point.

"However, in the developed countries we need to encourage some realistic, long-range planning. In the United States there are a handful of businesses that see mining on the moon as a profitable venture. They have drawn plans for new structures that can quickly be built on the lunar surface, and enterprising inventors are designing futuristic machines for mining. At one time we thought there was no water on the moon. Now the possibility of ice at the poles has reawakened the dreamers.

I use the moon, but it is not the only example.

"I submit that while such dreams are important, it is also important that we not follow these fantasies too far into the financial world. Our first priority needs to be to spend enough on the details that will enable us to survive. It seems foolish to pursue pillaging the minerals on the moon in a lethal atmosphere at the expense of ignoring our own atmosphere as it too turns lethal."

At this point, Brian sat down after introducing his brother, the scientist. Harold began to explain an agreement that would soon be introduced to the countries wanting to help the earth survive.

"The Global Environment and Atmosphere Doctrine (GEAD) will be written and signed by the countries that are serious about the lives of their citizens and the future of new generations. Initially, the administration of the doctrine will be a responsibility of a full-time staff housed at Urgent.

"There will be grants and loans to participating countries that improve the success of the long-term plans. Monitoring the terms of these financial and logistical arrangements needs to be done at Urgent. The authority to police the doctrine will be included in its language as will the system to resolve disputes by a new legal agency and court.

"We anticipate that countries may even wish to transact business through this new court in the interest of inter-signatory support and independent examination of the outcome of the exchanges. It would benefit all countries if they did business with each other. Our legal team is taking a wide view on drafting the initial language, as you will all see.

"We will distribute this information electronically unless you tell us otherwise. Further examination and changes and introductions are most welcome. Before we leave this room, we ask each of you to complete the small form inside the cover of the brochure you received.

"Obviously we need to know the correct electronic address. This address will have the highest security. This will be a visionary group of individuals within a select group of countries.

"Our communications with individuals on this list will be rare, but every message will be important."

SIXTEEN

•—• •• •••— • •—• •• •—

Donald Watson was a conservative politician. His father had taught him that progressive ideas and trends were immoral and not to be trusted. There was sin in not governing with an *iron fist,* in letting the people think for themselves. The good people of Wisconsin had elected him to the Senate three times. Those mandates could only mean he was doing something right.

Lately his job had been getting a little confusing. He was used to citizens confronting him as he approached the Capitol or other government buildings. Why were they now spending days in front of his office carrying those damn banners? Different groups began appearing on different days, as if someone had choreographed this protest dance. Local issues meant the most to him - he could identify with a desire to raise the minimum wage. Who didn't want a raise? But these tree-huggers and their huge, environmentally driven emotions were just too much for Watson to relate to.

The green issues were explained to him by the lobbyists representing the oil and gas interests. He understood them. He had enjoyed many afternoons with mining executives, flying in their jets high above their holdings.

Back on land, his staff could be counted on to wade through the confusion. Only donors with deep pockets were allowed to meet with him while Congress was in session. Naturally, when it was not, he was away at his family retreat in Florida.

The current congressional session involved his TSA committee. Transportation issues were always a highly visible subject, particularly when vehicle efficiency was involved. Ever since the 1980s the government has set mileage and thereby emission standards the new vehicles must meet. His committee was again reviewing those standards.

As science had revealed more detrimental components to emission gasses, the more the public had wanted to see vehicle exhaust cleaned up. The fuel efficiency of cars and trucks had improved, thus reducing the amount of pollution the engines spewed into the atmosphere. The fewer the molecules of nasty vapor, the cleaner the air – that made sense. The public wanted to clean up engines.

The automobile industry, and it is a large one, pointed out that more exotic and complicated emission gadgets must be paid for by the consumer, and thus add to the price of the car. That statement made sense too. The industry wanted to leave things as they were.

Senator Watson was on Capitol Hill because his committee had an important meeting. His vote would be pro auto makers, as it always was. Donald Watson favored big business when his decisions were based on counterbalancing statements.

However, he had been elected Chairman of the committee and should at least glance over some of the briefs his aides had prepared. His fellow committee members were deep into the final language on this issue, and he wanted to be able to hold up his end of a conversation.

He opened the large accordion folder and fingered the first item in the file, a sealed envelope with his name written on it. There was something familiar about the handwriting. Inside the manila envelope was a smaller letter-sized envelope that had not been sealed. Donald unfolded the single sheet of paper it contained:

"Dad - when are you going to grow up?"

"Sandy . . .," he whispered.

He had not seen, or even heard from his son for six years.

The Senator recalled that after getting over the shock, and working through the anger, he and his wife had talked about the young man's disappearance at great lengths. The couple had agreed that Donald's political leanings were one small cause, but that his inability to listen was actually a more important part of the problem. These conversations had resulted in the Senator undergoing two years of psychological counseling, but to what end? There was no one, other than his wife, to talk with.

On the QT, Senator Watson had asked a member of the intelligence community for help in locating his son. He had not filed a formal, missing person report with the police because of the adverse publicity. But he did need to know if the young man was still alive. One full year had passed before he heard from an investigator. The informal meeting was set, nothing in writing, and the politician would never forget that feeling when he was told there was no record of his son being alive. The investigator had continued;

"It is curious, though, that we have uncovered two similar cases of children of prominent politicians who have completely vanished. We will be keeping our eyes open because it is highly unusual – to simply vanish.

"Normally a credit card is used to buy gas in a neighboring state. Everyone that gets a job has to file a Social Security number with their employer. Most individuals have bank accounts. All these norms have been violated. We can find nothing."

Now he had heard from his son, and on the very day the Senator received his test results from his oncologist. There was nothing to do about the medical news, but the family issue demanded action.

The immediate response was to try to determine how he received the package. His staff advised that it had arrived in the official mail from the Madison office. He was told the envelope was delivered by a courier service with no return address.

Now he was even more curious. The Senator began

to review the file contents. The entire package contained original articles and newspaper clippings pertaining to the advantages and disadvantages of clean car standards, a thorough analysis of the very topic his committee was discussing.

Watson decided to check the validity of some sources and science. He called his staff together and told them, straight out, that he wanted to learn more about this. The stunned look on the collection of young faces amused the politician, and he mused aloud,

"I've never said that before, have I?"

He assigned them some research:

- Get information to confirm the integrity of the Union of Concerned Scientists, as they had written some of the material.

- Gather the names of the states that have followed California into setting the most stringent emissions reduction goals.

- Find analyses from the Air Resources Board that include data and financial impacts of those goals.

- Check with the EPA and get US vehicle emissions numbers.

"I just read that the automobile is responsible for twenty-eight percent of the total fossil fuel emissions for the entire country. Is that right?

"In other words, I need proof that there is a benefit to Wisconsin residents if this state signs on to new clean car standards.

"Let me share something with you while you are all in this room. This will be my last term in federal office. I have spent too many days away from home, and too many hours in smoke-filled rooms taking meetings. Long before many of you were born, I began my career in local offices and knew most of my constituents and their needs. I seem to have lost that connection. A package has arrived on my desk that asks me to open my eyes a bit and do some searching – maybe even some soul searching.

"I am not going to spend this last term following the party line. I want to do some real work and go out with my newfound head held high. You can help me with that grand finale. In fact, this might be fun.

"Talk with whomever you wish, that's OK. The staff at other offices may not believe you at first. Don't push it. The votes will speak for us. Those of you that can't stomach this change of heart can come and talk with me. I will do what I can to get you another appointment. To the others - go home, get some rest, and let's get to work."

The office now empty, Senator Watson phoned his wife in Madison and shared the good news – they had contact with their son. He heard her weep. They reminisced about what Sandy had missed during these past few years, including his dad's attempt to be more open-minded.

"To that end, I plan on staying in Washington tonight and this weekend to crunch these numbers. This file Sandy sent has almost one hundred pages of – wait . .What the . . ." he again whispered.

"Donald?"

"Sorry - that kid. The very last page in this package is an analysis of seventy-five years of tidal charts of the waters in front of our Vero Beach house. The data is calculated for West Palm Beach, but that's close enough. Looking at the high and low tide numbers over that many seasons leaves me convinced. He has illustrated sea level rise without a doubt. That clever young man.

"Now I know I need to get to work. Oh, and we are going to need to sell the Florida place."

At the large wooden desk in his DC office, the Senator began doing his own cursory research. The subject of global warming led into greenhouse gasses, which segued to man-made emissions. He zeroed in on a report about something called short-lived pollutants.

Everyone had heard about CO_2 and automobile exhaust. This publication suggested that in the long run, man had to control, even reduce, CO_2 content in the atmosphere. This must be a continuing practice with ongoing expense. However, it need not be the only action.

There are greenhouse gasses that do not last as long in the environment and may help cool things down while we corral CO_2. Methane, ozone, soot, and hydrofluorocarbons (hfc) only last 12 years, one month, weeks, and 15 years respectively – these were short lives compared to CO_2. The control of these lightweight warmers might prevent one-half a degree C. of warming over 30 years.

The Senator read that the US has partnered with other countries to form the Climate and Clean Air Coalition. He looked up that body to analyze its members and workings. They appeared to have agreed to target hfc's and study the rest.

"What study?" he asked out loud.

He reviewed the list of sources of all these contaminants and felt that diesel engines spoke the loudest. The soot from diesels, along with campfires and forest fires, was the second largest contributor to manmade pollution, behind CO_2. He saw no reason not to address this and continued digging, and thinking:

Forest fires are impossible to control once they start - educate the public about controlling fuel for a potential fire, and police it. The Forest Service might coordinate with local law enforcement to help with manpower.

Campfires - the same: education and policing.

Manufacturing processes spew these compounds into the air when making certain products. There would be too many independent facilities making glue, shampoo, soap, and the like to police.

Diesel engines, though, are widespread. Big, offroad rigs are fewer in numbers but probably have bigger engines; he could look at them later. Top priority should be truck engines. The millions of diesel-powered trucks on US highways alone must be a significant factor in soot concentrations.

Both new and used trucks were problematic. His committee was writing language for rules that would govern new equipment. Why not get truck makers to help write some pollution language? He made a note to get that process started in the future when his staff had time. Next, he would consider how to deal with the trucks on the road.

It was an earth-shattering event when Senator Donald Watson prowled the halls of Congress, after hours, talking with security guards. He was looking for some-one who had, or knew, the mechanics of trucks. He questioned a few of the personnel and finally found a guard that had experience driving big rigs. The guard was off duty in 30 minutes. They agreed to meet in the Senator's office.

A confused staff entered an even more confusing scene when they got to work the Monday morning. In the center of what used to be called the bull pen was the Senator's large oak desk and his overstuffed chair. He was surrounded by a few aides and empty chairs awaiting the arrival of other workers. The desks that had occupied this space were positioned around the perimeter of the room. He instructed them to get wa-ter, coffee, tea, whatever, and a notepad.

"We are going to write a bill. Among yourselves you will divide up the duties and areas of responsibilities for this effort. Right after lunch, at one o'clock sharp, the people with supervisory roles will meet me here and tell me what is going to happen.

"Our aim is to reduce emissions from trucks. Dream up a catchy title. This legislation will be bipartisan. Find two more co-sponsors from this conservative party and then get an equal number from the other party. You have heard me talk about the leanings of my fellow politicians. Talk with their staffs, get some support, and be prepared to tell me all about it.

"As I see it, we need to clean up the exhaust from commercial trucks. Find out how many there are. New trucks will be phased in by the manufacturer to meet certain emission standards. Leave the new vehicles to me and my transportation committee. I need you to concentrate on the huge used truck market, and that will be tricky. What should we set as a target mileage? Say, define our truck as a commercial vehicle that travels 50,000 miles per year on public roads. Then we need to set emission targets.

"Detroit will give you emission numbers on new engines. We need to write the rules for the used ones. Assuming our goal is to get dirty engines off the road, what is dirty? Where would we check emissions? These are long-haul rigs that cross state lines millions of times a day. In which states do they check emission for trucks?

"Could we use a handful of various locations for the certification of before-and-after measurements? With today's technology we could track the emissions of the truck from testing facility to testing facility. We could amass accurate emissions data on either side of an engine replacement.

"Not all engine swaps will be easy. The mechanics doing the conversions need to be vetted and charge reasonable prices. Let's say we guarantee to buy the retired power plants from the truck owner or mechanic. How much do we pay for it? Where do we take it? Call some steel plants and find out what they pay for scrap steel. That is one source of revenue. How do we fund the rest of it?

"Get creative in this area. Look into a possible tweak in the tax code. Either give some tax credit to the engine makers or a big tax break as incentive to the truck owner, then find some money to balance the books. We might raise the fuel tax on these more fuel-efficient engines. Find other money, though. We don't want the truckers to break even, they need to come out ahead.

"OK, that's it for now. Get to work - and thanks."

As the staff dispersed, the Senator heard the murmurs. He knew his appearance was part of the chatter. He did look a bit ragged. One reason was because he had not slept in his own bed for the past two nights.

Only he knew that another reason for his exhaustion was a recently diagnosed and growing tumor.

SEVENTEEN

— •• — — — •••— • •—•

The lookout high above the canyon floor had always been Edward's favorite place to contemplate. He came here every year if possible. He could still remember the first time; he only imagined what a village might look like, situated far below him. When Marina White-horse had told him the vision his dad and some rich guy had cooked up, he was amused. Then it really happened.

Harold Knight and Junior, as they used to call Edward, had passed by this overlook on that horseback ride they took when plotting and dreaming what the village might someday become. It was now obvious they were not very big dreamers. He remembered the reservoir as it was and thought today's deeper version was much more useful. They had to trade some land with the parks department in order to get title to much of what they had flooded, but that trade had been worth it.

He could not remember if they had contemplated two large suspension bridges spanning the wide canyon. However, he was certain that the first bridge they built ten years ago was along the highway extension that had been negotiated with the Wyoming Department of Transportation ten years before that. That crossing was the southern route, now connecting the town to the area near the new technology campus.

The taller second bridge also provided the roadbed for the light rail system. Like the trolleys of old, with rubber tires and overhead electric power, the coach ran above ground in a loop from the airport on the West plateau to the northern edge of the village. Then it dove into a tunnel just before the canyon rim. Exiting the tunnel, the transit vehicles continued onto the bridge deck built beneath the upper, exposed auto and truck lanes on that new canyon bridge. At the east end the transit line disappeared into another tunnel and continued deep into the maze beneath the industrial acreage of Urgent.

Eight years ago, the scientists had begun testing their launch system and the power controls. The large, deep launch barrels had been uncovered and they started the construction of the above-ground vertical rails. Then the systematic testing with fake and prototype vehicles began.

The new bridge was near the launch site at the north end of the mill complex and was temporarily closed to all traffic before each test, during the final countdown, and for five minutes post-liftoff of the space vehicle. Foremost, it was an irritation to wait on the bridge for the launch test while enduring either the hot summer or freezing winter days. Those familiar with local traffic drove south to use the old bridge. For those living in the new west side neighborhoods that were growing in the ravine south of the airport, that was now a long drive.

Once underground, beneath the steel mill and its ancillary buildings, the transit system followed a route that covered more than twice the distance it ran above ground. The warren of labs, studios, and assembly areas extended beyond the visible walls of the mill and surrounds. Even the tall transmission towers and wind generators had underground access. Edward could see the strategically placed tall towers that were bladeless.

These unusual structures were known to be filters for the surface air around the acres of solar cells and reflection array. Few knew they were also filters for the intake air used by the massive underground chamber. The collection of subterranean experiments required large quantities of fresh air.

Reining his horse into a U-turn, Edward looked west towards the high country. It might have been his imagination, but he thought he could see the tall antenna array situated near the Platform Communications building. Casual visitors to the village rarely drove this far up into the hills. They could not see the impressive collection of devices that would aid in communication with space platforms. Those that flew into the West plateau airport had the best view of all the *dishes* surrounding the PlatCom center.

A smile graced Edward's face as he visualized the cabin near the edge of a pond which he knew was half a day's ride farther west. He was thankful he had decided to share that retreat with Ruth. She was now his wife and the mother of their son. The cabin was a special place that had a romantic impact on that budding relationship.

He fondly remembered when Ruth and her traveling companion Courtney returned from what might be considered a sting operation on behalf of the young growing village. That team of young people had been in the field for a few years, silently slowing the opposition. Their work had been critical, and Edward had decided to recognize that fact by sharing the cabin with them. He knew they would honor his privacy and be thankful he took the time to debrief them.

The younger residents of Urgent were not aware that the early growth was not widely known. The founders felt that interruptions caused by visitors, well-wishers, and inspectors should be kept to a minimum. In fact, as was the case before WWII at Oak Ridge, Tennessee, even the workers were not aware of everything that was happening. Naturally, any leaks in the secrecy veil resulted in an immediate response from some conspiracy theorist or glory-seeking politician. Urgent had built a team to creatively intercept those individuals. Usually they never even knew how they got distracted from their goal of interrupting the Wyoming project.

Diverting his attention to the gully in the south, he noticed the Tribal Facilities building with its brightly colored new wing. What once had been an old, drab structure used to house equipment and a coffee pot was now a modern meeting place for members of the nation.

Harold Knight and Edward and Marina Whitehorse had first met there almost 25 years ago to talk about the likelihood of being able to develop this project. They had to pack their own lunch. Now the building could seat, and the kitchen could feed, over 200 at once. In fact, Edward knew that his dad, Chief Joseph, visited the cafeteria every morning to have coffee with other old-timers.

Three generations, he thought. My ten-year-old son Pope is on track to be the next chief of our nation. My family will have led this people for three generations if he becomes chief. Is that good for the nation?

His thoughts were interrupted by a siren. He saw no vehicles on the new bridge and knew immediately what time it was. A launch was ten minutes away. Edward often projected himself into precarious situations. Pretending to ride in the nosecone of some future rocket was not an unusual thought.

He would leave the solid ground of Wyoming and gain altitude, noticing the atmosphere on the horizon getting bluer. The projectile would nose over and begin to travel in an orbit around the planet with the entire grand vivid views of the world. His alma mater, MIT, was near the Atlantic far below. He knew there was a large project in the forests of Alaska and saw the trees. Half a world away he saw similar efforts beginning in Western Australia.

Turning his imagination towards the heavens, he saw the growth in the shield as it had been described to him. He recognized the tall, spherical tower on one side that anchored the large shield. Fuel tanks stacked on fuel tanks, all interlocked to form a work platform to be occupied by humans or robots. Someone would throw the first switch on the computer in person, then leave.

Ground operations would get control and the only thing moving would be a carbon dioxide powered robot. He could see the robots fastening sections of the shield together as they were delivered by the daily arrival of space vehicles. The robots would refuel at special ports on the space platform. Any machine in need of repair would dock itself in a designated garage on the platform, and its replacement would fly out to join the team.

Another siren signaled the end of the bridge closure and the end of Edward's daydreaming. He needed to return the horse to its stall and hustle over to the main auditorium building. He wanted to be there when Leah wrapped up her first lecture to the new students. As Chief of the Nation he attended important events if at all possible. This was an event not to be missed.

The daughter of one of Urgent's most influential families was speaking to the incoming students at the new Wyoming Institute of Science and Technology – WYIST. These were not just new students, but the first students. The grand opening of Urgent's higher education facility had been long awaited. The fact that Leah was in charge brought tears of joy to Edward. Her family was his family's closest friends.

One last glance down at the village and Edward

smiled as he noticed the landscaping around the homes and walkways. He thought of young Leah and their brief conversation the day the big mill was turned on; could that really have been 16 years ago?

Edward, his dad, and Bo Elliott (the major building coordinator and Leah's dad) had decided that she would get the honor of throwing the switch to initiate mill operations. The entire population of Urgent was at the ceremony and immediately partook in the celebratory barbeque. No one noticed Leah taking Edward aside and innocently asking if the mill would stink.

He replied by getting down on his knees to be at eye level with the seven-year old. "I think we need to plant some flowers to make sure all people can smell something sweeter than a steel mill. Can you help me with that?"

"Sure."

She dove into the landscaping issue before the day was over. For years, Leah could be found in the village digging in the dirt, or riding in a truck full of soil or full of plants. The tree-lined gullies in the high country had better soil and Leah convinced her dad to get some - then some more.

A few willing adults began giving her books about plants, how they grow and what they smell like when flowering. When one variety did not survive the cold or the heat, she replaced it with a hardier version or changed the environment. Small arbors began appearing in the village to give shade to exposed street corners. Colorful, short fences blocked some of the wind that whipped down from the high mountains.

Edward knew he had Leah to thank for the sweet

scent of a mock orange in spring, partially masked by a collection of nearby tall pines. Many walkways and building entrances were adorned with clumps of lavender that when brushed up against, released a pleasing aroma. Above all she had decided where to deposit hundreds of shade trees.

Over the years her dedication rubbed off on some of her peers. She began an unofficial committee to keep eyes on the village and watch out for diseased plants, insects, and the outcomes of periodic extreme weather events.

Now, however, she was devoting considerable time to the new institute. She saw the future of higher education in the community and needed to spend less time on plants in order to contribute more time learning how to become a good teacher.

Edward turned the horse's head and nudged his well-worn boot heels into the animal's sides. They bolted for the barn at a gallop. He climbed into a wheeled vehicle and drove to the WYIST campus. He would not miss giving her a well-deserved hug at the conclusion of the first lecture in her new career.

This young woman was the future.

EIGHTEEN

— — —   — • • —   — •   • —   • — •   — • •

"Welcome to the future," she began, and the room became silent.

"To those of you that know some of the background, I'm sorry about the following boring words. We need to convey some history to everyone in this room, then we will all take a tour."

As she gazed at the eager young faces, she was reminded that she was not much older. Had she actually finished college she would have been out for two years, while these freshmen were just getting started.

"You are the first group of young people to have this opportunity. This building, the others on the campus, even the program of study are brand new. I have the honor of presenting this orientation to the first class of students to attend the science school at

URGENT LAUNCH

Wyoming Institute of Science and Technology:WYIST. My name is Leah Elliott and until further notice you might call me the dean of this place."

She noticed a few looks of surprise as her new students settled in.

"This institute has been established to provide you and those who follow with the knowledge to continue the work that has been designed here. I know that sounds strange but there is so much research taking place within one mile of you, that the results of those experiments demand a new type of labor. As we develop new technologies, we must also develop the people behind them. Many of you will continue the research while others will perform that labor. You will make that choice.

"Thirty years ago, the Native Americans of the Wind River Indian Reservation agreed to dedicate this land to the protection of the planet. These natives, many citizens from Appalachia, more from the Deep South, and a quiet collection from laboratories around the nation have made an extreme effort. The community is called Urgent. The land is still the Wind River nation.

"As quickly as we could import the talent, we began building experiments and bringing in equipment to perform all research in-house. I say we because I live here and am a member of this community. You are here because you have expressed an interest in some or all of the subjects we investigate."

Leah asked for a show of hands of those interested in the science disciplines - materials, chemistry, cryogenics, agriculture.

There was quite a wide range of interests in the room.

"As you can see, there is not a single common denominator that we could call the major interest within your group. We will be asking all of you to get a working knowledge of everything, and to specialize in at least one subject. You will be exposed to science you have no interest in. Keep an open mind. We anticipate your curiosity will be piqued and you will want to learn more and want to examine how it all interconnects.

"At a glance, it is obvious that we dabble in power production. The wind turbines are sort of a give-away, as is the massive size of the solar cell field and the reflection array with its collection towers. There are two hydroelectric dams that are not as visible, and a nuclear reactor that just recently came online. You will be touring these facilities by this time tomorrow and expected to make some notes. That will be your first class.

"You are going to have an all-day session with the scientist responsible for keeping it all running and all up to date. One day you may attend an international conference with him in some foreign paradise. Power generation and efficient consumption will continue to be a major issue throughout your lifetime. Following a week of classes and an analysis of your basic math skills you will be transferred to another scientist.

"Consider yourselves the baton in a relay race. We have over twenty different sciences guiding our researchers through twice as many experiments. As previously mentioned, you will get to know a fair amount about everything. This will be hard work and involve long hours. Trust me when I say I can guarantee the reward. This work pace and ethic is how this community was built, and it has served us well. I'm not prone to getting personal but let me share my story.

"My mom and dad met on this reservation. They met when Urgent was young and have never left. From the time I can remember, I have never rested. Not that kind of rest - I mean having tons of time with nothing to do. I didn't watch television. I went with dad to a job site, to watch the meteor showers, to build a fish ladder, or to analyze the best route for the railroad tracks to reach the north end of the mill. In fact, we have never owned a TV.

"When it came time to go to college we sat around the table, talked for hours, looked up subjects on the computer, and decided my time was better spent learning more here, at my own pace and from friends. I did leave home to get the general knowledge under my belt. After two years at a public university I returned home, to the reservation.

"That was how I received my formal education - the informal still continues. Don't misunderstand, I'm not a smart person. But I know a lot. Something always sticks when you are exposed to an excessive amount of everything. That's exactly what is about to happen to you.

"Later this afternoon we will meet again in this auditorium, and you will learn the layout and workings of Urgent. This orientation will include descriptions of halls, maps of tunnels, stairs, and elevators; this can prevent you from continually getting lost.

"If you look out that window you can see the large,

open field with the steel mill on the far side. In the winter it helps to know that you can get from here to there without going outside. See that field of wind turbines about a mile to the east of the mill? There's a tunnel to that area too.

"In fact, beneath the mill, this closer field, and all those wind turbines and the solar mirrors is more infrastructure than you see above ground. You need to be familiar with it all. You may have heard that we have a launching pad near here. That fact will be evident in ninety minutes when today's launch test takes place. Soon you will know how to get to that site and, more importantly, when not to even try.

"We are going to break for lunch now. Staff members are standing by to help you to find the dining room and your own dorm room.

"Welcome to Urgent."

After giving her pep-talk, Leah was hungry but did not want to eat in the cafeteria with the new students. There would be hours of Q & A later today, and on subsequent days. Her office in the administration building had a small well stocked fridge. Scooting around a couple of young women, she bounced up the back stairs and into the tidy office.

Furnishings were simple – desk, fold-out couch, large monitor and small refrigerator. The monitor was old-fashioned, but she insisted on a screen that would allow her to view the data privately, even with a student sitting across the desk. Today's holographic systems just filled the room with image, and everyone could see the entire display.

Leah could work anywhere. She had a desk at Tribal

HQ, and a closet next to her dad's lair, both with large monitors. This was one consequence of spending 20 years *terrorizing* everyone. Another consequence was that no doors were locked to her. If she didn't know the code for the keypad, she could buzz Tom Lacey or Fitz to have the door opened.

Ever since she could read and write she was allowed into any lab and her many questions were always answered. The *off-limits* areas were clearly marked. She later learned that these restrictions were safety issues, nothing else. The community was hers to roam.

The education leaders of Urgent had considered this the purest form of education. Long before the founders began formal education, Native Americans had learned in this manner. Many of those now educated natives still believed this hands-on approach was the best way to teach and learn.

Leah had talked about science with many scientists during her short lifetime. They often referred to DARPA as the epitome of hands-on learning. In the late 1950's this agency was formed to concentrate on space related needs. The United States had some complex problems and no specific entity to study, then solve them: enter ARPA.

Later our Defense Department took it over, identified specific issues and, after adding the adjective "defense" to the name Advanced Research Projects Agency issued instructions to "fix it". The researchers knew the goal but there was no road map leading them there. Every DARPA project was complex. Every project was completed with an unusual amount of cooperation, trust, and creative thinking.

That was exactly how WYIST expected its students to learn. Leah began the afternoon session with statistics and facts:

" - - Three point nine million square miles. According to one source that is the area of land we should plant trees on in order to help with the climate crisis.

 - - Three hundred billion tons is the maximum amount of carbon we can emit into the air and still keep global warming in check. At our current emission rate, it will only take ten years to reach that mark.

 - - Since the turn of the twenty-first century, every year but one has been the warmest year on record.

 - - At current warming rates the planet will experience five feet of sea level rise by 2100. We know that today one hundred million people live within three feet of sea-level.

 - - Two-hundred thirteen million tons is the anticipated crop loss each year due to larger hungrier pests. In addition, rising seas continue to inundate farmlands, and warmer temperatures will result in a five percent crop loss due to drought and parching.

 - - Twenty-three million people have fled their homes because of environmental degradation.

 - - Two and one-half billion people live in locations in which demand for water exceeds supply.

 - - Ninety percent of all urban dwellers live in polluted places.

 - - The North American wildfire season arrives earlier, lasts longer, and is more severe than ever.

 - - There is a summer shipping lane open through both the Northwest Passage and the Northeast Passage.

URGENT LAUNCH

"What do all of these statements have in common?" Leah asked.

"I mentioned earlier that this community was built on one simple premise – to save the planet. Actually, to save mankind is the more accurate statement. The planet did just fine before man and will continue to be all right after we are gone. The research and activities in Urgent are dedicated to giving man a bit more time on earth, time to figure things out.

"The problems I just identified do have fixes, however they will take serious effort and time. We have already put our *army* to work collecting, propagating, and planting trees. To limit the amount of carbon we burn and put in the atmosphere, would mean we leave half of the remaining oil, natural gas, and coal in the ground. With science we could limit insect reproduction. With money we can get water to more people.

"We don't have all the answers yet and that's where you come in. All these problems are being presented to you to study and solve.

"No one in this auditorium is paying a penny to be at this institute. Room and board, meals, transportation, and entertainment are all part of the package. You will be *living* your learning experience. Since all your previous schooling has revolved around classes, the absence of bells and schedules will be foreign to you. At Urgent you will study challenges.

"At the far end of Lab Row is the green garden where they are looking at plants and trees. We have modified the genome on some vegetables so they grow faster, but now we want to know how they react to a longer growing day. Some grains can yield three crops per season if they have light all the time. Can our modified crops do that?

"Those dedicated scientists are also attempting to coax trees to grow faster and spread out a larger canopy. The best way to add oxygen to our atmosphere is for trees to turn the combustion waste product, CO_2, back into carbon and oxygen. Trees emit oxygen through the photo-synthesis process and trap the carbon. Can we hurry things up? The answer is yes, but we need to experiment with more species.

"Closer to the central steel mill, you can find the Robot Lab. We have custom-made helpers to work in space that we need to talk to and control. We also need to design the next generation. Technology keeps marching on, and that progress often means an increase in reliability and dexterity of the small machines.

"In a couple of years, we will meet the stars at fourteen-thousand miles above the earth. We will begin building a space shield beyond the International Space Station. At that distance, we can send an order to a robot and expect response in a second. A few years after that we will start moving the entire shield deeper into space, towards the sun. When we need to send signal four times farther, how long will it be before we can expect a response? What about fifty times farther out? The farther from the planet we travel, the more the robots need to be independent.

"The temperature team does most of its work deeper underground, although the entrance is on Lab Row. Below the temptank, along a massively insulated rectangle, is a series of workbenches and machines that are integral to experiments with super-cold and super-hot temperatures. While the finished solar shield will always be in the hot sunlight, except for the odd passing planet or asteroid, it will get cold when it orbits through earth's shadow as the shield is being built. We need to know the reaction of every component to extreme cold and heat. There are labs conducting experiments in thermochemistry that may have application in the reactor and turbines.

"Farther down Lab Row is the pressure vessel and its technicians. Extreme pressure, or lack thereof, vacuums, can also affect materials. In fact, some alloys only come into being under extreme pressure. We make wafers for our electronic components that have layers of various elements which are formed by pressure and vacuum.

"The large, central section of this complex is Power Central. Liquid sodium in the temptank stores a massive amount of energy in the form of heat. This is transferred to water which makes steam that turns the turbines. The dams have water driven turbines, and the fusion reactor uses atomic energy to heat the sodium. There must be a massive collection of pipes, valves, turbines, and electric power leads connected to all this. It's there in the Power Central.

"Naturally, power consumers are close to all that power generation. Directly above is the steel mill that runs on that electricity. Obviously, the research complex and the community buildings use that power. Once a week, a huge jolt is delivered to test our rocket launch ideas. It's not the typical rocket-launch explosion because the launch system is electromagnetic.

"That's sort of the quick verbal tour of this area. Let's get you better acquainted with your surroundings, then each other."

The students gathered around the staff members that had earlier taken them to their dorm rooms. A series of electric trolleys waited for the students in front of the Auditorium building. Soon the trail of curious minds was under way, destined to experience an hour-long scenic tour of the community.

Leah walked out the same front doors and turned left, toward the mill, and the new visitor center. She knew that there was a stairwell in that building that led down to a tunnel and transportation.

At the base of the stairs she found a community cart, jumped into it, and drove toward the research complex. On the north side of the buildings on the surface was the first of a series of wind turbines. The foundation of that tall structure was larger than the others in the row. This was because her father had built a cavity in the foundation.

Beneath the large concrete overhang was an old weathered picnic table surrounded by clumps of lavender and other aromatic herbs. A soft, well-tended patch of grass was under the table while Japanese tatami mats softened the three walls upon which they hung.

It had been a long first day.

Leah was there to meditate.

NINETEEN

━━━ •━• •━ ━• ━━• • •━━• ━

"Those hypocrites," shouted Tom Lacey to no one in particular. Randall James was the one that brought him the news, but he was not angry at the messenger. He was angry at the government of Brazil for thinking they could breach the deal and void the contract, without thinking about the repercussions. It would take work but there would be consequences. Lacey could guarantee that.

The electronic research at Urgent was under the purview of this man. Years ago, he had been involved in research elsewhere, and not too many years ago, working for Urgent elsewhere. After a series of false starts he had managed to move everything to the Wind River site. Now, safely ensconced below ground, his responsibilities had grown. His computers were in touch with other machines and with lower life forms such as flora and fauna. He was the data center waiting for the space exploration high above the planet, and working with the small member-owned bank up on the surface.

Eavesdropping had always been his forte´. The smooth, constant growth of the community had been partially come about because Lacey knew what his opponents were planning. He had thwarted many attempts to impede the progress of work being done. His staff was able to monitor the calendars of senators and the cell phones of their secretaries. He was patched into the non-secure lines of the various alphabet intelligence agencies. Computers sounded alerts when specific buzz words were overheard. He even kept the bank records for hidden team members.

That had been an unusual request from Harold Knight a few years ago. Urgent planned to bring on board a full-time researcher, but "we want no electronic record of his being here." They were looking for a way to pay this individual and guarantee his future.

Lacey knew the place to start was the Wyoming State Bank because it was totally controlled by Urgent and its citizens. But how does he get paid? Does he get an account number? How do we credit interest?

The answer had revolved around arranging a safe deposit box, putting that box number as a payable in the payroll ledger, and physically printing share certificates in the bank – like bearer bonds. The person presenting the certificate to a teller at the bank would get cash, no questions asked. This was a unique banking arrangement, and had been for almost ten years.

Now there were three such accounts.

That challenge had been a pleasure to resolve. Today's will not be pleasant at all. He had just been told by Randall James, the senior researcher in Lacey's operation, of a transmission he had intercepted.

The President of Brazil had asked his brother-in-law if he thought they could operate the fusion reactor on their own. The Urgent consortium had built the reactor near the Amazon rain forest and its purpose was to deliver power to the facility connected with the reforestation project. Tom knew this line of questioning could not be allowed to continue. The dialog had to stop.

Large reforestation efforts involved paperwork. To protect the interest of the Wind River nation, the United States, and the ForCI project, Brazil had signed contracts. After the documents were executed, the land was titled to ForCI, and the fusion reactor leased to the host country.

Actually, the electricity was rented while the physical reactor was still owned by the Urgent group. These contracts also stipulated that the reactor would be located on ForCI land, not on land under title to the host country, providing further safeguards.

Lacey told Randall to get Brian Knight here ASAP. He also cleared his large monitor of the data from another project and pulled up some itineraries, disclosing the whereabouts of Eduardo and Javier. Finally, he needed to consult the files of the universities in Alaska and Canada and of the Universidade Federal do Para in Brazil.

Local time in Wyoming was afternoon, which meant

the people he wanted to speak with in the various offices were not at work in Brazil. He would ask Randall to get up early to do that. They got Edward White to agree to a quick meeting in Bo's lair. Lacey went over the situation.

In the usual arrangement, he would wait for Brian Knight to arrive from his office out West, but Tom wanted to expedite all communications. He began:

"We have just picked up some chatter between the President of Brazil and a relative about what it would take to run the nuclear power plant we built near the rain forest. Edward knows how complicated this is, but it's not the manpower that bothers me. It's the fact that they are even thinking of breaching our agreement.

"We have built a small community down there as part of our reforestation efforts. There are buildings which we own, an electric grid that extends well into their territory from the small patch we own, and millions of trees at stake. This does not count thousands of student-hours spent in planting and tending those seedlings.

"All we want to do is help the planet and be left alone. Brazil must think the electric power plant is worth more than we do. Regardless, they can't have it - period. What I want you to know is that tomorrow we will be driving that point home.

"Very few people are aware of the fact that many of the students working in this exchange program are hand-picked. While we advertise it as a large class, a cohort so to speak, it is a specific group with specific talents. We have sent along a few students that have military experience, even special forces training.

"They are able to defend themselves or really hurt others. There are at least four in each class. They may or may not know each other, it doesn't matter. These men and women can be useful, even without weapons.

"The most interesting aspect of this project is the exchange of students. We always trade our students for theirs, thus everyone has a foreign experience. This project has the Brazilian class helping in Alaska and in British Columbia, totally under our supervision and a significant distance from home.

"Those involved in the project know where the foreign camps are. What they do not realize is that the back-grounds of students that came from Brazil is far from ordinary. We have hand-picked the offspring of five prominent politicians or their relatives. I can give you the titles of the government offices their parents or relatives hold. The fact that we recruited these kids is unknown.

"My office spent long hours combing through the university records and political archives to locate targets with college aged relatives. With the help of the university staff, we offered each of them this unique class. With few exceptions, they don't even know each other either.

"What I intend to do is get Eduardo and Javier in the loop on this and continue to watch the chatter in Brasilia. They are smart people, and I suspect they will decide it's too complicated an issue, and too risky, to steal a nuclear reactor from a US concern. Brazil did sign on to the Global Environment and Atmosphere Doctrine (GEAD), which contains language about noncompliance. I trust they have read that recently.

"That's my hope. If this idea goes any further, we have our messengers standing by."

At this pause, Edward couldn't resist. "Tom, this is unbelievable. How long did it take you folks to determine who to recruit, and then get results?"

"From start to finish, the Amazon research took over a year," Tom replied. "But there are others and they are ongoing. Each presents unique problems, consider:

-- China is a massive country with only twenty percent of the land covered by forests. Plus, they have twelve universities, but they are scattered over two-million square kilometers of area - and then there's the communist thing.

-- Indonesia has less than one-million square kilometers of area and nearly twenty-eight colleges that study forestry and engineering. That's a better prospect. Plus, they are dealing with the oil palm frenzy.

-- Mexico is only about a third forest and they have eleven schools that could help. We would need to study the prevailing winds and atmosphere to pinpoint potential reforestation pockets.

"If we can increase the size of an existing forest and get it to a level at which the weather is positively affected, we can proudly go on to the next country. There is an advantage to cooling down an area by planting a bunch of trees.

"However, if that advantage is lost because that cooler air is blown over a hot desert, we might need to look elsewhere to start. The forests of the US and Canada, below latitude sixty degrees North, temper and carry the weather across the North Atlantic. Even though they consist largely of evergreen trees, that is an important function. We could work in Canada for a while.

"We might return to the Amazon as a mid-planet exercise and further our work in Australia to have a greater impact on the Southern Hemisphere. Personally, I like the idea of working in a friendly English-speaking country where they know they have a heat problem and seriously want to fix it.

"Now back to your observation Edward, we can selectively recruit in any of these countries."

Brian Knight and Myrlene flew in the next morning. Edward asked Sandy and Bo to join them in Bo's lair. They wanted privacy, electronic security, and needed to be near Sandy's lab.

Tom Lacey explained the situation to the newcomers, including his wish that the threat die-down. He had asked his staff to task at least one more satellite to monitor *traffic* near Brasilia on all bandwidths. This would automatically add emphasis on communications that were encrypted or low-powered, such as Citizens Band and short-distance signals. Tom finished voicing his concern and asked Sandy to share his thoughts with the group.

"Tom and I want to get your input on the security of an invention we have running in Brazil. In other meetings, I may have touched briefly on the audio laser experiment we have been engaged with in our Ag Lab. Not that sound might help the plants grow, but that certain frequencies might be an irritant to pests. To carry a sound with a laser is to pinpoint the audio.

"Normally sound is radiated from the source: you can hear it as long as you are within the ever-expanding *cone of sound.* We can now get a laser to carry some sound along that narrow band the laser uses. The sound is only heard when one is in close proximity of that invisible light line. Our experiments at Urgent have focused the laser across our crops that are growing beneath the solar array.

"We have planted a variety of vegetables and trees at a number of different times. This yields green things of different heights growing in our test garden. We have purposely imported a variety of insects into fenced-off sections of the garden and turned on the audio laser. I am proud to say we have encouraging results. So successful in fact, that we have scaled up the experiment in Brazil. This is in testing mode in the rain forest and we are trying to keep the lid on this invention.

"Our concern over this threat from the Brazilian government is not so much for the trees, or the insects, but over the experiment and the proprietary rights. We need to retain full control over this technology and all data derived from it. If there is even a hint that the Brazilians are overrunning our compound, we must dismantle this system and bring it home."

Myrlene was the first to respond, with a question about the size and location of the equipment. She and Sandy had helped with the design and logistics of this installation, but were not very familiar with the site.

URGENT LAUNCH

After hearing his answer, she felt confident that the location had been well thought out. The fact that the local farmers could not see the equipment unique to the experiment would mean they had nothing to tell the local police that might be asking questions.

The Urgent researchers would have time to remove any evidence if inquiries went farther than local police. If disassembled, these parts would be lost among the other parts gathering dust in the warehouse they had built earlier. Even if the compound were invaded or impounded by the government, the pieces of this machine would make no sense to anyone once the components had been mixed in with other electronic discards.

Bo Elliott cleared his throat, signaling his intention to speak. "Leah has told me about this new device, but mostly about the success you have had with the large conifers up north. Weren't you concentrating on controlling the beetles?"

"That's right Bo," said Sandy. "Our first real-life experiment was in the Tongass reforestation project. We worked our way through a few laser setups until we determined that opposing, undulating waves were the most effective. Very few of the little creatures liked to cross the wall of sound we created.

"Each laser is the source of the light and sound beams which extends from the ground to the treetops about one mile away. We have cut a slash in the damaged forest and installed the devices at each end of the slash. When two lasers are pointed at each other and both are oscillating up and down they discourage a major percentage of beetles from crossing the open area. This keeps them confined to the area of forest that is already dying due to beetle damage and will ultimately save more of the healthy trees in Alaska.

"I should mention, though, that due to the way the jungle grows, we are trying different laser placement in the Amazon. No perfect solution has been reached yet, but we keep trying. If our beams are interrupted every couple of months by fast growing vegetation, we need another plan. That's where we are now."

"Am I to understand they have a beetle problem in the Amazon?" asked Myrlene.

"No - but they do have poachers and black market loggers."

She looked at Brian.

Brian ignored her gaze and brought them back to the topic at hand – overheard conversation in Brasilia. They decided to wait and see the nature of further conversation.

Fortunately, there was none.

TWENTY

The shells of reusable spacecraft must be made of a very specific alloy. During launch and reentry into the earth's atmosphere, friction creates extreme heat. While in space it may also experience extreme cold for a long period of time. The aerodynamics of the craft might cause shuddering and set off low-speed harmonic vibrations. Touchdown could result in an impact and the stresses related to that. The materials scientists who created an impermeable skin that withstands those numerous forces had done a lot of homework.

One such shell was being fabricated in the fourth level below ground at the research facility of Urgent. The team was designing cages, or crumple zones, to surround precious electronics. They were working backwards from a frame that could take the thrust of liftoff and the compression of landing.

Also in the works, was a half-pipe shaft structure to attach to the stationary vertical frame rails that pull the vehicle to 800 mph at launch. That exterior frame had better be well assembled. Its purpose was to guide, but not touch, the companion magnetic channel formed in the sides of the craft. The half-pipe design provided for a protected area of magnetic interaction for those few seconds that the internal magnet was lifted by the external force at an ever increasing rate.

The technicians had determined that the rocket mounted channel could not be entirely made of steel, or any material that would be attracted to the magnet. They could not take the chance that indirect but weak magnetism could briefly pull down on any part of the vehicle – thus slowing the ascent.

Their solution was to build internal electromagnets, spaced at specific intervals, and have the computer time the magnetic impulses to guarantee that the external forces were always in sympathy with the internal forces, and pulling the load up. They placed a layer of beryllium, which does not have any magnetic properties, between the magnets to create a magnetic dotted line running up the side of the vehicle.

The composite alloy that made up the tall half-pipe shaft was similar material. The scientists had devised a scheme to stack layers of the two materials into one tall piece of electronic wizardry. Set into the tall, thick covering of alloy that did not conduct magnetism were contrasting bright discs of electro-magnets. The "firing" sequence of the magnets in the half-pipe guide outside the rocket was electronically controlled to coordinate with the exact location of magnetic attraction inside the vehicle. Ground based and on-board computers would control the timing of these events to the nanosecond.

The lack of flammable fuel was one advantage to this particular design. The small craft did have three external booster tanks, evenly distributed around the perimeter, but they would not burst into flame. They were loaded with cold, liquid gas.

Countless hours of research had gone into finding a fuel for these daily launches that did not involve combustion. It was illogical to save the atmosphere by having spent rocket fuel contribute to air pollution every day. The solution was liquid nitrogen with a smattering of liquid oxygen when needed. Both these gasses can be cooled to the point where they become liquid. On the Celsius scale, minus 120° did the job.

Slightly opening a bottle of frozen liquid gas starts a well-known process – it boils. At that boiling point (for water this is 100°C) the liquid immediately turns into a gas and wants to occupy a lot more space. Liquid oxygen for example wants to grow to 50 times its liquid size when exposed to air any warmer than minus100°C.

When attached to a vehicle, such as a rocket, this controlled explosion produces thrust to keep the projectile moving. Using frozen gas in this application would be ideal, because as the package got higher off the ground, the more the gas could expand. Our atmosphere is half as dense at 100,000 feet up as it is on the ground.

The light, slippery space vehicle would continue to gain altitude even though the content of the booster tanks was being depleted. There was less atmospheric pressure resistance on both the vehicle surface and on the escaping expanding gas. Naturally, it would take a complicated series of electric valves to allow the appropriate portion of the gas to escape from a booster tank and provide controlled ascent.

A smaller compartment inside each external tank was a storage area loaded with a reserve supply of compressed gas, high-pressure CO_2. This power reserve would be used for:

-- A second boost to reach altitude,
-- Vehicle maneuvering, and
-- Robot maneuvering.

Therefore, the booster tanks accompanied the shuttle on the entire trip. The load of pressurized carbon dioxide was actually cargo to be left in space before the vehicle returned to earth – it was fuel for the robots.

The booster tanks were fabricated to be easily removed from the rocket body. The control wiring passed through the skin of the vehicle beneath the tank attachment point. Once the tanks were removed, the space vehicle could then deploy its reentry control surfaces.

A wing would hydraulically extend out from the rocket body at each of two attachment points previously occupied by external tanks. The third location housed the opening where the tailpiece (complete with moveable rudder) would move into position. What formerly looked like a missile now looked more like a short-winged glider. These control features, coupled with GPS navigation and a backup closed circuit video feed peeking through the window, meant the craft was now able to return to earth.

There had been an issue with the window – the team had an ongoing argument with the designers as to the need for this luxury. Regardless of the logic behind that discussion, the decision was always the same – install a window near the nose of the craft, triangular in shape and about two feet on each leg. Plans proceeded on schedule – with a window.

The first prototypes were closely monitored for balance and overall weight. The immediate goal was to produce at least eight such craft. The assembly crew would later be adding landing gear and a heat-resistant belly coating to keep things a little cooler during reentry. If possible, the staff wanted to reuse the electronics and other internal components.

Deep in the complex of laboratories was the single-room computer center. Sophisticated, fast, barely taxed supercomputers were in contact with people and sensors all throughout Urgent. In fact, most of the soft tasks surrounding the entire project were performed in that room by a machine the locals called *Dave.*

The name was an homage to a famous outer-space movie with an on-board computer gone wild, named Hal. However, Urgent already had an important Hal, so they interchanged the computer's and human's name in the movie. *Dave* was now the grounded computer standing by to go rogue.

In their workroom closer to the launch point, the team was finishing the assembly of the external booster tanks. Engineers had sized the tanks so they could bring two back inside the spacecraft when it returned to earth. The vehicle was more than twice as tall as an external tank but only as big around as a small car.

To return two booster tanks per trip they needed to be stacked. There was no room for them side-by-side. *Dave* was working to resolve the balance and weight issues. Assembly of the basic craft continued apace.

The early experimental launches did not require any landing gear – they used parachutes instead. Each subsequent liftoff was from a point higher than the previous one, meaning the propulsion system had pulled harder and the launch speed had increased. Scientists took care not to make great leaps in either force or speed, and all results were carefully examined. Soon the taller launch rails began experiencing alignment problems.

The test schedule was slowed down to allow the technicians to experiment with a variety of guidewire configurations. Using only three wires to maintain exact spacing along all axes could be the problem. The force vectors for these wires and their anchoring locations were carefully analyzed, as the rocket and tanks needed specific clearance.

Seven hundred feet is an impressive height for any structure. Even though they were only running tests, the guide rails required a red navigation warning light. The magnets were providing enough thrust to get the test vehicle five miles above the flight path of any passenger airline. Parachutes were not totally trustworthy at this height, but aerodynamics guaranteed that they would deploy before the package crashed into the earth. It was time to back off on the power of the magnets and test with the added weight of landing gear.

The materials team had continued to experiment with metallic properties, even during the series of launch tests. One new discovery produced such favorable results that the scientists immediately called Hal. There was a new skin on the way. Lighter and stronger than the one being tested plus it had a unique feature – ripples.

Many classes of science students had been taught about the design of fish scales as they relate to underwater speed. The scales cause the flowing water molecules to release from the fish profile for just a short time. Millions of tiny, quick releases result in the fish using minimal energy to swim. The materials scientists had worked with the alloys team to print a new skin with ripples. They had yet to test it in extreme cold, but in theory it would be no more brittle or fragile than the old skin.

Dialing the magnets down and using the new skin material, they decided to run a test with the rails still at 700 feet. They discovered that this version yielded an equal altitude as the previous test. The new skin also resulted in 10% improvement in exit velocity, plus it was cooler at launch – all significant advances.

The team knew it was time to give a heads-up notice to the private launch company to prepare for the manned flight. Advance notification was mandatory. The two launch facilities needed closer coordination as the date approached. NASA also needed to be in the loop. Their Human Exploration and Operations section would be informed since expanded communication and tracking needs arose whenever a human went into space.

Upper management at Urgent was notified before the 800-foot launch. The team wanted the old-timers and younger decision makers to watch this event. All around the nation citizens rearranged social and business calendars. The underground control center was standing room only, as was the viewing area across the canyon. Speakers had been installed on the multipurpose light poles so the public could listen to the countdown. There was a single weather-related pause due to some wind gusts, but they quickly resumed the count.

To those in the viewing area, the liftoff was little more than a whisper, except for the sonic boom. That sound was dwarfed by the sheer magnificence of the rocket quickly gaining altitude. Few had been that close to an object traveling at more than 500 miles per hour. The projectile was out of sight before a viewer could start a conversation. In fifteen seconds it was at an altitude occupied by passenger airplanes and would not be seen from the ground until the parachute deployed. The two-thirds power demonstration had been impressive.

The spectators cheered because they had seen a successful launch. The scientists cheered because they had not lost the spacecraft.

The weight of the landing gear was a concern to the team. Before the next test they wanted to confirm

Dave's calculations regarding the weight distribution, overall balance, and speed at the top of the towers, or exit velocity. The wheels and the mechanism that lowered them were in design.

Gravity and other forces affect the structure of landing gear. Strength of these moving parts was more of an issue than the strength of other parts on the space craft. Material science came into play in defining the construction of the wheel-hubs, supporting struts, and other components of landing gear. To save weight and maximize strength, the team decided on 3D printed titanium. The subterranean lab could print with other materials, but the availability of titanium was the deciding factor.

The upcoming test was the first real-time run-through with all systems. This launch was to include the Steam Assist Start – the SAS.

The maneuverability of the robots at the future shield had been in question. It was not a design issue, but a fuel concern. The robots used small, short squirts of compressed CO_2 to do their job. When low on fuel they returned to a specific pressure tank to top off. What if those tanks ran low?

To alleviate this concern, a new launch feature was added to the first moment of lift. A high-pressure steam-powered platform would move the rocket initially.

At its boiling point of 100 ˚C, liquid water transforms into a gas and wants to occupy a space 200 times greater if not contained. If not allowed to expand, the gas creates quite a pressure inside its container. That pressure would be used to kickstart the vehicle, meaning a savings in the amount of compressed CO_2 needed later to achieve orbit.

This pressure used to overcome inertia would be created by superheated steam. The craft would be resting on top of a large piston, and start to move as soon as the superheated steam was released into the pressure chamber below the piston.

Once moving, the rising piston top would cause a reduction of the pressure within the chamber. After a second or two, more steam would be injected into the chamber, increasing the pressure again. This allowed the initial thrust to build on itself momentarily. Naturally, the programmers needed to design a new launch sequence for the electromagnets, taking the SAS into account.

Without prior notice and with little fanfare, another 800-foot test launch was scheduled, and it was to be the last. Success of that trial run confirmed the calculations of the computer and the scientists were left without need for an incremental test. Any more power or height would result in more speed and the spacecraft would be launched.

Trusting that they could retrieve the craft, the scientists notified NASA of the upcoming event and advised that no human would be on board. The ground crew slowly increased the rails to one thousand feet in height.

Five more guidewires were attached to each of the three rail structures at midpoint and two more stretched from the top to the ground at a point farther around the launch cavity than any previous wires. They did not want to risk any movement. From a distance of one mile the launch site looked like one large piece of string art.

With five minutes to go, they quickly chilled the booster tanks with a through-flow of liquid nitrogen then filled the tanks with their *pressure solution* of both liquid N and O. In accordance with the time, direction and telemetry data, all agencies with the appropriate equipment watched the next, unannounced liftoff of:

Urgent – Vehicle One.

Perfect!

TWENTY ONE

━ ━ ━   ● ━ ●   ━ ━   ━ ━ ━   ━ ●   ━ ● ●

Mechanical and structural engineers had worked long and hard to accomplish something no one yet had – to design a space refueling station. It would be less like a station to receive intermittent services and more like those dreaded oil platforms anchored at sea – a nucleus of all activity.

They initially thought they could begin this undertaking without sending a human into space; that proved to be wrong. To accommodate man meant a change in the design of the stellar platform and the need to use a different launch vehicle. A human-friendly environment required cargo capacity for oxygen, water, waste storage, communication, and nutrition. They had gone elsewhere to find a suitable launch vehicle.

The delivery of the basic platform structure would

provide the foundation from which to expand. The scientists at Urgent were responsible for that. The engineers had repeatedly been reminded of the goal of this effort – to build a shield.

The stellar platform would provide a place to anchor the shield. Plans called for special fittings to be attached at various places along one side of the platform. The shield sections would snap into these fittings.

Because of the shape of the launch vehicle's cargo bay, the fundamental shape of the stellar platform would be tubular, not unlike a massive, steel thermos bottle. Future unmanned launches would transport pieces to be snapped onto each end, extending the platform in both directions. Attachment points along the length would provide options for future structures.

There were entry ports into the platform, on the side opposite the attachment points. Initially the long tube would be airtight, providing a living environment for humans. Once the assembly was completed, the solar collectors displayed, and the mechanics turned on, man would leave. Then the cavernous tube would act as a series of exterior garages to provide storage at the platform.

An external fuel tank and electric pump were the final components to be attached to the platform. Soon, more solar panels would be needed, but there was time for that. More important would be the communications between *Dave* on the ground, and the computer on the platform. All signals needed to be perfect before the first section of shield arrived, along with the first COTs: Carbon Dioxide (CO+Two= COT) powered robots.

The Urgent scientists had put robot design high on the priority list since human would not be present during this interminable operation. They had long planned to capture all the CO_2 they were producing in the village and use that compressed gas to power the space robots. Yet they had no plan for how many of these little helpers they would need power for.

They did, however, produce a simple list of the traits each (or some) must have. To help spread the shield, the COTs must pull, squeeze, turn, back up, detect electricity, and detect magnetism. Dexterity was limited to snip, grab and twist motions. The unit had an arm on each corner and a wing-span large enough to securely grab a corner of a shield frame.

Rectangular in shape, the COT was the height and width of an average household refrigerator, but only as thick as an inflated car tire. Along the back side were the ports for CO_2 hook up, electrical fast charge fitting, and overnight security snaps. Both the top and bottom were covered with solar cells. Midway along each side and at each corner was a small pressure port for maneuvering. There were also ports on the top and bottom, at each corner. Communication was limited in range, but a fail-safe homing program was built in.

Projects have checklists and drawing boards. The stellar platform was no exception. The timing of man's presence on the platform was the most hotly discussed item on that list. It had been agreed that less was likely to go wrong if a human were to monitor the arrival of the first vehicle, but how much longer would life support be needed?

Vehicle One would contain the first section of the shield and arrive with four COTs on board. Plans called for the small craft to dock, nose first, into the base of the platform and shed its external tanks.

The tanks would be tethered to the vehicle and allowed to float free. Small hydraulic arms could then direct the leading edge of the shield out into space, and the COTs would take over. An accordion fold allowed for easy deployment of the entire length, until the fine wire attached to the last corner of shield was taut. The shield would then be fully removed from the spacecraft and unfolded along the axis perpendicular to the direction the spacecraft pointed.

With the shield material no longer inside the vehicle, mechanical arms would rotate from their rest position, bringing a telescoping pole into the hatch opening. These arms would extend, as if offering the pole to the COTs. Two COTs would then attach themselves to the pole and inject high-pressure CO_2 into the pole causing it to telescope to a length of ten times the original dimension.

The design called for four such poles on the rotating frame inside the vehicle. The COTs would snap two together and fasten the top of the unfurled shield to this sturdy rod. The remaining two poles formed the basis of frame for one of the sides of the shield. The COTs would gently unfold the accordion-folded shield along this axis and snap the lower corner to the bottom of the frame.

Two sides of the initial section of shield would then

be fully deployed and attached to a rigid frame. The other two sides were anchored by COTs until their position and any motion were stabilized. The next three launches would each bring a section of shield and frame. The assembled four quadrants would form the basis from which the space shield would grow, and became one solid corner to which the debris filter was also fastened.

Space debris would always be a threat, even after the manned Space Shuttle had left the platform. The stellar platform would be equipped to detect and position the threat of these objects. One or more robots could be deployed should any large pieces of junk threaten the platform. Yet to be field-tested, version 1 of the Defense Robots was on the drawing board.

With shield deployment completed, the COTs were programmed to maneuver each external tank into position next to the main tank at the top of the platform, hook up the pump, and transfer all CO_2 into that fixed reservoir. Two of the empty tanks could be loaded into the returning vehicle after its wings and tail were extended into position and locked. The third tank would be placed near the outer solid corner of the shield frame, making a surplus tank dock. This vehicle itself was bound for earth at that point. The COTs were to be programmed to return to the garage, one at a time, for a full charge of CO_2.

To accommodate future growth, the side of the platform that faced the sun had been designed with special openings. Urgent personnel felt it likely that humans may need to visit the site in the event of an emergency. Knowing the likely mode of transport and

URGENT LAUNCH

Stellar Platform components

1 - Sparrow Vehicle One remains anchored at platform.
2 - Booster tanks used as fuel depot for COTs.
3 - Telescoping poles define perimeter.
4 - First 4 panels of shield material form solid corner.
5 - Next shield panel begins checkerboard pattern.

size of vehicle, the engineers designed hatches, attachment points, and life-support ports into the platform. For safety sake, the warmer side was favored over the colder option. It would be more likely that space debris would be reaching their location from below, the cooler side closer to earth. Design special openings into the other side.

Harold Knight enjoyed a close association with NASA and their science through his connections with the scientific community. While a part of the public record, the intimate details of many ingenious experiments are omitted in announcements delivered to the public because of either complexity of design, or lack of column inches. This was the case with the short article Hal had read about debris in space; he wanted more information.

He learned that NASA had mounted a debris sensor on the outside of the International Space Station. The sensor was still working, even though it was beyond the anticipated life span of the project. He had long been interested in space debris, specifically, the amount of junk likely to be encountered at different altitudes.

Harold asked his scientists to team with NASA to match the design, materials, and elements of electronic transmission of the NASA shield. He then directed his engineers to design the first section of the shield to specifications that would allow simple COTs to secure a debris filter to monitor whatever might impact the shield.

The experimental sensor was a series of layers which present themselves to a piece of junk. The front layer was a thin film with acoustic sensors and a grid of resistive wires. These components measured the time and location of penetration, while a change in resistance on the grid when lines were broken provided a size estimate.

The sensor also measured the velocity with which debris struck. Behind the first layer was a second thin layer of film with more acoustic sensors to measure the time and location of the second penetration. The computer calculated debris speed from the time and distance between the two impact points. The final layer filtered and stopped debris of a specific size and measured the amount of energy in the collision. Hal knew that an accurate data gathering operation would be critical and, from various altitudes above the earth, wanted to guarantee that signal would always reach his base on planet earth. Where they were going, there would be a significant number of metal pieces flying around at supersonic speeds. They would need to both find these objects and learn to mitigate damage when struck by them.

The International Space Station (ISS) was in an orbit 240 miles above the earth. The stellar platform was positioned farther away from the planet. The difference in distance made it necessary to build a new debris filter on the ground and transport it directly to the stellar platform by way of the Urgent launches, even though Hal had negotiated with NASA to buy theirs.

Harold Knight knew he could remove the debris sensor from the abandoned ISS if need be. The lunar orbit is 240,000 miles out, and the moon might provide an interim staging ground for supplies. What if they removed the debris sensor from the ISS and stored it on the moon? That possibility deserved further thought.

Closer to home, the team was discussing options of the dates for launching the prototype Defense Robots – DefBots. In designing the debris filter one oft-spoken truth was that any sizeable piece of space junk could quickly cripple or eliminate an entire satellite station. Pebble size debris would be stopped and analyzed by the filter but what about larger pieces? DefBots were to be deployed to capture or redirect big wandering objects.

Scientists in the laboratory had affectionately called their invention a space wrecker. While nearly the same size as the COTs, the DefBots had more sophisticated navigation and propulsion systems. The wrecker was faster and bigger that a COT and could shove an entire satellite out into deep space.

Through its power from the sun, it could gently encourage an object out of the way. Its hi-capacity CO_2 tank delivered a powerful up-front burst of thrust when needed. The most dramatic features of the DefBot were the new communications package and laser.

The robot could change its alert level in response to input from an outside source or from its own sensors. A signal of impending danger from the stellar platform would prompt a response as would a random object located and identified by the wrecker itself. Without input from another source, the DefBot would remain docked, but it had the capability of looking for trouble.

A scientific field called Mechatronics provided the

researchers on the ground with solutions to hands-off problems relating to robotics, automation, sensing, and systems control. These answers applied not only to construction in space but also defense. DefBots carried a laser powerful enough to melt any man-made material within a five-mile range.

The proposed supply of DefBots had been recently revised upward because of increased worldwide activity in satellite launches and the ever-changing orbit altitudes of these devices. There would be Defense Robots stationed at all stellar platforms.

The wreckers would even remain with the shield sections as they transitioned deep into space and began casting a shadow on the planet from a sun-synchronous position.

TWENTY TWO

• • — — • — — • • — • • • • •

The small, single engine plane made an investigatory loop around the mesa, then touched down on the crude runway. It had not rained for months, and the dry Australian soil was perfect for a makeshift landing field. The pilot taxied towards the short row of trees in hopes of encountering some shade.

A structure similar to a double-wide mobile home stood on the far side of the trees. Two young people came running from the trailer and met the passenger as she jumped down from the wing. Myrlene was still spry enough to easily jump that far. Once the propeller stopped, Leah approached, gave her guest a hug, and welcomed her to the outback. "This is a first," offered Myrlene.

As assistant to Brian Knight and liaison to everything, Myrlene had flown to Australia from Borneo.

This was a brief courtesy visit before she continued the rest of the way around the world and back to North America.

The original itinerary had called for her to visit the various reforestation plantations ForCI was managing. She had taken a tour of the young project in Gabon and was taken aback at the lack of progress in India. Her visit to Borneo was to see again the devastation man had caused and to, again, be not-so-softly told to mind her own business. However, the landing in the outback was to deliver a personal message.

"The fusion power plant at Urgent has had a successful burn of almost a complete minute. Your dad is now convinced that he is in way over his head and wants you to return with me. As you know, the next phase of our long-term strategy is to take our technology to the places that need it. We have partners standing by waiting for electricity. Our team has sent one reactor to the Amazon, capable of only ten seconds. In arid conditions such as this place, that's not good enough.

"They are working hard to get this machine to become self-sustaining. The next step is a quantum leap in building and learning. He wants you to learn about it alongside him, because he has no intention of traveling to sell *this stuff*, as he calls it."

"Can I have a day to say good-byes?" she asked.

It would take a day for her to visit the people and places involved in the Aussie project. As with all ForCI forests, this one was massive, so walking was not the preferred mode of transportation. Small electric four-wheel, brush scooters held two passengers and a small load in the rear bed, they looked somewhat like a short, small pick-up with no cab. Traveling on balloon tires capable of scrambling over roots and downed tree limbs, it had no steering wheel, only handlebars.

The terrain changed as she began leaving the cleared mesa around the landing field and descended towards the river. The young trees were obvious, as was the large solar array encountered long before entering the old-growth forest. Acres of solar panels gave a dark foreboding appearance to the desert plain above the river canyon. A close inspection of these flat panels would reveal small trees growing in the shade beneath them. The watering system fed by the river and a series of electric pumps was virtually hidden above the small seedlings.Many thousands of solar generators delivered sufficient electricity to power the community, pump the water, and shade the young trees.

Previous seedlings were closer to the river and stood tall and healthy as a vivid example to their younger brethren. The forest was getting larger, one generation at a time, always moving away from the river. The Aussie project was one of the many steps being taken by the ForCI group to grow more trees and return O_2 back to the atmosphere. This exercise was also a mission in keeping this forested part of Australia from joining the adjacent desert plain.

Forty percent of the planet was arid hardscrabble when the ForCI group first appeared in this valley. Any increase in the amount of inhospitable land meant that what was previously farm or forest land disappeared. The group intended to use all its efforts to maintain the useable agricultural portion of the planet.

The age of the reforestation site was easily determined by examining its size. The new forest in Western Australia was the third in the ForCI portfolio, with the Amazon site being second and Tongass the first. This southern hemisphere forest was larger, primarily because they knew what they were doing when they started. That had not been the case in Brazil.

The first misstep had been in manpower. The team now knew that the university, its students, the curriculum, and the faculty HAD to be organized on day one. In Western Australia, Perth University had been recruited by the ForCI consulting staff. They had needed a one-year period to get it all in order. This was not too bad considering that an entire army was leaving campus for three-fourths of an academic year, yet was still entitled to receive teaching, books, room and board, and light entertainment.

The students began research in the biology lab while still on campus. The experiments conducted at Urgent on photosynthesis and photorespiration were brought to Perth and explained to the faculty and students. They began their own testing and genetic designs, addressing the native species only. Beginning with the dominant trees in the existing forest, the study was revealing data about the growth rate of those trees, before and after genetic modifications.

Further trials were needed to determine if similar but less abundant species could improve the yield. Western Australia is home to sheoak, karri and spotted gum and these hardwood trees were indeed hard, tall, and slow growing. Was it possible to plant a forest of paulownia, for example, that grows more than twice as fast? As word got around campus of these efforts the environmental purists awakened and became vocal. They were given a promise: "If we can save the planet, your grand-children can come in and cut down these non-indigenous trees."

A further advantage of a shorter, big leaf tree like the empress tree (paulownia) was the extensive foliage. The species could add one foot each month to both the height and diameter of the tree. The greater the area of green leaf, the more the photosynthesis; and the greater the mass of material that is composting in the soil when it falls from the tree.

The dirt along the edges of many forest areas is less nutritious than the floor of a forest with a heavy canopy. The quicker that condition can be improved, the sooner human management of the forest can end. The more decomposing leaves on the forest floor the better. This is not only a matter of nutrients, but moisture retention. Soil with biomass holds water much longer than sand.

The students knew they needed sun and water in order to grow anything at a faster rate. Sun was abundant in the outback, but water presented a challenge. The Urgent researchers, again, came through. They helped the students install a watering system that brought life to the experimental plants and also all students' lodgings. Even in Australia, this experiment was expedited because the cost to the locals was zero; Urgent paid for it all.

Leah Elliott asked one of her friends to show Myrlene to the guest cottage and wandered over to one of the electric buggies. She hopped in and headed deep into the forest. The path she followed became more pronounced as soon as she entered the old, natural forest, with its dense underbrush. Her route took her away from modern civilization and back in time. She wanted to say good-bye to the local aborigine families that had been such a help.

The clearing was vacant. Three days ago, she had eaten with them in this very spot, and talked forest and animals. She had listened to their stories and learned of their ways during many meals over many months.

Earlier, they had spoken of leaving this forest since her work was done. Leah had no idea why they shared that information, or the source of the knowledge that she was about to fly home. She did know that the indigenous peoples were able to predict events that were not evident. When that visit ended, she departed as she always had, with a friendly wave and a "See you soon."

Working from where they had built the fire, she examined that edge of the meadow and soon found the map. To the typical tourist this would look like a bunch of dots in the sand. Leah knew it was the visual aid, supporting a conversation the family had before they began the next day of traveling. She was able to decipher their intentions and motored off.

Leah followed the trail until the battery level indicator on her dashboard reached the half-way mark. It was not a good idea to go beyond the half-way point in any venture if the return route was the same. She held a brief argument with herself – the sentimental half won. She decided she would allow herself fifteen minutes more to follow the path on foot, and left the cart behind. Leah knew the aborigine were not prone to long good-byes, nor would the family be slighted if there was no farewell at all. It was she that wanted the closure.

She saw movement in the underbrush up ahead just as she was nearing the end of the time she had allowed herself. The land was rising slightly, and she could clearly see motion. She stepped up the pace while climbing a slight rise, thinking her friends were causing the commotion. The pack of Dingo's saw her at the same instant she saw them. They dropped the kangaroo carcass they were tussling over and headed for the fresh meat – Leah.

There was no time to return to the vehicle; what was option B? A large Australian blackwood tree was blocking the view of some of the wild dogs. Thinking quickly, she grabbed the machete that was fastened to her belt and jumped as high as she could into the mature tree. She then reached down and hacked off all lower limbs. Dogs could not climb trees, but they were strong and smart. Her idea was to give them no purchase above the ground.

The dogs surrounded the tree, jumping and howling. Leah climbed higher and cut off a couple more lower limbs. She double checked the strength of her perch, and settled in. For how long she did not know, but she did know she could not climb down to retrieve the phone/radio she had carelessly left charging in the rig. The other weapon on her belt was a pistol.

There were more dogs down there than she had bullets, so she took deep breaths and started focusing on her surroundings.

Four years ago, as she was preparing the curriculum for the first group at WYIST, she had an opportunity to spend hours of quality time with a researcher from Australia. Leah had become enthralled with this country. As usual, when she grew interested in a subject, she would study it.

Leah began spending hours at her computer and much of her spare time in the library satisfying her curiosity about indigenous peoples; after all, she was one. She learned that the peoples along the Peru-Brazil border are not likely to log large swaths of forest and sell the timber to a mill. These natives hunt and fish and are somewhat nomadic. There may be warfare between groups, but not with the forest.

In Australia the aborigines are also nomads. They inhabited the entire continent for hundreds of generations, perhaps thousands. Evolution resulted in a people acutely aware of the land and the animals. Although seemingly impossible, there are stories of aborigine families crossing the massive desert. Where did they find food and find water? There are also stories of an uncanny ability to sense the pain, joy, and suffering – the feelings of other members of the family who were not within sight. This was almost like mind reading but on an emotional level.

After what seemed like hours in her tree, but probably just one, the dogs stopped jumping and for an instant went on high alert. Noiselessly, they ran off into the forest. Leah was fairly certain she knew what was about to happen. She could see aborigine families above the scrub brush, clicking their spears against the shields they carried.

Without ceremony, she climbed down, helped the last few feet by the eldest son. They walked with her to her four-wheeled cart and continued as far as the place of their previous supper. The family decided they would spend the night there and told her they would be gone the next morning.

Tearfully she hugged every member of the group and bade them farewell. Soon she had put the dense old-growth forest behind her. Her thoughts drifted to what had just happened. What a confirmation of her relationship with that family – they sensed her distress. This had been a life-changing adventure, and a real good-bye. Her eyes swelled with tears.

Myrlene was resting in her small quarters when she heard a knock on the door and a small voice whispering, "It's Leah."

They hugged again. No mention was made of the encounter with the dogs. The excitement for the rest of the day would be getting the class together.

"There is a lot to say and I could use your help," Leah said.

The building that housed the mess-hall/classroom-auditorium was built from six modular units. When the tables were stacked out of the way, there was seating for 100. To include the faculty was to create standing room only, as in the case of this gathering. Leah had called them all together to wrap up her latest visit. She felt it important to acknowledge their hard work.

URGENT LAUNCH

"Well, here we are again. I seem to be bouncing in and out of your lives every six months or so. I may be away longer this time. I'll know more later, but we need to be together one more time.

"It has been a joy and honor to share your progress and your success. Based on the stories you relayed to me, it's safe to say that each of you had a different vision of what this experience would be like. Based on these same stories, I know you all value your efforts and take pride in your work.

"You have helped us save a bit of the environment and truly have changed the future. The hundreds of thousands of new trees within sight of this building are adding oxygen to the atmosphere and also helping create an improved climate over this part of the continent. Science has taught us that respiration of trees releases airborne molecules that invite clouds to form.

"You and I are too fragile, short lived, and just plain short to see these changes. But trust the experts that say the moisture added to the atmosphere through this process will be carried across the continent. Maybe someday even across an ocean. Closer to home, we can rest assured that our efforts will increase summer rains and subsequent runoff into the river. Regardless, we have used local water and sunlight to shade a bit of Australia and change the climate for the better.

"At the back of the room is Myrlene, my friend and companion on the next leg of my journey. We have been asked to help with the completion of a major experiment started years ago in my birthplace of Urgent, Wyoming. Many of you have heard about it.

URGENT LAUNCH

Many more will learn more in the near future.

"We have a group of scientists, not unlike the scientist that came to help us get this forest started, who are now making electricity from seawater. I am going to help those wizards put together a portable version of that invention and bring it back here. This won't happen in the near future. In fact, all of you will have graduated before this happens.

"One exciting element of this project is the need for manpower. Each of you is a college student with a familiarity about going into the unknown; otherwise you wouldn't be here. If you still have that spirit of adventure when we meet again, I may have an offer for you. Just as Australia is a long flight away from my birthplace, we could be asking you to venture a great distance from yours. I trust you talk about the future with your friends and family and confide in them your dreams. I suggest you bring this topic up before too long so that you don't send them into shock.

"I would anticipate that we will have five major reforestation efforts underway before we mobilize the new power system. That means we will need manpower to travel to these locations to train the power plant operators. We will need to train those trainers. That's you.

"Young people such as yourselves are the face of the future. You will help build these forest programs which will help save the planet. Your education and enthusiasm are the foundation of this project and will be the building blocks of our future endeavors. The hope is that you will grow into the generation that unifies the world and is not afraid of that unity.

URGENT LAUNCH

"We old folks tend to bring prejudices and preconceived notions and other baggage with us. There is not enough time to turn around past generations. Our leaders decided the better option is to better educate the new ones, and that's you. We are counting on you and your discoveries. More important than adding to the field of facts, those discoveries will advance the field of wonder.

"Now I'm done talking. Myrlene and I will be sitting at the head table to chat with anyone that wants to wander by. Give us ten minutes to set up the dining room, then you can break into your usual two shifts for dinner."

During the next hour Leah did not have time to finish even a salad. She was approached by a parade of her students, some in tears, others with smiles on their faces and gratitude in their hearts.

Many of these young people had been transformed by Leah and the ForCI group,

as had Western Australia.

TWENTY THREE

•—• ——— —•—• •••• •

"Roger that." Crackled the voice he heard through the headset, confirming what he had just told them.

FJ Guindo had announced his sighting of the wandering sparrow – Urgent Vehicle One. It was just a small dot of color in the emptiness of space. He was thinking that white would be easier to see. However, his was to be the only manned mission to the stellar platform, so what difference does it make from here on out. Future *sparrows* (space arrows) would be unmanned.

The instruments on the panel below his window had first indicated he was getting close. The signal reflected off the destination had been guiding his chartered Space Shuttle for a few orbits. Standard operating procedure was to slowly close the distance on any object traveling through space, if you eventually wanted to be going the same speed. With no reference points, like the car in the next lane or a billboard, a pilot cannot judge the speed by looking out the window.

It had taken five orbits since an uneventful launch to commence the pacing of the target. FJ (he was only known by his first two initials) had finally gotten to sleep on the last orbit which meant it was a short nap. The first trip into space was not one that normally induced sleep. It was necessary to get some rest though since hard work was coming up. FJ was used to hard work, and sleeping when absolutely necessary.

His job during the past few years had been in the Tongass National Forest in Alaska, helping the ForCI group with the reforestation project. The administrators of the exercise were white collar thinkers and had designed the curriculum believing that their college-aged students would provide all the labor. Right!

Who had to clamber over downed trees and large valleys to reach and therefore define, the limits of their new chunk of forest floor? Exactly who knew how to operate the chainsaw needed to de-limb the downed trees and pull those heavy pieces off the soon-to-be path?

He never complained because he enjoyed hard work. As an ex-jock he had the physique for it. But it always amazed him how the architects of educational projects thought them so simple, while the engineering required totally different thinking and effort.

There had been a one-hour discussion about the history and goals (and a brief description of the chain-of-command in Alaska) when Dennis Hall, the boss at ForCI, had asked FJ to take a supervisory role in the Tongass. In preparation for being thrust into space, there had been a week-long series of classes delving into history, communications, guidance controls and safety: followed by a week on weightlessness training, physical tuning and mental exercising. He was better prepared to do nothing in his space capsule than he had been to "Run my ass off in a national forest..." as he once described his job.

"Houston," radioed the astronaut, "It looks like we will need one more go around to reach the same altitude. What do you make of the speed difference?"

"On the next contact we can match speed and prepare to dock," was the reply.

"Oh good. I get to watch the world for a couple hours longer."

"After one hour fifteen we expect you to start looking dead-ahead."

"Roger."

The launch of Vehicle One from the pad at Urgent had actually been a test. The contents were somewhat low in value to the mission, knowing that they might not be retrievable. Meaning, during this flight, the docking and capsule control became more of an exercise than subsequent dockings would be. Vehicle One's cargo was still useful and would be reclaimed.

The contents of FJ's vehicle were all too valuable. His life-support and the nucleus of the future stellar platform were on board his private Space Shuttle, as was a robotic, telescoping arm with which to remove items from the cargo bay. That same remote-controlled device could reach the hatch of Vehicle One.

Between them, the two cargo containers held the main shell and one more length of living quarters. The two cylinders would be mated, side-by-side, and the structure loaded with breathable air. FJ would then close the cargo bay doors and reposition the private Space Shuttle with its nose at the base of the unique platform. He would be able to slip through a hatch into the newly built quarters after flipping a couple of switches. Then the hard work would start.

He would have five days before the air in the stellar platform was stale, toxic and unbreathable. He would *have* to be on his way back to earth by then, traveling in the Space Shuttle which made its own oxygen.

Each trip to space had so many components that were unique and finite, the venture was never without checklists. The astronaut had an electronic version and a paper copy while the ground crew provided further redundancy. The first item on the list would be announced as soon as FJ entered the new quarters, and so it would continue.

The growth of the space shield was to be controlled entirely from earth. Robots, called COTs, would be the labor employed in the weightless environment. Frequent sparrows, as the new vehicles were called, would arrive from earth with cargo requiring some handling. The robots had been built with capabilities needed to work with that cargo yet plans also called for the ability to reprogram these helpers from earth. Before FJ flew back home all these capabilities needed testing. He would double check the video links between the cameras mounted on the platform and those carried by specific COTs.

The astronaut was trained to program revised instructions, or transmit a work-around command when performance of a COT was substandard. A true fix would entail bringing the COT inside the crew quarters and replacing either components or the entire COT. Orders were to leave with at least six COTs in perfect working condition.

In addition, all cameras had to function. This was defined as transmitting with earth having directional control. One set of joysticks was on the ground and FJ had another. The process of ticking each camera and COT off the checklist took most of the five days.

The return to earth was as uneventful as the launch had been. The private firm that had contracted for this space delivery had done everything asked of them. On final approach to the landing strip in California, communications were handed-off to the local tower. The air traffic controller introduced himself and advised that there were a number of folks and a few press people ready to welcome the astronaut back to earth.

"A quick look at my orders show that you do not want any photographs. Is that right sir?" the tower asked.

"Affirmative."

"OK, when you land and bring the craft to a stop, we will send a van. Do not take your helmet off, leave the visor down and walk directly to the waiting vehicle. This will obscure your visual ID and get you out of the public eye quickly. We will handle the publicity."

"Roger - and thanks."

The anonymity requested by the space traveler was an ongoing attempt to avoid sending a message to his ultra-controlling father. FJ did not want to be located. He wanted nothing to do with the paternal way of life he had been born into, nor the name of that family. His identity would be his own and he wanted no influence from any family ties.

Francis Jesse Guindo was born in the United States, but not conceived there. His parents immigrated from Mali. Not knowing the sex of their unborn child, they used a unisex name when registering. His father had accepted a position at a university in the eastern United States. The move had been rushed to get him to campus before classes began.

The institution was conservative in nature, which fit nicely into his father's views. There was never a college *right-enough* for Dr. Guindo, but the small religious compound named after its evangelical leader and founder was a good place to start. He had not taken long to nudge his students and family to even more conservative views. Except for his son.

As a high-school student he had been exposed to students from other schools during sports activities. FJ had grown to like sports. At one competitive college event, an opponent, also a black kid, started talking about schools, varied interests, and mentioned the upcoming talk about green power to be given by some Indian guy at the community center. FJ went to listen to that talk since he had always been an advocate of sustainability.

It is there that he met Edward White, the Urgent representative lecturing about alternative energy. FJ was taken by Urgent's communal philosophy and un-believable dedication to saving the planet. He knew he had found a home. The logical next step for this growing young man was to move to Urgent and sign on to help the forest.

His experience at varying specialties had yet to make him feel inferior, as he had always felt when growing up. He was never good enough while under his father's roof, yet was congratulated by fellow workers at Urgent for his achievements, even in the lowly Ag Lab.

The Tongass project led by Dr. Hall and the space junket that Harold Knight controlled had been won-derful missions. It was odd to him that the most meaningful involvement was the smallest and least well-known: being one of Ruth's Flyers, yet that is what got him the new job.

There was a legend at Urgent about the early days when the community was just getting off the ground. As is the case with anything new, there was an out-side element of naysayers that did not want progress. Growing a Native American reservation was a bold idea. Too bold for those that wanted no progress in the arena of minorities and greenies. Urgent had ele-ments of both.

To silence the voice of those anti-growth folks, a small team of dedicated young people was asked to slow the opponents down. There was an unlim-ited budget, unlimited help, and a communications intercept as good as intelligence agencies had. Give them a target and they can tell you when and where lunch is. Rumors were that this went on for almost ten years and they only hurt one guy. FJ knew that Sara, his peer in the Tongass Forest, had been part of that team over 18 years ago. He did not know that the leader of that task force was known as Ruthie and her team members known as flyers.

Each of them could fly a drone like no one else on earth. Ruth and her team had such hand-eye coordination that they could control underwater toys, airborne helicopters, and model planes, two at a time. It was unfair for any of them to enter remote-control vehicle contests, or on-line gaming marathons.

FJ encountered Ruth in the solar cell field one afternoon, quite by accident. She was involved in an aerial inspection of the wind turbines and literally stumbled over him. FJ had been on his hands & knees making a visual count of the insect population beneath the solar panels.

He asked if he could learn to fly "that thing" and they arranged to meet at the airport up on the West plateau. They hopped into a reservation Jeep to get out of the way of all air traffic. He learned that she was the daughter-in-law of the Chief. She learned that he had an uncanny aptitude for flying drones. His concentration and coordination were a joy to watch.

They returned to the hangar and she offered him a cold drink. As they got acquainted Ruthie knew this man would be a real asset to the community. She suggested he meet her husband. He confirmed that Edward had basically recruited him. What followed was a series of meetings that resulted in FJ being named the first astronaut and the lead pilot in the building of the shield.

He was also put in charge of building a ground control center.

The Urgent communications team knew to locate stellar communication headquarters a few miles away from any source of stray signal. To also gain a bit of altitude, the stellar platform communications center, PlatCom, was built west of the airport, farther up in the high country above the plateau. It was rough terrain but ideal for the purpose intended. Resident quarters were included.

His dexterity at controlling the COTs proved invaluable. At times he called for a programmer or a number cruncher to join him at PlatCom and help him troubleshoot. Sara was his favorite assistant because of their history, his unspoken admiration and her ability with data. They would watch the COT reaction to a command and then talk about ways to improve or better control what they had seen.

While it seemed simple, the COT duties of attaching pieces of a rectangle to other rectangles were a bit complex. Slowly, the remote control signals were improved and the shield expansion was proceeding at a faster rate. FJ could even count on a few hours of sleep as part of this daily routine.

During one lazy morning, FJ recalled the afternoon during the construction period, when Edward had taken Ruth and FJ horse-back riding. Ruth had known where they were going and was pleased her husband was about to share. The log cabin was located in a dip in the meadow, a few miles beyond the building site. It had been his family hideaway for generations, and was the place where Edward and Ruth fell in love.

URGENT LAUNCH

They had dismounted, admired the scenery and gone inside the small building. Edward had explained to FJ that this was the closest safe house should he ever need to escape his workplace. A quick tour of the accommodations had included location of firewood, rations, firearms, and the front door key.

His quiet reminiscing was interrupted by a call from the visitor center. Actually, the student at the desk had been instructed to call Pope, who had then called FJ.

"A young woman claiming to be your sister is at the visitor center."

TWENTY FOUR

The video monitor had been quietly providing white noise, and was turned to the University's cable channel because of the science hour. She had always tried to watch this locally produced, albeit slightly stolen, program to keep herself informed. As a serious college student, she did not have much connection with the world outside the campus. The science and political programs were the only visual luxuries she allowed herself.

Wait. Did she hear what she thought she heard?

She knew the program would be repeated again before the station signed off for the night. Maybe she could get in an hour of exercise at the gym and watch the rerun during dinner. Her mom would call during that second hour and Elizabeth could eat while listening to her mother's nightly, mostly one-sided conversation. They would agree that dad could not talk because he had an important meeting to get ready for, or he was not home yet due to his attending an important meeting.

Mrs. Guindo would offer how proud she was that her daughter was attending the most prestigious school in North Carolina, notwithstanding the fact that her husband was the Provost at that very same institution, the one their son had transferred from the year before he vanished. With these obligatory topics covered Lizzy could bring up the weather and then close. That would leave ten minutes before the program ran again.

She increased the volume slightly and decided to record the audio with her communication device. With her closely cropped head leaning towards the speaker she heard it again. In the background, behind the voice-over of the narrator, was the radio response from ground-control to the astronaut: "Roger that, FJ." For a moment her breathing stopped. *How many FJ's are there?*

Elizabeth was ten years younger than her brother Francis. Over the years they had developed the typical sibling love/hate relationship. He had an annoying little sister who always asked silly questions and got in the way. She had an annoying brother with good grades who some teachers expected her to duplicate. They loved each other too. That relationship gave each the stability and trust to experiment with independence and try to live the American dream.

Their grandparents remained in Mali and comprised

a typical Middle Eastern male-dominated household. When their parents came to the United States, they were too old to break completely free from the patriarchal mold. Although both were professionals, her real worth was never honored by him. The children knew they were *not* going to treat their spouses, if they ever had any, as their parents did.

After high school, Francis, now called FJ by everybody, toed the family line and enrolled in the institution in which his father had a leadership role; that lasted two years.

Twelve years later, Lizzy, as she was now known, was enrolled in that same university. She did not know why, but before she even graduated high school, she had lost her brother. He had vanished from her life, and from her parent's lives, without warning. She knew it was to escape their parents. She agreed that a new life was the only route to sanity. A mixture of hate, jealousy, love and curiosity often kept her awake at night. Mostly she was jealous. FJ had escaped.

Lizzy was a virgin, "So why does dad always give me that acidic abortion speech at least once a week?" She was a straight-A student that did not deserve to be watched, questioned, and constantly asked about her studies. Mom's money was the same color as his, yet she was not valued or entitled to drive or spend evenings with female friends, let alone buy any fashionable outfits.

Worse, though, was her father's meddling call to each professor she took classes from, every other week to check on her progress. And he wondered why she had moved out of the house and into an apartment "closer to campus" and then taken a year off before returning to classes, she thought to herself.

Now there was a chance that she could find her brother. This was her first clue to his whereabouts, and she was going to pursue this lead. She knew how to use the computer, and there were computer gurus in her math class who constantly bragged about their hacking abilities. That materials science course she was taking just for fun had a few geeks as well. This was the most enthusiastic she had felt in ages.

The devious plotting required to be away from campus during spring break was unsettling but necessary. She needed at least a week and a car, maybe even a train ticket. Without much difficulty she contacted members of a club that followed NASA and space flight. These students confirmed that the footage she saw was from a space flight, launched by a private company, but funded by that Wyoming space shield enterprise.

Dogged investigating dug up websites, internet links and details about the Wind River Indian Reservation/Urgent that convinced her she was getting closer to finding her brother. She remembered his interest in sustainability and environmental issues. The project in Wyoming dovetailed perfectly with those interests. There was no doubt about the need for a trip to Urgent.

What should she say? Would he be glad to see her? Is he secure in his new surroundings? Do his studies continue? ... and on and on ...

Lizzy spent the first night near Cincinnati, the next in Kansas City, and the final night at a motel in Cheyenne. She anxiously drove into Urgent the morning of day four and followed the signs directing her to the visitor center.

"As good a place as any to start," she said to herself. After she told her story to the young woman at the desk there was a long pause. This gave her hope. She was asked to take a seat while a supervisor was called. The desk clerk reminded her, "Security and all, ya' know."

Instantly, she recognized her brother by his gait. That walk had been etched in her mind. She ran past the desk, across the lobby and down the short hall. Public decorum be damned, she shrieked and cried and gave him a long tight hug.

It took FJ five minutes to settle his shock, return the joy and calm down this vivid display of affection. He led her to a chair at the edge of the reception area and introduced her to Leah, his emergency support system should he have needed it. He did not, and Leah excused herself.

The small talk portion of their reunion was ending when FJ asked if she would like to join him for lunch. "We can continue in more comfortable surroundings."

The visitor center was in the lobby of the new administration building of the university. FJ led them to an elevator. He entered a code into a keypad and the machine transported them to an unmarked lower level where his electric cart was waiting.

The trip beneath the large common area of the campus took ten minutes. They found two seats at a secluded table in the scientists' dining room and continued their two-way Q&A session. It took the entire lunch hour, and then some, to catch up on years of family news. The older brother was not confident in his interpretation of Lizzy's relationship with their parents, her interests, or her long-range plans, until she mentioned the intriguing materials science class she had taken. FJ asked about that course.

"Man, it's so cool. The professor has all kinds of degrees in metallurgy and things, but admits he fell into materials science. He says to understand the elements and the materials and how they all fit together is to understand everything we see and touch. I must admit that he makes a dry and academic subject really interesting. I'll probably take another semester from him."

"Lizzy, there is someone I would like you to meet," said her brother.

Harold Knight's laboratory was known as a confusing, but receptive haven. When he was on the premises, he had an open-door policy. FJ checked with Brittany in Hal's office near the mill. She confirmed that Hal was in his lab and would let him know he was about to receive visitors. He was not advised that his guest was a budding materials science student.

FJ assumed the common area of interest would help his sister find the older Harold, and Urgent itself, less intimidating. What he had not expected was instant bonding, and a grand tour of the underground that took all day, dinner, and well into the night. All the while FJ could have been elsewhere; he did not need to be by her side. He set Lizzy up in a guest suite for the night.

The following morning the siblings ate, talked about long-range plans and finally addressed the question of where to go from here? Unfortunately, this brought her to the point he knew too well.

"We both know our father and his attitudes," FJ began. "Actually, I guess his beliefs control those attitudes when his children are in the conversation. We can't change that thinking; God knows we both tried in our own way. I reached the conclusion that vanishing was the best course of action. I'm sorry you and Mom got caught in the middle, but I retained my sanity and Dad is now convinced he was right all along – that I am worthless and disrespectful.

"Whatever you decide to do with your future, I ask that you not tell anyone where I am. Neither Dad nor I is ready for a reunion. It's hard, but I can't come to you either. I can't take the chance that I'll run into him, or one of the faculty, if I visit the campus. It's too big a risk."

Both were quiet for some time, then Lizzy spoke, "What if I disappeared too? What if I joined you here and finished my education?"

FJ was astonished. The consequences brought fear to his face, not because of any threat to either of them, but the heartbreak their mother would feel. He immediately tried to think of an alternative. Lizzy knew not to speak when he adopted that blank stare, minutes passed.

"You are my only sister, and I love you a lot. When I think of your future, in that setting, with that man, I fear for you. Physically, he won't do any damage. Mentally, I think you are at great risk. Socially, you have no future. It will destroy Mom but I agree; you should think seriously about moving to Urgent.

"I am completely offline technically. Dad couldn't

find me even if he tried. We could set you up too. But think long and hard because for the foreseeable future you can't go back."

"Listen FJ," she replied. "I have a couple days before I need to get back to class. Do you think I could see a little more of this place? You know I'm the curious, scientific type and all I have seen so far is the most spectacular working lab I have ever encountered. I'm dying to know what else ya' got down here."

"I think we can arrange something," said her brother. "I have some work I need to do at the office but let me find you a tour guide."

Remembering that she had already met Leah, FJ activated the search feature on his communication device by speaking "*Dave* - find Leah." From across the breakfast table, she heard both sides of the quick conversation. As arranged, she returned to the guest suite to wait the appointed half hour.

"Good to see you again Ms. Guindo," said her guide as she opened the door.

"It's Lizzy to anyone that is a friend of my brother."

"Lizzy it is. One quick question first, although I think I know the answer - can you walk this tour or would you rather ride? It will take a few hours."

The two women exited through an unadorned, unlocked door Lizzy had not noticed on the far side of the guest suite living room. They entered the long hall. Leah proceeded to show her what was behind every door along that corridor.

They entered a few laboratories and met scientists who were more than happy to share their research with the inquisitive college student. She engaged each researcher and continually asked relevant questions. This curiosity impressed Leah, who was not easily impressed.

At one junction in the subterranean maze Leah mentioned that they could find food "that way" and directed them away from the wider and obviously older tunnel. This new brightly lit hall was of taller construction, giving it a more open feel, and with signage. Leah opened the door labeled *café* and they ascended the stairs.

Instantly Lizzy knew they were in the same building that housed the visitor center. The massive windows and large collection of whirling young people could only be a school. They followed the students through the cafeteria line and took their loaded plates to a table in the far corner, away from most ears, to begin a meal together.

"Lizzy," she began after an obvious break in the eating. "Less than five years ago we opened the doors of this institution. The Wyoming Institute of Science and Technology was the logical extension of the education process we believe is needed in our endeavor. I'm sure your brother told you of our mission. I can confirm to you that this is all about saving mankind and the planet.

"We call WYIST a technology center because science is too often viewed as only research. Not that the general public cares, but our recruiting efforts of both students and faculty must be honest and truthful. We are more than research; we are action too, and most of the tenured university faculty researchers in the US know it.

"You could call this a private institution in that it is funded by private foundations. We do not bother with that wicked series of hoops that lead to accreditation. That's old school (pardon the pun) and it just doesn't matter. We are one of a kind, and no board or jury in the land can tell us if we are doing our job right.

"We find the talent, put it to work in the most effective and engaging manner, and nurture those individuals with never-ending challenges, honors and other rewards. To us, degrees don't matter, slight infractions can be overlooked, personal history is just that. Teamwork, effort, and enthusiasm are the tickets to success in this community, and we need success.

"The last time the temperatures in the Arctic were a few degrees warmer than they are today, the sea level was over 13 feet higher than it is now. The Union of Concerned Scientists keeps reminding us of the trillions of dollars in coastal housing that will be lost if the oceans rise that much. We are always looking for dedicated talent to help us curtail the climate change causes."

"FJ explained some of this to me," she responded, "but he has yet to explain how he so thoroughly dropped out of sight. I would like to know more about his escape route so I could consider following suit."

"Oh?" questioned Leah as she raised her eyebrows, "I was toying with another idea."

"Please do go on."

"I was going to offer you a position on the faculty here at WYIST."

URGENT LAUNCH

It was Lizzy's turn to raise her eyebrows.

"I'm only 28 years old and living in an apartment with two other girls to save money while I finish getting my doctorate. How can I possibly transition into being college professor now?"

The response to that question was life altering. Leah began,

"Let me explain what I see and know. First, though, you need to know that I am only a couple of years older than you. So, don't think youth equals ignorance in my book.

"My primary reason for believing in you is your insatiable curiosity. During the half day we have been visiting scientific professionals you have continually questioned them, in their own jargon, and about details within their specialties. You are like a human sponge.

"WYIST will soon start the new school year. We divide the year in half, and I propose you take the first half getting acquainted with our community and the campus. We could give you some fancy title along with the keys to the city, but in reality you would be an entitled student. Entitled as in you would have a key to and security access to everything. In this five-month period you would also design the course you want to teach."

"And I suppose," Lizzy interrupted, "you will tell me that a teaching certificate is not required."

"Right you are. At least that is the correct answer for this Institute. I do the hiring, and you are hired."

"Well, Leah. That's a flattering offer, but I need to connect with my brother and run a few questions by

251

him before I can give you a response."

"Understood." said Leah - then, "*Dave* - find FJ."

The brother and sister met back at the guest suite. After he heard her story, FJ did admit that he was surprised at the quick action taken by Leah. He also admitted that his view of her as an older, but still younger sister whom he had not seen for five years, could have tainted his image. He had grown to know and trust Leah, therefore he quickly embraced the decision to offer his sister a job.

The siblings returned to a somber mood when Lizzy asked a few questions:

-- What should she tell their father?

-- Should she disclose the location or go underground?

-- How would she continue to hide her brother?

They agreed that Leah should be brought into this conversation. Over dinner in the underground dining room the three decided to be open about Lizzy's new position, with no reference to FJ needed. He would stay hidden.

"OK - I'll do it," said the new faculty member, "although I need to return the borrowed car and get another one to drive me and my stuff back out here."

"How much stuff?" asked Leah.

"Really just clothes, books and a few cooking things."

"FJ," said Leah, "Talk to Edward and find out if we have a plane in the neighborhood. Also, she will need some help with all the packing and loading, and you can't go. If Pope is feeling up for a trip, we could use his strong back. Leave the car here and buy it from her friend."

Lizzy had never been in a private jet. When Leah had mentioned a plane, the image that came to mind was a small, single-engine design like she saw at local airstrips. She was in awe when she arrived at the airport the next morning and saw the jet. Waiting in the customer lounge for the clearance to board was a young Native American man. He quickly introduced himself as Pope.

"I won't bother you with my given name," he said. "Everyone just calls me Pope."

They got the all clear to board the aircraft, and Lizzy and Pope took their seats. She was a surprised to see that a couple was already on board. Pope made the introductions to Brian Knight and Myrlene.

"Yes," Brian replied after being questioned. "I am Hal's brother, and this is my partner."

The conversation continued after the din of takeoff. Lizzy heard that the flight plan called for one stop in Maine then on to North Carolina the next morning.

"Sorry about the delay," Brian said. "We have an important session scheduled with Sean that will continue until you return to retrieve us. You can fly out to North Carolina in the morning and transact all your business in the daylight. Then come back to get us, spend one more night, and on back to Urgent the following morning."

Lizzy was self-confident enough to not worry about the sleeping arrangements. She trusted her brother, and these were his friends and associates. Brian and Myrlene were courteous and included her in the conversation. Even the testosterone-ladened young Pope was a perfect gentleman.

She decided she would deliver the news to her father in person the next day and enthusiastically relate her joy in being offered a job at this new institution.

She would *not* tell her father about spending the night at the compound of a former President of the United States.

TWENTY FIVE

•••• •— •—•• •• ••—• •— —••—

Willard Graham sat across the desk from Emmet Fitz-patrick just as he had hundreds of times already in his short life. Both had started working for the bureau at about the same time, but in different offices. Fitz had been transferred by the FBI to their Los Angeles agency and was in position when the younger Willy was brought in. Fitzpatrick had been Graham's boss.

"In the past, you and I have investigated numerous white collar and industrial cases," Fitz began. "We know how the businessman thinks and how they try to skirt the rules. Interpreting their intentions, meeting them face-to-face is where I need help.

"Recently, the large conglomerates and international concerns have begun to watch our growth. We have had some indirect contact and more than one 'Let's get together' inquiry. The science team here at Urgent has been looking to me to respond to these contacts. I just don't want to go out there and meet with these guys. You have always been good at it and still operate on a lot more social cylinders than I do."

"Show me what you're talking about, Fitz."

"Actually, when the time comes, you will be showing me what I'm talking about. I need to create a system, a program, a manual illustrating how we can negotiate with executives and big business to allow both parties to benefit.

"As you know, our mission is to save the planet. These early steps are huge. Our daily launches to the shield have been happening for three years, the ForCI projects began fifteen years ago (with Australia reforestation being just two years old) and our fusion reactors are now running better each year. Any one of these represents a lifetime's worth of work.

"With each advance we receive 'hits' and visitors from outside the nation. At first, we could easily refuse an arrangement with any firm that did not deliver an employee-owned location. As our accomplishments became more complex, so did our potential partners.

"To date we have not entered into any large-scale business agreements, but we foresee a demand to do just that. One of our latest patent applications drew enough attention from the defense industry that it reinforced our belief that we need to get organized.

"The technology we have developed in our magnetic launch system is totally unheard of. Harold Knight has received at least two different requests for a meeting to discuss these inventions. His delay tactics worked for a while, but he just told me that it's time we do something positive.

"I admit that I am at a loss as to how to go about this, and need some help."

"Fitz," Willard Graham responded, "When it comes to delegating, you are the best around. I have never had any trouble following your orders and can't imagine having any second thoughts today.

"When we approach a negotiating table, we will be accompanied by knowledgeable individuals, as we have always been. We will follow our script and monitor everyone's reactions. High-powered negotiations take more than one meeting. We merely change supporting actors as the stakes get higher. Ultimately we are in the room with decision makers on both sides."

"I appreciate your confidence," Fitzpatrick replied. "To remain informed, I will do the preliminary investigative work from my office down the hall. I need you to coordinate the efforts of all parties and report to me. Any decisions reached by your team will most likely be rubber-stamped, but I need to see it all. Please understand, everything we have done for years in building this community has been unique. Before I got here, they were managing by seat-of--the-pants. There is no blueprint for anything Urgent has accomplished.

"My brief experience has given me some insight into what works and what may not. That, again I'll say brief, institutional memory is all we have. We follow my instincts on all issues until our successes allow me to back-off and turn the decision-making over to you. My constant chats with Edward or Pope guarantee that the Native Americans are in the loop on everything. The Native American ethos will be represented too.

"We need to establish targets that potential partners can set their sights on rather than continuing to fight these negotiations on a case-by-case basis. Please ask your team to establish ground rules we can publish to inform potential customers and partners what we demand, or at least expect, of them. We are not going to engineer and produce a special alloy for an arms manufacturer. Nor are we about to schedule an experiment from big oil to hitch a ride on our next launch.

"Another item on your team's agenda is to meet with experts in the field of psychology and learn all you can about reward. Not all people jump when you throw dollars at them. There are those who have serious ego issues and those who are always in some sort of major competitive event. You need to know how this works so you and I can find the hot button when we need it – what do we push to encourage a decision.

"There are decisions made at the board of directors' level that are the not the product of democratic action. It is possible for a minority of the directors to swing a vote. It sounds crass, but our goal is to be able to better see when a bribe of a certain personality type might be effective."

"No offense, Fitz," said Graham, "but meetings such as these will be few and far between. Most of the research I can do from my desk, only hitting the road for two or three sessions per agreement. What else can I do around this place?

"I accepted your offer of taking up residence here at Urgent with the understanding that you needed help. We have spent a decade teaching me the ropes, having me meet the players, and flying around the continent getting acquainted with important people. Other than contract negotiations, what else can I help with?

"You know I no longer play with exotic cars. That wreck two years ago at Watkins Glen cured me of trying to keep up with younger drivers. Granted, I do still buy and sell fancy imports, but that takes less time than it used to, what with better computers and a more developed network out there. I would like to get even more involved in our community."

Fitzpatrick was hoping Graham would ask for more responsibility. Such a request not only confirmed Graham's dedication to his job, but confirmed his attitude and work ethic. Willard Graham had been known as someone who was always moving. He kept a pace more furious than all his peers, albeit only equally as effective. Fitzpatrick knew there would be wasted motion by the now out-of-shape Graham, and he didn't care.

"I'm glad you asked, because I would like you to assemble a management team and take on one more task. All of you must be visionaries and have top security clearances. This new project needs to be top-secret for a while. Let me tell you about the *spirit capsule*."

Within the hallowed research halls of Urgent were

hundreds of young people, and seasoned scientists as well. All vocational specialties have their own vocabularies; specific words for specific items or compounds, or just verbal short-cuts. Spirit Capsule was the in-house identity of a new project.

This project had been in design for years. The engineers knew that significant progress on the shield would be needed before the next space adventure was launched; and adventure was an apt description of the Spirit Capsule. This was to be a manned vehicle designed for a one-way trip.

Many cultures honor space and the heavens. Some of these societies do not fear death. With these facts in mind, the engineers asked a group of project managers if a percentage of the populace would be interested in viewing earth from above as their last living act. The next step was to pose this question to the Chief. Native American response to this proposition was positive. Many seniors in the community also thought it a great idea.

"We will be keeping a tight lid on this during our planning stages," said Fitzpatrick. "We want to make this an extreme honor, like earning the Nobel Prize. Sure, it will take money to buy the vehicle, but to earn the right to fly needs to be a big deal. Your team will be tasked to determine what it will take to earn that right. Some rich executive giving up three-fourths of his or her salary is not what we should be looking for. Has that executive convinced their board that they need to undertake some major *green* issue, and at what expense?

"Neither your team nor folks at Urgent can hypothesize all the scenarios that we will see. You will design this project to get creative juices flowing in others. Next you will design a non-discriminatory process by which you can choose the passenger. Then you need to figure out how to make it public.

"You have been around DC and New York long enough to know the negative landmarks. The doomsday predictions, the countdown to Armageddon, the national debt clock: all these show the public that they should fear for the end of their world. I want us to have a public face with the opposite indicators. I want to show the public the progress."

"Like you want to build some pie chart in neon on Times Square to give people hope?" asked Graham.

"I don't really know, but I want you to think about such a project. To get you started I will contact Sean Crockett and ask him to join us. He no longer enjoys flying, which means it may take him a while to get here. In the interim I would like you to contact Brian Knight who will travel with Myrlene, and Randall James from Tom Lacey's office. These are all well-informed senior citizens. You will be surprised at how worldly our active Urgent participants have become, even though they rarely leave home."

It took two months to coordinate calendars, but the former President and other individuals managed to set aside two days to meet, not including travel time. Bo's lair, the multi-level complex next to the dining room, had been reserved for this group. The guests were lodged in guest rooms below ground.

After introductions and brief remarks, Emmet Fitzpatrick confirmed that he had other, pressing issues to contend with. "Not that this group needs leadership anyway, but Willard Graham will keep you on topic and well fed." They chuckled. Fitz left the room.

Even though the entire session would be recorded, President Crockett's aide, Mark Madison, advised he would be taking notes and likely asking questions:

"The President and I work best when working from my scribble rather than some screen." There were no objections.

First the group had to agree on a bit of parliamentary procedure, like how to stop each other from talking and when to break for one reason or another. Graham thought a good beginning would be to brainstorm some examples of people or projects that might qualify for the proposed honor. Mark Madison decided his notes should include a number for the ideas, and a code indicating whose suggestion it was:

1-M   There is a mayor in a town in the Sun Belt who found funding for a roofing plan. All flat roofs in the community were converted to vegetable gardens, including a watering system.

2-R   Many communities have taken up tree-planting in a big way. How can we recognize, maybe even quantify, those efforts and include them in our analysis?

3-M   Didn't I read someplace about a city that is distributing free rain barrels to all homeowners?

4-P   I know of at least two Fortune 300 companies whose boards have come down hard on executive compensation. With a dividends-be-damned attitude, one has lost a CEO over the issue, but the spot was vacant for only one month.

Interestingly, the stock lost less than one percent.

5-B   What about the person that invented that dead-zone cultivator? The planet has twelve million square miles of dead zones in the sea. A well-placed university professor helped her class launch a machine that controls algae growth in the dead zones in our coastal waters. She used her contacts and a couple of grants to outfit a floating platform with a system that reaches deep to harvest algae, transforms the biomass into fuel in a digester, then uses the fuel to power the engine that propels the platform. They guide the contraption via GPS from her classroom. Call it a self-propelled, perpetual ocean filter. Her class concentrates on the massive seaweed bloom that shows up every year and extends across the Atlantic from the mouth of the Amazon River to the upwelling along western Africa.

6-P   We have heard about at least one governor that has signed legislation requiring an increasing percentage of new car sales be green. Are there other less populated states following their lead?

7-M   It is not well known, but Detroit is on the cusp of a program of education that might revolutionize the area's summer curriculum. An enterprising stadium manager, whose job it is to operate the venue (not related to any specific team) began a foundation funded by the owner of the dome, the owner of the team that uses the venue, and the rich athletes that play there. Rumor has it that a million dollars from each (which won't be missed - and is tax-deductible) amounted to a $25 million fund.

This money is being used to establish a summer science-fair with a sports twist.

R asked what athletics had to do with a science fair.

M "As I understand it, the pros will hold a morning sports camp with every student at least getting some exercise. Afterwards, in the afternoon the students present their team science projects to the same referees. Science in all disciplines will be encouraged, including those related to agriculture, animal husbandry, health care, and anything green.

The organizers want to invite every school district (particularly rural) in the region, and it's all free. Local hotels will provide off-season housing. The kids, chaperones, and athletes can all eat in the dome.

8-W Along those lines, the auto racing industry has introduced an electric car element to races. How has that worked and what effect did it have on engineering advancement. Is any of this an altruistic effort, or is it all to just keep selling tickets?

9-P At some point we will need to look at a politician or two. Don't misunderstand. I'm not addressing this subject because I used to be in office. Holding that high office should, in my book, exclude one from receiving any honors. The public deserves perfection and hard work. It goes with the territory. I'm referring to those in Congress and state politics that have dedicated their lives to public service and have done an outstanding job. Between doing what they are paid to do and then spending countless hours campaigning so they can get elected to continue doing it is a tremendous effort. Those that are super productive and still patriotic deserve special consideration, not today obviously, but one day.

10-R   There are large cities that have transitioned to an all-electric transit fleet and completely removed fares. How can we recognize them?

After a relaxing dinner in the dining room, Sean Crockett used his text-book gaze to silently silence the group, and then he began to speak.

"I'd like to toss into the hat the name of a young man whose very name I can't remember. Mark will look it up and give it to you. I did not mention him earlier because I believe there is time before he needs to be nominated, and/or needs to fly in a Spirit Capsule. At least I hope there's time.

"None of you was present in the White House at the time, or even aware of the conversation. My administration had just issued an executive order forcing the states and the nation to honor the obligation we have towards education. We declared a State of Emergency and ordered various committees to write new rules and others to figure out how to audit the Department of Defense and fund the mandates we put in place. One particularly creative staffer came up with the idea of a tax-code suggestion box.

"We tried it, and it worked. The concept was simple, the results were astounding. The bright minds of all those college graduates created revenue from places our conservative old-timers would never have thought of. Changes were happening quickly because there was no lobbying allowed during the emergency. We locked the IRS folks in their offices and asked for fast action. That's exactly what we got.

"Six of the eight years I was in office were under the emergency. We saw the fast-tracking of new rules about electronic trading on the stock markets. We introduced a tax on those transactions that brought no value to the market and tightened up on stratospheric compensation of hedge fund bigwigs. Our young minds solved some of the overseas investment mysteries which indirectly led to unearthing several large money laundering schemes.

"The audit of our bloated defense system released sufficient funds and we were able to jumpstart major education reforms nationwide.

"I would like to recognize that young man for his insight - someday."

When Crockett stopped, another member spoke up:

11 - R In keeping with the topic of "someday," we need to honor the architecture student that came up with the attic agriculture idea. The brilliant concept of building gardens just below the roof in commercial buildings was a response to the fact that urban waste heat warms the winter air in cities by one degree.

Electric motors and furnaces and other equipment give off heat that can be retained and allowed to drift upwards. She designed buildings with internal channels that encourage this heat to stay inside the structure and help grow vegetables above the top floor, below the roof.

12 - B We have already agreed that politicians are doing their job if and when they pass a law that benefits the public. All laws should. However, I want

to add the name of a Senator who did the biggest turn around in recent memory. Watson from Wisconsin wrote a bill to get dirty truck engines off the road. He took it from scratch all the way through Congress.

Randall James took a quick visual lap around the room. When no one else spoke up he acknowledged, "You do know that he is the father of one of our finest scientists?"

All eyes were now on Randall as he explained,

"We cannot put the Senator on our list. He is too ill. But please; this is not common knowledge and not to be mentioned outside this room. Sandy Watson is one of our sharpest agriculture researchers and a friend of mine. I know for a fact how sick his dad is."

The President took the lead again and asked if there were any other ideas. He got no response, so he declared the first brainstorming session over. He turned to Mark Madison, "I would also like to contact Edward White."

The former President wanted to catch up. He had last enjoyed Edward's company at the presidential retreat on Mount Desert Isle ten years ago. The newlywed Native American had been about to inherit command of the Wind River Reservation.

Crockett's impression was that Edward was quite capable of the job at hand. The President wanted to let him know he was thinking about him. Randall James knew that the evening was over when the president's aide gave a thumbs-up after talking with Edward over the phone.

Brian excused himself to find his brother. He offered his hand to Myrlene, they rose and walked

URGENT LAUNCH

across the dining room toward the doors leading to the research facility.

The Knight siblings had briefly spoken earlier. Brian knew he would find Harold in his elaborate quarters deep inside the complex. Once in the underground tunnel, Brian approached the cart station and placed his thumb on the scanner in the center of the console. Soon a green light indicated recognition of an approved operator.

The brothers had not seen each other in over a year; for Myrlene and Brittany it was almost five. Myrlene had never been so deep into the tunnels. She had not seen, let alone imagined, a living space below ground as attractive as Hal's compound. They entered a small foyer and Brian explained, as they turned left, that Harold's unique lab was through the oversized door to the right.

Part small-project laboratory, part utilitarian home, the surfaces were all unpolished stone. Interior partitions were more benches and cabinets than walls, with wireless electronics pleasingly placed. The large monitor along the biggest wall displayed a scene of an ocean beach; its display changed every fifteen minutes.

The four adults sat in large, well-cushioned chairs at a highly polished, circular wood table with a spiral design around the center. Myrlene asked about it and Hal explained that his computer had designed and carved the table to his specifications. Push the right button on the remote and the spiral design began unwinding (at least that was the illusion) until the table was almost twice the original diameter, with a lamp rising up from the hole in the center. The base of the lamp filled the hole.

Brian knew of most of the workings at Urgent. The brothers still talked regularly. However, the success of the college, its students, and lecture series were one subject that needed attention today. Harold offered his limited knowledge, quickly summarizing by saying that Brittany had spent more time exploring the new facility than he had. In fact, she had helped design the new administration building, complete with visitor center.

Brittany picked-up the explanation with details about the curriculum, core faculty, visiting professors, explorations and student perceptions. She outlined the growth in number and ethnicity of students, and the increase and variety of subjects to be studied. Her voice took on a unique tone of pride as she explained that there were no adjunct professors.

"The real scientists from Urgent's laboratories were at the front of those classrooms." It was obvious to Myrlene that Brittany was more than just observant – she was involved.

Brian turned to his brother and began a second subject, "Tell us about the launches."

TWENTY SIX

•• —• •••— • •—• —• • ••• •••

There would be no fanfare, no blaring trumpets or marching bands. The decision to launch senior citizens into space would not be celebrated in that manner. The somber last rites would always be spoken of in a solemn tone. Only Native Americans were initially to be offered this journey aboard what was publicized as a Spirit Capsule.

The senior population was now a major factor in the Urgent cultural mix. Most of their children had not been participants in the growth of the new community for a variety of reasons. Many had left the reservation to pursue a normal, urban life. This created an age gap in the demographics of the Great Plains Native Americans. However, the grandchildren of these aging tribal members had been attracted to the new Urgent offerings.

URGENT LAUNCH

They had chosen to return and get an education. These thirty-somethings had been the generation to conduct the death and dying conversation with the senior citizens. Native Americans and non-natives alike were welcomed at the gatherings celebrating the hereafter. The Spirit Capsule was known to all those on both sides of those end-of-life talks.

The physical container was built at a facility adjacent to the steel mill. It had been designed to launch via the sparrow's cargo doors. Its air-tight window aligned with the one on the sparrow providing the occupant a view. The actual construction of those final chambers might have been done by a relative of the occupant. The worker would be proud of his/her part in the task at hand. The older traveler would be proud of the younger worker

It was considered an honor to travel in the Spirit Capsule. The founders of Urgent believed their offer of this honor would be kept confidential. They would not allow public disclosure of the names of the people receiving the offer. A celebration of life ceremony would be held after launch while the capsule was still in orbit.

Former United States President Sean Crockett was a member of this older community. He knew his dying wish would be made aboard a Spirit Capsule but not in the near future. His interest in the visit today was to spend time with Edward White and get first-hand information about his father Joseph, the Chief of the combined tribes on the Wind River Reservation. One great national leader was wanted to honor another, and they both were getting old.

URGENT LAUNCH

While Crockett had been solving man-made problems in his role, Joseph had been building a new future. The dreams of both men were intertwined but they had never met. The Native American community felt that their leader would appear weak if he visited Washington, DC to confer with the US President. The former inhabitant of the White House had received non-stop negative press after he announced the State of Emergency those many years ago. He dared not leave his post because of the frenzied activity and ongoing opposition.

Now Urgent's Security director, Tom Lacey had been had been a confidant of the Chief's since before the first blueprint of the village was drawn. The two men knew each other well. Lacey recognized that Chief Joseph would be the first to fly, if he wished. This offering was a secret kept from the Chief until Lacey thought the time was right. Sean Crockett was also in the decision-making process on that timing. He had long wanted to speak with Joseph's son about the timing of that Spirit Capsule conversation. These best laid plans were moot when Mark Madison delivered a hand-written note from Chief Joseph to Sean Crockett asking for an audience.

Edward had suggested that they all get a good night's sleep and meet for coffee first thing in the morning. "I'll call Willard Graham and Randall James and tell them of our timing. See you in Bo's lair at nine." As other guests headed for their reooms, his aide excused himself to take the President for an evening drive around the grounds.

The morning conversation involved serious aspects

of future space travel. It again brought security to the forefront. Emmet Fitzpatrick was to physical security what Tom Lacey was to the digital safety of Urgent. Both were invited to join the President and Edward. FJ Guindo would sit in as the seasoned space traveler.

After quick introductions President Crockett began the meeting by explaining the process by which one ends up inside the Spirit Capsule. Edward explained the selection committee and its criteria to everyone in the room. Tom Lacey spoke to the absence of publicity and asked that they discuss the physical properties surrounding the capsule and the space traveler.

"Once the shock of launch subsides," Lacey said, "the traveler is conscious for more than two complete orbits of the planet. During that time the passenger can leave a message just by speaking. We use a secure space-to-ground communication channel that cannot be overheard by anyone. This one-of-a-kind recording is given to whomever the traveler suggests, or maybe stored in our archives. If we are instructed to share the message we will do so."

Emmet Fitzpatrick added his knowledge about how the body reacts to the lack of oxygen, and what the medical profession surmised the pain level was.

"I have studied various methods of execution during my days in law enforcement. In usual circumstances there is not a severe bodily pain that one feels during asphyxiation. It's the apprehension that causes the most stress. We could add any number of gasses to the capsule at the last minute to reduce that apprehension."

"For the most part," said Edward "my people, particularly my father, the Chief, do not fear death and would not be overly excited. Perhaps we could ask him to record his feelings for all to share and study.

"Just out of curiosity," he continued "I assume we are monitoring heart rate or some other vital sign."

President Crockett mentioned a conversation he had with Hal about that very subject. "Telemetry will consist of a wireless connection between the space vehicle and the traveler, which transmits vitals to ground personnel. Only when there is no sign of life for at least one orbit will they open the hatch and release the Spirit Capsule into space."

Looking at FJ the President asked, "I assume this is your job."

"Yes sir," he replied. "We have had the ability to monitor such signals for some time now. We rely on a decision made by both Sara and me in our analysis of the data we receive. Both of us have undergone appropriate medical training in interpreting the digital telemetry.

"If the need arises, we have the channels open between ground and the sparrow to actually listen for sound. We will make a copy of the recordings from the entire flight and lock it away for safe keeping."

FJ concluded by reviewing that the sparrow, having released the Spirit Capsule, would make one more orbit and dock at the stellar platform. While it was the standard space vehicle, it had no outside booster tanks or load to deliver. But it would pick up cargo bound for earth. Having just completed a most honorable flight, the sparrow would return to be reused.

Tom Lacey then asked how they planned to approach the Chief with an offer to travel in the Spirit Capsule.

"I can talk with him about that," announced Edward.

Sean Crockett knew the old chief had thought this all through the night before, but would later act surprised. The two aged leaders had met at Chief's insistance but soon realized, despite having never met, how well they knew each other. It had been a short session at Tribal Facilities and a meaningful farewell.

TWENTY SEVEN

•—•• •— ••—• •• — — •

"My name is John Saddey and I demand to talk to whoever the hell runs this place," the overwrought man exclaimed.

"Mister Saddey," said the young woman. "Please calm down, lower your voice, take a deep breath and tell me what 'this place' means. You are at the desk of the gift shop which is within the visitor's center for the space launches which are part of the surrounding community called Urgent."

"I'm sorry," he replied, after taking a deep breath. "It's just that I have been driving around this complicated area for two hours and really must speak with Mr. Edward White. I was in Casper on other business and thought I would just drive by on the off-chance I could watch a launch and talk with an executive.

Mr. White's is the only name I know."

"Mister White does have an office near the mill complex in Urgent," she gracefully said. "Let me see if I can contact that office for you."

It had been a long day for the overdressed businessman. A day earlier he had finally been given the go-ahead to approach the scientists at Urgent. He got very little sleep that night because the lengthy negotiating session with the major aircraft manufacturer headquartered in Chicago. A schedule change, charter flight, and scientific homework also kept him up into the early hours.

Edward and Brian Knight had long known this day would come. It had been two months since the news release about the new skin on the space vehicle. Word quickly spread through the scientific community that FishHide, as it was now known and patented, was dramatically improving performance of the spacecraft. Inventing the product was one thing, mass producing it was more complicated.

The construction team was rapidly producing mass quantities of the new skin at a multi-level structure they had built on the north side of the temptank. As with the shield material, but not publicized, the FishHide was cured in the extreme heat environment surrounding the temptank. This production process made the manufacturing of this simple looking material more complicated than it appeared to be.

Mr. Saddey was well known in the world of mergers and acquisitions, particularly in the niche of scientific breakthroughs. University labs were his playground. He was proud of his ability to recognize the value and application of scientific discoveries, specifically compounds that were potentially wonder drugs. The normal results of his hard work took years but finally surfaced as a new pharmaceutical. His interest in this particular new product at Urgent arose from his love of airplanes and the physics behind flight.

It was an uncomfortably hot ride to the architecturally striking WYIST administrative center. Thankfully the center was air-conditioned, as was the elevator. Once he entered the subterranean world with its dark tunnels, non-reflective walls and unusual sounds and echoes, he lost track of direction.

When the situation called for it, John Saddey could tap into his ability to quickly read, interpret and react to the verbal and nonverbal language of people he dealt with. He was being escorted to Edward's office by a member of Emmet's security team, but Saddey gradually became more involved in examining his surroundings than watching his guide; the unfamiliar was dampening his power of observation.

The guide and driver, Randall James, was purposefully making conversation peppered with scientific questions as he drove through the labyrinth of underground passages.

"That's our agriculture lab in that room. Do you ever think about how plants and trees grow? Those white coats are our scientists in cryogenics. Did you know liquid nitrogen freezes at below negative 300 degrees? The massive machines in that lab test stresses and breaking points of various materials. Did you know that the alloy wheel on your car can actually leak after a few years? Our institute now has over one-hundred classes. Have you seen our catalog?"

The guest did not interpret these questions as anything other than small talk. However, based on his answers, Randall was entering data into the communications panel on the console of his electric cart. Due to that input, specific members of the Urgent executive staff were being called to Edward's office.

When the small cart pulled up to the simple non-descript door, John Saddey was thinking that this spur-of-the-moment meeting would yield a one-on-one dialog with some geeky scientist who would be overwhelmed by his negotiating prowess and quickly agree to something leading to a significant bump in Saddey's income. His expectations were about to be shattered.

Edward White's suite was the showplace of Urgent. Whenever negotiations or important meetings were held with guests from the outside world, this office was used. More like a residential great room than an office, the physical space was an attention grabber. The conference table in the center of the room was circled by 18 matching chairs, yet it did not dominate the view.

One wall was made up of a solid black monitor while the others were polished stone. These white and gold speckled surfaces were complimented by a ceiling of similar colors, but with a large wide streak of flat black running diagonally, to the left and away from the entrance. The mirror image of this streak was in the floor. Saddey would later learn these were sealed seams of coal.

The near side of the coal seam, on the left of the

room, was a sitting area with over-stuffed chairs and sofas. It was obvious that the black and white hide covering the furniture was real animal skin. In addition, there were eight side chairs with identical upholstery strategically placed around the room.

Randall James motioned for his guest to approach the people now rising from their seats in the small, intimate seating area. Introductions were made to: Tom Lacey, communications guru; Harold Knight, lead scientist; Mr. James, data management: and Edward White, Chief. They all took seats in the comfortable setting and allowed their guest to take center stage.

Saddey began immediately, "I have been asked by a client to determine the feasibility of merging some of your projects with theirs or even buying your technology outright. The client is in the aerospace industry and your rippled metal sheeting is the product of particular interest. Technical papers explaining your accomplishment detail a minimum of ten percent less friction drag in your launches of the space vehicle. My client is anxious to test this product in a wind tunnel and possibly on a new aircraft they have in pre-flight production."

"Mr. Saddey," Edward replied. "You may have heard that Urgent conducts business with outside firms if they agree to one of our guiding principles: that we partner only with employee-owned businesses. How do you think your client would respond to such a demand?"

"We are dealing with a major public corporation with thousands if not millions of stock-holders," Saddey said, "and a large board of directors. Their normal business functions are managed by qualified employees executing decisions made by that board. They are slow to react to an outside stimulus."

"Oh John," interrupted Tom Lacey, "let's stop being coy. We know who you represent, and we know what they do. Sure, they have a big board, but those board members are hungry for this new technology. If they could improve the performance of their missiles and rockets, the defense arm of the company could renew government contracts for years to come. This would keep the St. Louis plant busy, add some much-needed overtime for the Long Beach facility, help with that Canadian operation, and keep a few folks on the payroll in the Macon shop that nobody talks about."

Saddey was momentarily speechless. He had never needed to familiarize himself with the physical operations of his clients. He also had never before encountered a party that knew as much about the opposing party before his disclosing the facts. How did the Urgent folks know such details?

Lacey allowed the quiet to remain for ten seconds, then spoke. "I believe we have an opportunity to bring your client to the table for a test run if they agree to also test a new business model. The St. Louis plant has a small research section with about a hundred employees. These geniuses researched and assembled the Cargo Aerial Vehicle (CAV) and the batteries that power it.

"We will agree to help your client install our revolutionary product on the largest, least efficient aircraft they make in exchange for helping us design and build an aircraft here in our complex. If they bring part of their team here to build a new experimental vehicle, we will take our new skin material to St. Louis and help advance the potential of your client's fleet. We can stipulate a probationary period of seven years within which time we will monitor the suitability of the product on the aircraft and the productivity of the employees.

"At the end of that seven-year period we would re-visit all aspects of the agreement, including whether we sell them the rights to produce our unique ma-terial. Throughout this experimental period, we will provide management for both projects. While not employee-owned, we can insure equitable compensa-tion this way."

"You really mean that," said Saddey. "You actually believe a massive, publicly owned defense contractor can spin off a new division and give control to you?"

"If I may, Mr. Saddey, it is already happening throughout the business community." said Randall.

"Around the Urgent complex we have lodging, re-tail outlets, fuel/convenience stores and more, with signage that looks similar to what you see every-where, but each property located on the reservation is employee owned. I know for a fact that numerous outside locations of those and other businesses have also transitioned to being employee owned. It may surprise you to hear that community goodwill and quality jobs have had positive effects on the percep-tion of large, public business.

"I'm sure you know this, but over the past years corporate profits have risen more than twenty times faster than worker's wages. Stockholders and ivory tower executives have bled corporations to the point where worker's wages are less than seventy percent of corporate income. That is a level not seen since after World War II.

"Without exception the public corporation that works with us to reverse this trend has ironically seen its stock price increase. The aforementioned goodwill is a realignment of profits that makes the stockholders money, predominately because one well-known outcome of all dealings with the Urgent team is a radical change in executive compensation. We insist on a realistic ratio of worker's average pay to executive income.

"In this scenario," continued Randall, "our proposal allows your client to use new technology without spending money. Their expertise will be brought to Urgent, but we will supply the labor and materials with which to build the new craft. The executive in charge of St. Louis research would be relieved of duties relative to the test aircraft and replaced by a leader of our choosing."

"Before you exhaust yourself thinking about others and how they make decisions, I believe you need to see our facilities," interjected Harold Knight.

He motioned for everyone to follow him and led the group to an almost invisible short, black hall at the far end of the dark, screened wall. A six-passenger electric cart was among the fleet of compact vehicles parked on the far side of that passageway.

Edward's office was beneath the southern end of the steel mill itself. The cart followed the corridor that ran beneath the mill then turned east. After driving for five minutes the temptank came into view, seen through large windows to the right. The cart stopped in front of a wide glass door.

Harold took one hand off the wheel and placed it on a black pad attached to the wall on his right, the door opened. The driver turned to his passenger, "FYI, since it looks like scales but is as tough as leather, the team now calls this material fish-hide."

They drove off to the left and after 30 seconds stopped at a wide platform which overlooked the floor of a cavern that was covered with freshly printed FishHide. Careful examination revealed the massive size of the 3D printer along the far wall and the special mechanism that moved the roll of material away from the printer, along the floor and toward a large chamber. Doors periodically opened on the side of that chamber and the material, riding on a unique remote-controlled cart, seemed to float into that cavity before the doors closed.

On the other side of the chamber other doors opened and the FishHide floated off to be unrolled and placed on racks beneath the temptank. Saddey learned that temperature inside the temptank room was over 700 degrees. He was told the FishHide was cured flat, in that environment for two hours. The material was then moved along to the assembly facility located in the next large cavern, back toward the mill.

"I believe," Harold began, "that you can appreciate the scope of our manufacturing process and why your client may want to consider our offer. No board of directors on the planet would approve the construction of such a facility merely to save a few percentage points of fuel cost."

"I agree," Saddey replied.

"Good. Let's return to my office," Edward said, "and talk about what we need your client to design and build."

They were seated around the huge conference table. The dark panel on the wall lit up as Edward began controlling what the group would watch. This presentation had been reviewed and fine-tuned by Urgent engineers involved in various aspects of designing the craft.

"We need to build an electric launch vehicle, and we want to do it quickly," said Harold.

He proceeded to explain that this aircraft needed to reach an extreme altitude, such as 14 miles or more, to release a payload at supersonic speeds; Mach 2 for example. Edward further confirmed that Urgent was finalizing the light-weight battery design and would be making perovskite solar cells to cover all horizontal surfaces.

"Neither of these new technologies has been widely used in flight before. The batteries weigh less than all other options at the moment, and the unique solar panels can be printed on a flexible surface. We have one of the premier materials science facilities in the country, so we can accurately calculate the weight of this craft and determine exactly how much power we need to achieve our goals.

"We can do most of the engineering surrounding the exterior covering and the power plant. The physical structure of the joints which handle the varying stresses is an area in which we could use your client's expertise. In addition, their fly-by-wire technology would be useful.

"As previously mentioned," said Edward, "this is a launch vehicle. We will have a piggy-backed load. Our scientists will get you the exact weight and balance of the cargo craft, as well as the weight of the battery pack.

"I can't imagine balance is much of an issue except at the moment of separation at supersonic speeds. Release of the cargo will create temporary forces in one direction, and an instant later a change of direction results in other forces. Your client's wind tunnel may be needed to properly analyze the divergent stresses present at that moment."

"Pardon me for asking, but how are you launching today?" queried Saddey.

Harold fielded the question. "Our daily launches are via proprietary systems. Special computer programs control the timing of three events before the vehicle even clears the tall guide towers:

First: An instant magnetic pulse that jump-starts the process.

Second: A super-heated, high-pressure steam reaction that increases acceleration for two seconds.

Finally: The one-thousand-foot magnetic force that takes us up to an acceleration rate of fifteen G's.

"The small, compact spacecraft is traveling at over twelve hundred feet per second when it clears the towers and has yet to use any onboard fuel.

"Two seconds later our *pressure solution* begins

its controlled release from the booster tanks. That initial thrust lasts for nine minutes, takes the craft through maximum dynamic pressure, and then the vehicle coasts for a few more seconds. When the next shot from the booster tanks hits (at about the ten minute mark) we are at the height where a small fraction atmospheric pressure interferes, and practically ready for orbit."

"That sounds like a well sequenced process," Saddey admitted. "What will you be launching that you can't already handle?"

"People." Was the reply.

TWENTY EIGHT

—•• •— •—• •• • —•

Many first-time visitors to Urgent noticed the routine, if not slow, pace of the citizens. School activities on playgrounds were obvious, and the electric coaches were seen scurrying around the town and across the bridges. What could not be seen was the continuous, hurried activity of growing the shield.

Each routine daily launch resulted in a return to earth by that same vehicle. Preparations for each such pair of trips were on-going and meticulous. It was a chore to clean, examine, re-load and prepare the returning empty spacecraft for re-launch. The returning sparrows that had carried a Spirit Capsule into space demanded more careful attention, since the messaging devices required proper handling.

There had been occasional gaps in the launch schedule during the early years. The brief interruptions were to resolve technical glitches and fix mechanical problems. The minor incidents had not been crashes and there was no loss of life. The shield was now in orbit around the planet and the daily arrival of material allowed its area to spread to a 10-mile square in only seven months. One reason for this rate of expansion was the decision to change the initial design.

The original plan called for a complete uninterrupted surface. The revised checkerboard-like assembly would still accomplish the desired goal once in deep space - provide miles of partial shade for the planet below.

A major program milestone was reached at the one year point – the decision to add a second launch site. To increase the size of this large shield area took many launches: one year had been needed to grow from 15 to 20 miles square at one launch per day. That was too slow. With two launch sites, and by building out different corners, the shield was enlarged quicker. Neither daily launch would endanger the other since the arrival times were staggered.

Locating two launch sites on different continents did keep the sparrows away from each other. The launch, flight, and docking timing was a challenge for the programmers working with *Dave*. The scientists at Urgent patiently waited for the engineers to program multiple launch site flexibility. Once accomplished, all systems were "go" to add one new launch site per year.

It had been ten years since FJ Guindo had established the stellar platform at, what was now, the corner of the shield. It was time for the mammoth installation to have another more up-to-date platform to anchor the next phase of growth. The team of scientists had called for a meeting with Hal, who then invited Edward, the Chief of the nation, since another manned mission was surely a national event.

The gathering in Hal's compound was not designated as classified, but he interrupted the small talk to remind them of the continued need for common-sense security.

"We need to talk about the future steps we can take to grow the shield. I won't say plans," Hal said, "because these future moves may be more dreams than reality. Regardless, please keep this to yourself. We don't need developers or governments misinterpreting our intentions."

The scientists and the Chief's family (Edward and Pope) began comparing notes and sharing:

"You all know," Harold continued, "that our building project in space is automatic. We have light, sleek space vehicles (sparrows) sent up to a stellar platform every day. We anchor the space shield and debris filter to that stellar platform. Our unique robots (COTs) then help the shield grow.

"Once the sparrows reached the shield, they automatically unload their cargo. The waiting COTs then snap the new pieces onto the larger area in a day. With the size now 100 miles on each side, the COTs must travel farther to refuel. The increasing maneuvering is takes time and is taking a toll on the reliability of the COTs.

"During the first eight years of daily launches, the shield has been held in a medium orbit near 14,000 miles above the earth. This distance was selected in order to place the shield above the orbit of the International Space Station and all its debris at 250 miles, yet below the popular 22,000-mile location of all geostationary satellites. The fact that the shield orbits twice in each earth day is one feature of this location."

As Hal took a breath, FJ decided to clarify the launch situation, "I just wanted to remind you all that our latest launch site is in Tanzania. We now have sparrows arriving daily from that location as well as from seven others.

Harold continued: "Right, FJ, Tanzania also sent extra COTs aloft, as is our *sop*, but distance to refueling is still an issue. I would like to discuss sending the first section deeper into space and concentrate on completing a second section of shield.

"The perfect game plan would be to complete section-two in space while designing COT V-2 and preparing to build another stellar platform. The Urgent facility could begin manufacturing a more trouble-free and flexible COT V-2. We would need them ready to fly with the first sparrows farther out to platform number-2."

"Yea." Said young Pope. "The guys in the communications and robotics labs have been working on deep space communications. They tell me they have a more efficient signal between the earth and the COTS, but need a redesign of the small robots. They would need another visit by a manned mission."

Hal chose to continue: "A logical approach would be to immediately start a second stellar platform. COT version-1 would continue to work with platform one. We will detatch and send section-one deeper into space. Remotely, the scientists would start and grow section-two for a few years at the platform number-one site..

Section-three would begin with the construction of the new platform and require another manned visit. The human would install the debris filter, launch the new COTs, and activate all systems aboard platform number-two."

Lately, Urgent's scientists had been insisting on better control. A push deeper into space could tax their decade-old communications system, and control was all about communications. Hal began to explain,

"In a non-human environment, communications efficiency is a two-pronged issue: speed and quality. Speed is a concern because of the distances involved. The signal from the PlatCom center on the high plain near Urgent reaches the COTs at the shield in less than a second. These signals travel at the speed of light and 300,000 kilometers per second gets to the shield at 20,000 kilometers fairly quickly.

"When pushing deeper into space, the time it takes for the receiving party to get input from the sending party can be problematic. This is referred to as One Way Light Time. The *owlt* to the moon, for example, is 1.3 seconds. To signal Mars could take 10 to 20 minutes. Any problem is compounded if the sender needs to wait for a reply, which is not the case with communications to the COTs.

"At present we are building the shield in a medium earth orbit. We plan to move the first section deeper into space to about 30,000 miles and study the shadow it casts on earth. It will take task-specific COTs to tug this large object deeper into space and then to slow it down in a controlled manner.

"To maximize the quality of those one-way signals, the input to the COTs will now be routed through the stellar platform instead of the COTs receiving direct instruction from the ground. With the stellar platform acting as a routing agent it can receive all transmission from the ground. The input can then be sent to individual COTs via direct, crisp transmission from the platform. In the rare case of needing feedback from the COT, this too will arrive quicker and with more clarity.

"Naturally, both stellar platforms will talk with earth but on individual frequencies due to the differences in *owlt*. This change in signal time will occur because we will build platform number-2 at 25,000 miles.

"Our team at PlatCom monitors all satellite activity near our stellar platforms. To date there has been no major concern. However, we recently realized that to move our completed sections into deep space, we must transit the satellite geo-synchronous zone at 22,000 miles. Watching the increase in traffic at this location is quite a wake-up call.

"There are thousands of objects of various sizes orbiting the planet at this altitude. Sure, space is huge and we should be able to move our large shield sections across this zone without incident. At least in the near future - but what about later? We are not going to take the risk. We will start our construction farther out and let the sparrows cross this busy area as they carry their cargo to the new stellar platform. For the forseeable future we will be building at two distinctly different locations and analyzing build rates and maintenance needs of both"

At this point Edward inquired, "What does it take to move this immense sunshade?"

"Edward, the special robots we have designed will be powered by both CO_2 and solar. They need to return to the charging tanks to top off with CO_2, and stay in the sun to charge their batteries. Between these two power sources we will have no trouble slowly tugging the shield deeper into space. It's the next step that is the challenge."

Hal continued: "At what point do we discontinue this process in earth orbit, scattering the shadow all around the planet haphazardly? At what point do we place the shield in a lock-step orbit with the earth around the sun?"

"That would place the shield in sun-synchronous position, with the shadow being cast at the same latitude on the planet as it rotates beneath the shield. Oh, and at what latitude do we put it?

"We have our brain-team of FJ and Sara working on the math. It's a complicated problem, maybe with no real answer. You can appreciate that the farther away from earth the shield sits, the smaller the force of gravity. We want to continue to make the shadow larger, yet the farther away it is from low earth orbit the longer it takes for the new shield sections to join the growing shield at the ultimate location. For that reason we plan on waiting for the completion of section 2. We will combine both finished sections and position them as one over the planet.

"Furthermore, we may decide that weaker gravity is not as important as shadow control. The farther into space we send the shield the longer it takes to see the shadow's reaction to orders. Remember, we are always moving the shield. What is optimum reaction time?

"The new launch sites we built over the years are all home to a nuclear reactor. That reactor solves the water and climate control issues of the region and supplies the massive amount of electricity required during each launch. However, we chose not to reproduce our manufacturing and assembly facilities in these locations. Should we reconsider?

"The rapid expansion of our launch capabilities has brought about a sparrow shortage. We have more vehicles in motion than we ever imagined, leaving too few in preparation for launch. We need to make more sparrows and fast. Are there any unforeseen consequences to expanding our foreign launch layouts to include an assembly plant? Please examine all aspects of installing an assembly plant at future launch sites and determine what we need," Hal said.

"In the past we have rerouted returning sparrows to a new site. Those vehicles have supplemented the supply we shipped along with the other materials. We backfilled our local inventory gaps with new product coming off the assembly line. Now we find that our production of booster tanks, sparrows and tower rails is still lagging behind the delivery. Regardless of the launch site, we have holes in the inventory and distribution.

URGENT LAUNCH

"Please consult with your team leaders to determine which facilities at our massive complex at the Urgent location need to be duplicated. Our 3D printing facility is easy to build elsewhere but the materials need to be made and prepared at Urgent."

Hal took a break from his explanation and approached Pope. Standing next to the young man, he placed his hand on Pope's shoulder and addressed the small group.

"We need to send a citizen into harm's way to help us grow, exactly as we did ten years ago for our first space endeavor. Any new stellar platform demands human involvement in the physical and electronic construction. We will program software, build new COTs, and design a self-unfurling space station but someone needs to flip the switch. Young Pope has agreed to go aloft – we just don't know when.

"We will contact a private launch company and reserve a spot on one of their vehicles. The timing will depend on the scientists in this room. When can we begin shield section three? How can we improve construction efficiency?"

Looking Pope in the eye, Hal added: "You will be getting a crash course (no pun intended) in astronaut school. Beyond just being in shape there are things to learn. Appreciate the spirit with which you are considered worthy of these lessons. You already know FJ is available to answer any questions and to share stories with you. He was the first to represent Urgent in an environment other than earth's.

"You will join an exclusive club."

TWENTY NINE

.—. . —.—— . ...

Young Pope was a little nervous. Not that the classroom at WYIST bothered him, he had been in almost all of them: however not standing in front. Professor Guindo had asked him to make an appearance and meet the students in her class. He had chosen a session near the end of her second year of teaching. Before his remarks began, she asked him to, "Drop the professor thing, I use Lizzy in here." Obviously, she was now comfortable in this setting. That thought put him more at ease. He took a deep breath, reminded himself that he wrote the lecture, and began.

"I'm sure many of you remember the fairy tale "Goldilocks and the Three Bears." You know that she breaks into their house and tries the bed and porridge of each of the bears with the evaluation being "too hot," or "too cold," or "just right." Those in the scientific community like to state that we live on a planet that's in the Goldilocks zone.

"Our next neighbor in one direction is 25 million miles closer to the sun. We can melt lead on the surface of Venus - it's that hot. In the other direction, after traveling another 50 million miles away from the sun, it's too cold. An average day on Mars is minus 81 degrees. So when it comes to supporting life, the earth is "just right." Let's take a look at other Goldilocks zones, within our own.

"The average temperature worldwide is fifty-seven degrees Fahrenheit. That would be the average considering cold at the poles and heat at the Equator. Between those extremes we often cannot live without clothing or shelter, at least not all year. Man is a fairly fragile mammal. It has taken us a long time to adapt to our environments.

"Long ago we determined that we could not exist at those colder poles. Even if there was easy food available, slow metabolism and the lack of thick fur and large feet would prove fatal. We let the polar bear and penguins have the poles.

"Closer to the Equator we learned to feed and dress ourselves as climate dictated. Layers of animal skins were worn or removed depending on the weather. We evolved to be able to chew and digest certain animals and plants. Other animals and plants had to be avoided by man; we learned which was which. This took a long time.

"Let us look at the growing requirements of that food. Set aside flooding and sea level rise and desertification for a moment. We now know that our man-made changes to the climate of this planet endanger our very existence because of the Goldilocks zones of our food."

Lizzy interrupted Pope and said, "That is the topic of your assignment this week."

Every student magically produced a recording device and placed it on their desk.

"Of the thousands of animal types on the planet," Pope continued, "man mostly consumes animals from the sea. All of those creatures have evolved to thrive within very specific temperature ranges, Goldilocks zones if you will. What happens when we warm the seas of the world as we are doing? Will the prey move to different areas? Can the predator adapt to those new locations to avoid starvation?

"One terrestrial example of this is the Grizzly Bear. In the search for food and a cold place to hibernate, this species has now wandered into the same territory as the Polar Bear. The Polar Bear in a search for food has moved south, while the Grizzly has moved north.

"Coral colonies dwell in the shallows of most of our oceans. While covering only one-tenth of one percent of the ocean floor, coral supports twenty five percent of all marine species. This is a major player in the food chain. When the seas warm, the algae that coral eat move on to grow in cooler water, and the coral starve. Dead or bleached coral colonies not only endanger the marine life that rely on the nutrition and camouflage, but will promote larger waves above. Studies indicate wave height of more than twice the normal, when coral reefs with their nooks and crannies no longer diffuse the movement of ocean waves.

"Warmer oceans also play a role in how fast storms move and how intense they are. Storms draw more energy from a warmer ocean. The atmospheric pressure between the poles and the tropics is reduced by warmer oceans and the storms slow down, they have more time to drop more rain. For decades the Inter-governmental Panel on Climate Change has produced a periodic report detailing the anticipated rate of ocean warming. Invariably the panel reports that the oceans are warming faster than predicted.

"Along the Pacific Coast we have another interesting situation. The sea otter has a serious appetite for sea urchins. However, our ignored planet has created a shortage of breeding ground for the otters. The polluted and infested coastal waters have affected mortality rates of adults. Fewer births and more deaths equal a population in danger.

"The urchin population has, therefore, blossomed. One of their favorite food is kelp holdfasts. Without an anchor (holdfast) to the sea floor the kelp floats free and dies. Without the otters to keep the urchins in check the large kelp forests are being decimated. Who lives in those forests?"

One young man's hand immediately shot up.

"Sorry," Pope smiled, "that was a rhetorical question. You all will get an opportunity to answer, though, since you will be asked to identify the fish that use the dense kelp as either a place to live, or feed, or hide, and which species rely most heavily on coral: then identify where they are in the food chain.

Without those species is there a risk of starving their predators to extinction? What fish rely on those predators for food?

"Beyond the broken food chain issue, we face species extinction due to loss of habitat. How can the ocean not be hospitable you might ask?

"Please look at the mighty salmon, the popular food of man and beast. Years of evolving have implanted into every salmon the need to return to its place of birth - to give birth. They swim up the very rivers and streams they were born in, lay eggs in shallow water, and die. Those eggs are nurtured by the cool, fresh water and hidden by rocks, branches and debris. After birth, the fingerlings swim out to sea and live for a couple of years.

"Melting snow and ice provide the cool water that constitutes a river. Rising temperatures and agricultural diversion puts this habitat at risk. Warm water is not going to accommodate the fish and shallow water gives them nothing to swim in. Where will they go then? Their gestation period is three to five months; where will these fish decide to lay those eggs when they have an urgent instinct driving them to one very specific point where the fresh water flows to the salt water?"

Pope picked up a framed photograph he had earlier leaned against the classroom wall. The large, color photo was a composite of many pictures which showed the planet without any cloud cover.

"Temperature and availability of water are the forces behind where our food comes from. The agricultural bands on our earth are well defined. When the average temperature in those areas increases five degrees, which is certainly within the realm of possibility, those plants need to be closer to the poles to grow in the same conditions. Pear orchards, wheat fields, vineyards: all are in danger.

"We are concerned about logging too because we need the trees. Coinciding with our need for food is our need for oxygen. The trees manufacture that necessity and we would be foolish to reduce our source of O_2. In fact, one last example of our Goldilocks scenario is those big trees and a pest that takes them down: the bark beetle."

As he spoke Pope referred to his photograph and pointed to the obvious lines of vegetation and forests on both sides of the Equator. Now he zeroed in on interior Alaska forests.

"A healthy evergreen tree has thick bark and a chemical defense layer beneath the bark which discourages insects from dining on either the outside or inside of the tree. When the tree weakens those defenses are easily overpowered by voracious bark beetles.

"A few years of drought brought on by changing weather patterns can weaken a tree, or an entire forest. Every 45 to 50 days one beetle can lay up to ten eggs beneath the bark. Those larvae hatch, eat their way back out of the tree, grow wings and fly to a neighboring weak tree, leaving a dying tree in their wake.

"Within one year there can be seven overlapping generations eating their way through thousands of trees. The beetle takes less than two months to start working on ending the life of a one-hundred year-old Douglas fir tree. Those trees within that forest provide the habitat for the beetle. Where is the goldilocks zone for the tree that takes years (not days) to evolve?

"Many of you know I had the honor of visiting our facilities in outer space. I took many pictures of the planet, my home, during my days at the platform. This image you see is less than five years old. After class I invite you to look at how much damage has been done to our forests. It's visible from space.

"Before I close I want to point out the clarity of this photograph. In reality our planet is actually as clean as is pictured here. The primary reason for that is our success in reducing the particulate matter in our atmosphere. It is comforting to know our years of work in reducing emissions and shuttering coal-fired power plants have paid off, but we can't rest.

"We know there has been a gradual warming of the planet during the past decades. That increased heat has caused sea ice and glaciers to slowly disappear; that we can see. What we can't see is the gradual thawing of the tundra and peat bogs that are now exposed to sunlight.

"These soils, particularly peat, contain massive amounts of methane. This is a gas which contaminates our atmosphere and remains harmful many years after carbon dioxide has dissipated. We have stopped logging and burning forests near other large peatlands on the planet. Naturally we get the occasional forest fire started by Mother Nature, but we largely have the human driven devastation have under control. It's just the problem of environmental degradation in the large lower polar regions that we can't access to solve.

"As I said, you can't see it but the planet you see so clearly in this photograph has an atmosphere deadlier than ever. The best possible way to clean this up is to continue on the path we chose 40 years ago. We must cool the planet down."

Pope closed and Lizzy returned to the front of the class.

"One of your assignments next week will be to write a report on how far we need to relocate our agriculture. We also need to know if there is room to do that without massive logging. I might mention that you will be getting a little help with your next paper from some experts.

"The Agriculture Lab at Urgent is in the middle of a few experiments that will help you determine why a Goldilocks zone exists for plants and trees, and what we can do to widen that zone. You will get an appreciation for the balancing act of life on this planet.

"Everyone in this class knows that Urgent is involved in trying to save our species. We are not waiting for governments to iron out their differences and decide who is going to tackle which problem. Our solution revolves around buying time by shading the earth and slowing the increase in temperature.

"A little shade, though, will not yield a breathable atmosphere. If we don't get these other issues under control, we had better plan on deserting this planet. The major unknown is the amount of time we have. That's where you come in.

"The curriculum at WYIST presents a student with lots of options. Those of you interested in materials science may be seated next to a future astronaut. Regardless of your area of interest, you will become acquainted with each other and work together. Our team in the Materials Lab is working hard to create the optimum shield material which the stellar platform team will install in space. Cooperation is crucial for success.

"We expect each of you to spend the rest of your working lives on your part of the solution. These solutions will be reached through education. Thousands of teachers are helping their students learn a little bit about what we face. Every student must mature and advance the cause. There is a massive student exchange program taking place around the world because this issue has no boundaries and every effort is a good one. We all can learn from each other.

"Here at WYIST you are learning the science which provides a big picture look at the work man can do. In less developed countries the students are waking up to some other aspects of our dilemma. Pollution, birth control, solar power, and desalination are just a few of the topics these young people are exploring.

"Any changes are a tough sell to their parents, but all are necessary. They can be trusted to carry the message and implement needed changes in spite of the obstacles the older generation presents. The more we help the less developed countries the quicker we can expect to see results, and we need results.

"But please understand that our primary mission is to grow the shield. The money and leadership needed to clean up our earth-bound problems must come from governments. This guarantees many years will pass before we see action.

The big countries have big, slow governments and politically conservative leaders who want to keep their jobs. The smaller countries do not have the money to lead such a massive undertaking.

"In 2015 the United Nations negotiated the Paris Climate Agreement and convinced close to two hundred countries to agree to emissions and temperature goals. Every year since then there has been a problem with one or another of the signors, in implementing changes and starting to live up to their part of the deal.

"The European Union had tried to agree as a 'united entity' to use 2050 as a target for eliminating fossil fuels. One country backed off a few years in. Then Britain did the Brexit move. Now here we are, well past that date and still, not all governments have had the nerve to deprive their citizens of oil and gas. We get numbers from the Integrated Carbon Observation System (ICOS) and they are not what they should be according to the Paris Agreement.

"I trust you see why we follow the course of action we do, and what has happened to the other players in this global issue.

"Thank you, Pope. See you all tomorrow. Now, let's get to work."

THIRTY

• ••— •—• • —•— •—

"As of this morning we are up 2.02 degrees. This is a
slight leveling off of the upward trajectory we saw on
the report of five-years ago. Naturally, it's too soon to
tell but at least we are not boiling the planet."

Sandy Watson had the honor of addressing the
gathering. This presentation was a rotating report
used to inform the principal supporters of the Urgent
project. This year the group had again invaded Mt.
Desert Isle, President Crockett's summer retreat. The
former leader was becoming frail and this arrangement suited everyone. He could stay home. Also "at
home" were the four philanthropists behind the project. It was telling that Henry, Steven, and Eduardo all
trusted their alternates to represent them.

Section One of the space shield was placed in a

307

sun-synchronous position 12 years before this meeting. At that time lead scientist Harold Knight had told the group that Urgent would begin to more closely monitor the average temperature and the carbon dioxide content of our atmosphere. Sandy was reporting the latest statistics.

"When realistic-minded citizens began listening to scientists early in the 21st century, the carbon dioxide content in our atmosphere was 375 parts per million (ppm), increasing at a rate of fewer than ten ppm every five years. Since that time the increase has been increasing, until the latest trend is a bump of fifteen ppm for the last five-year span. Science does not want our CO2 level to reach 450ppm."

Myrlene was seated next to Brian Knight and raised her hand; "Has our shield been up there long enough to yield meaningful numbers?"

"Before I answer, I want to caution everyone that it's too soon to look for concrete results. Our first launch of shield into deeper space and in lockstep with the sun was an object only 100 miles square. Our launch rate and payload average for that first section resulted in a nine-year effort to reach that size. One hundred miles by one hundred miles does not cast too large a shadow on the arctic. But it's a start."

"To now answer your question - yes. Seven years ago, we did move Section Two of the shield deeper into space to join Section One at 30,000 miles. These first two shield fragments have been coupled together so they move as one when needing to be realigned. This combined section has been positioned to cast its faint shadow on the planet at the sixty degree or so parallels, or more towards the poles. The COTs that travel with the shield are constantly moving it and helping it remain in position as the earth's rotation causes the planet to go through daily exposure to the shaded sunlight.

"Our scientists feel that winter will take care of itself if we can prevent some of the ice loss in summer. We help minimize ice loss by reducing the intensity of sunlight during the hottest part of the summer day. Locating the shadow above the Arctic, or below the Antarctic circles, means the shadow's path around the top of the planet is shorter so our small shield is more effective. In the land of the midnight sun, we are in position to block more of the sun's rays because of longer days. We are confident our placement is the ideal location.

"We started nudging Section Three into deep space one year ago. That section will be placed near the combined section but will not be attached. We will be experimenting with re-positioning the two sections and gradually moving the shadow by leap-frogging the sections: first move one to the new position, then move the other to the far side of the first, and so on.

"As the planet orbits the sun, the tilt of its axis creates longer and shorter days during different seasons, at a given latitude. That 23-degree offset is something we need to take into consideration when determining what to shield from the sun and when we will leap sections. We move the shield a little every week, but the major shift from shading in the Arctic region to placement above the Antarctic is a semi-annual event.

"As the shield grows, we intend to lengthen it more than we widen it, that is; more growth towards the equator. We would like to influence ice melt in that direction rather than stretching the shadow around the planet and creating much shorter summer days.

"The 2.02 degree rise in temperature we just measured is not reflecting any meaningful trend. Over the years the earth has experienced swings in that indicator, but we definitely have a gradual upward curve on the graph. During the past 50 years we have seen almost a quarter of a degree real rise in the average per decade. Scientists do not want to see us get to three degrees."

Brian Knight, obviously nudged by Myrlene, spoke, "Back to the shield for a moment, is our rate of construction improving?"

Pope was near the head of the table and the leading expert in the shield's progress. "Let me respond to that question with a complicated answer: yes - but. It's hard to tell because we keep changing things. As previously mentioned, the combined section of shield is in position at 30,000 miles. Right now, it is all alone and the only sun-synchronous section.

"The next piece, however, is larger and will join the first at that position before the year is over. We got that done quicker than the first, and it's a bit bigger, because we used a new version of our assembly robots; COT version-2.

"We designed a new stellar platform, introduced better robots, and brought a larger shield piece per shuttle. The rate of growth of Section Three was increased by twenty five percent. We are about to do even better," Pope said, and they believed him. Everyone in the room knew that Pope had been the astronaut chosen to organize the foundation of the new stellar platform, the anchor for Section Three, three years ago.

"The engineers have been working closely with material scientists to design and make a larger and lighter shield material. I believe our future sparrows will have a cargo of one square mile of shield. That is a further improvement of fifty percent. Consider this the ultimate, for the moment.

"We have achieved this rate of construction by adding to the number of launch sites, and improving our cargo capacity. We accomplished this feat through standardization of our structure, and infrastructure. The sparrows, launch tubes, vertical rails, electronics modules, and so on, are the same size at every launch site. However, our efficiency in growth is beginning to cause traffic problems. Not problems on the ground, but at the active stellar platforms.

"Each shield section begins growth by anchoring two long poles to the stellar platform, extending perpendicular to each other, defining the direction of the perimeter. As new pieces of shield arrive, they extend the perimeter in both directions. We then direct the sparrows to the area inside that corner and the COTs begin filling the inside space.

You may recall that we create a checkerboard pattern, allowing equal-sized empty squares to form between solid shield pieces. We fill from the perimeters toward the inside. This results in a diagonal sawtoothed shield edge.

URGENT LAUNCH

"Our traffic problem is here, along that edge. In the past, to speed up the building rate, we have added one sparrow arrival from one launch site every time the diagonal distance between perimeters increased by five miles. Our logistics team had analyzed travel patterns and timing to arrive at that launch frequency. The arrival, unloading, COT activity and departure routes were analyzed by *Dave*. If we get any more efficient in our shield construction we will need to rethink all launch schedules. Too many sparrows unloading near each other presents potential problems.

"Pardon the stupid question, Pope." The former President said, "but can you see it on the ground?"

"Mister President, it's so cool. We have a before and after series of photos taken from a satellite." He retrieved the photograph from his e-file and activated all the monitors around the table, including the one in front of the President.

"Look closely and you can see the blurry shadow edge as it crosses the glaciers in Greenland. Our early efforts are small plus, there are a lot of direct rays peeking around the shield edges because the light source, the sun, is just plane huge. That being said, we can see the difference in the partially blocked sunlight as it heads for the earth."

"I can see it," whispered a withered Sean Crockett.

At this, Dennis Hall spoke up. "You do know that there are millions of people on the ocean's edge who want you to hurry up. The seas are continuing to rise, and the resulting exodus causes an immeasurable amount of pain on both the migrants and the communities on the receiving end."

He paused. "I'm sorry. I realize the cautionary approach we have to take, and I understand the consequences if we go too far. As I work with these reforestation projects though, I have a constant nagging feeling that these young people deserve to see some results. Sure, they see growth of the trees they planted. Of course, they move on to work in other jobs, most in the environment fields, but wouldn't it feel great to show them a picture of a Polar Bear returning to the sea ice."

"Yes, it would," said Sandy. "In fact, it would be great to show them a picture of sea ice as it used to be. Unfortunately, that will take some time. When President Crockett and the elders started this project 45 years ago, the world was half in denial and half in study mode. There was no forward momentum. We took action, and in that time have been on the edge of significant changes.

"Not that we made these changes, or get credit for them. Hell, we don't even want credit. We are happy when our involvement produces an increase in momentum towards a better system. Consider:

-- Today's education system in this country is vastly improved.

-- We have won some battles in income inequality.

-- The massive reforestation projects Dr. Hall was just referring to have been spawned by us.

-- Our collection of fusion reactors is scattered around the planet providing power to millions who never had it before.

"Many of our launch site/reactors have caused the shut-down of hundreds of coal-fired plants. These changes have put thousands to work in hundreds of villages and brought value to millions of lives.

"Yes, there are still millions out there living under constant environmental threat and living without electricity and clean water. We know the sandstorms in the Sahara have gotten worse and that hurricane season in the Atlantic is longer than ever. On any given morning we may be talking with the Egyptian government and that afternoon listening to the World Meteorological Organization (WMO). But our number one priority is, and always has been, to address climate change.

"Eduardo and Javier are the tree and water experts. At Urgent we handle the off-planet projects. For now, the rest of our planet's problems will need direct help from other sources, or they must wait until indirect help trickles down from our efforts. The public benefits from our myriad experiments in agriculture, materials science, and robotics research. We will continue that research, but our priorities cannot change."

Javier raised his hand and Sandy acknowledged his silent request with a nod.

"As for the reforestation programs, you all know we have been working closely with the International Institute of Tropical Forests. When we first contacted them, they had been studying areas in our hemisphere, near the Caribbean. Since then we have, together, helped efforts in Western Africa, fine-tuned an Amazon forest and launched projects in Australia and Indonesia.

"When we began the forestry consortium, the

Urgent community was in chaos trying to relocate friends and family of the founding workers. Our tree work was not overly organized. We had some questionable success in the Tongass National Forest, but we got better. It is difficult to estimate the total amount of forests we have turned around, but I would guess tens of thousands of square miles.

"Local projects are the actual success story that reinforce our efforts. I can proudly say that our university student exchange system is healthier than it has ever been. These students have planted millions of trees and inspired their classmates to do the same. Local student involvement, although not as organized as our foreign exchange classes, has still delivered the labor to lovingly plant thousands of square miles of trees.

"Before this meeting I spoke with our education coordinators. They are pleased with favorable numbers as we track the exchange students that graduate and then return to the classroom as teachers. Even in the US our statistics on college grads that evolve into teachers is very encouraging. We know that those young people with a positive exchange experience want to teach other young students about that memorable overseas program. The more worldly our teachers are the better."

Myrlene interrupted, again. "Pardon me Javier, but are you involved in water scenarios as well?"

"Only to the extent that it involves desalination and making enough electricity to operate the water purification plant. We knew early on that we needed to get water to the trees we planted if they wanted it. We built desalination facilities to help water the young forest and deliver fresh water to the workers at the site. The growth of plant, animal, and insect loops soon made it clear how critical the water was at every location. That famous web of life was evident once the water was abundant.

"In a location such as the rain forest we had sufficient fresh water to aid in our reforestation plans, but we needed electricity. In Western Australia we purified more water than needed because we did not trust the natural system. How fortuitous, since six of the first nine years of that program were the driest years on record. Please recognize how drought prone that country is."

"Boy, can I vouch for that," interjected Leah. "I have experience in that land when it's hot. We began our reforestation effort in Western Australia fifteen years ago. It was hot then. The World Meteorological Organization (WMO) crunches numbers from other scientific groups and extrapolates patterns. That source, which tracks the heat and moisture levels of various lands, has warned of the continued brutal heat in Australia.

"Although we can now say there has been no extreme rise in temperatures during the past two years, the heat in Australia and parts of inland China is still unbearable. Our shield may be helping but for many it's too late. Millions have or will be displaced. The trend of the immediate past indicates a leveling of heat in China. I would guess we did that, but until it starts actually cooling, we have no reason to celebrate.

"ForCI has ongoing reforestation efforts in Western Australia. That location is changing, and will continue to change, the environment across the outback and ultimately the east coast too. As for China, the Chinese have started their own programs and we do not have total confidence in their enthusiasm.

"The ForCI workers spend days conditioning the land, before and after planting trees. The future of the forest without man's help is bleak if the new forest is not supported by reconditioned soil. We don't know if the Chinese are that dedicated.

"Most of you know we also try to build in a solar cell system that shades the young trees and contains the almost invisible plumbing to periodically deliver water to the seedlings. In fact, our new sites are home to quite a number of proprietary secrets.

"In locations where we only need electricity, we get primary power from the sun, wind, or both. Regardless, the first use of this power is to route incoming water through an electrolyzer. This machine splits water into hydrogen and oxygen. The hydrogen gas becomes a remote, all-weather battery that is used as fuel in making cheap, 24/7 electricity. We can drive water pumps, light homes, and help schools in the neighboring villages. The oxygen is released into the atmosphere.

"Our latest effort is in Gabon, in an area bordering the Republic of Congo, that has been illegally logged and slashed for years. Brian Knight can speak to the salesmanship that went into getting the go-ahead. I'll just say it was beautiful and will be well received by the populace"

"Thanks Leah," responded Brian. "It is a good story, both from the standpoint of patience and making connections. As luck would have it, Javier and I were in the UAE about six months ago. The mission was to talk with the royal family about signing onto the global environment network (GEAD) then using some of their money to start a forest in their sand. During that conversation the prince told us that he had just sold an investment to an industrialist from Gabon, for cash.

"It was a lot of cash and the prince did not want us to know any more than that. Yet he remembered that his buyer had been complaining about the relationship his country had with the Democratic Republic of Congo. Something about illegal logging on both sides of the border they share. This theft disturbed the businessman. We got the OK from the prince, and set off to contact this person and offer our services. My thought was that we could police the forest, and in fact enlarge it, in exchange for a moratorium on all logging of healthy trees.

"The prince let us use a plaza in the palace as a place to meet. I believe it was this opulent setting that helped convince the Gabonese to at least listen to the message in the GEAD papers, and helped the prince see the value of doing the same."

President Crockett asked Brian, "I'm not familiar with that part of Africa. Please explain the situation."

"Mister President. This old growth rain forest reminds one of the Amazon. You see that much green and it's that dense. However, when you proceed east, through the Congo and into the DRC, you find refugees, oil palm plantations, and lack of all vegetation in places.

This speaks to an area that has seen many types of conflict. If we allow the desert, or savanna, to take back thousands of miles of this precious forest we run a severe environmental risk. As of today, they have plenty of water and the ethnic tensions have settled down. However, makeshift settlements on the riverbanks and upstream mining and logging are endangering the water quality of the great Congo River basin.

"We explained to the Gabonese how our teams of students, with the help of the locals, spend thousands of hours scurrying all around a project site, totally confusing any adversaries. No poaching, illegal logging, or burning occurs while we are working on our end of the bargain.

"He asked us if other countries had agreed to such an exchange. In respose I told him the story of the Chinese early investement of $50B from their infrastructure fund, but only after tens of thousands of their citizens had been flooded out of coastal cities. We further described how we helped them relocate villages near the site of new reactors farther inland.

"I told him about our transactions with Malaysia and their commitment for $25B from the new community budget. Then mentioned the Philippine's decision to take $10B away from the funds earmarked for the New Clark City. Those dollar amounts seemed to have an impact. We parted company with an understanding that we were invited to Gabon to continue the conversation."

"So . . ." asked Myrlene.

"Signed and sealed two weeks ago," replied Brian with a bit of a grin on his face.

THIRTY ONE

—• ——— —— •

Chief Edward and his son Pope were on horseback racing towards the cabin on the high plateau. The two had just left the PlatCom center to visit the family home and debrief each other on the shield progress. FJ Guindo, their mentor of an hour ago, was still hunkered down in the Platform Communications building trying to get the COTs to behave. When the Whites left the building, FJ and Sara were side-by-side, sending messages to two non-responsive robots at the stellar platform.

There were wooden chairs on the front porch, facing the pond which had been stocked with fish. They were not there to fish, though. Edward began,

"It is important that I tell you again how proud I am of you. Your trip to the new stellar platform was a total success. We will now build the shield faster and protect our planet better than before. Your efforts are worthy of our people."

"Dad, I completely understand your pride in our nation," said Pope, "and I honor our ancestors and brothers in this great nation. But you need to recognize that I have a different definition of 'our people' than you do. Urgent has matured to the extent that we have citizens who were conceived and born here and are as much a part of our being as you and I.

"You have walked the streets of our town and know as well as I that people of all colors now call Urgent home. Parents of scientists may have been born in India, those of our faculty team may be from China, but all ethnicities now live here. The mission I undertook was to benefit all mankind and if it brought honors to Urgent that's all the better. The honor goes to all who are a part of this community.

"Accolades notwithstanding, there is still work to be done. You heard FJ talk about the recent numbers he received from the World Meteorological Organization. The latest five-year trend for both temperature and CO_2 content is encouraging. My internal optimist wants to activate a worldwide megaphone announcing that the planet is cooling.

"The WMO, however, wants to wait a couple more years before they trust their findings, we can't tell anyone. The work we are doing with that shield has always been a race against man's mindset. We can't mistakenly allow the earth-friendly momentum of that groupthink to return to complacency."

"I know," said Edward. "Even with the seas constantly rising, the past forty years have been a tug of war with the rest of the world's leaders. I have truly been amazed that our scientists have been successful at negotiating with those ten countries for the installation of the nuclear reactors and eighteen launch sites. We could not even count the number of coal-fired power plants that were either taken off line or never built. Even some African and Asian cultures stopped burning wood when we got them electricity."

"Yeah," said Pope. "It's just too bad we couldn't help get air-conditioning to some locations. Millions in upper China and inland India and Africa will never get back to their homelands in their lifetimes. I'm not even convinced that their parched land can be helped. Hell, look at our prairie out there."

"We are devoting our lives to the cause of preserving our species." said his father. "Right now, that does not include our high plains environment but it may be possible one day. We will keep feeding the buffalo and preventing any hunting on this land. I remember when you used to ride up here on one of our ponies and swim in that pond. We want your grand-children to have the same opportunity."

"Thanks Dad, I know, and as I said, I do have hope. Part of the report we received from the weather folks contained up-to-date images sent by the satellites. I zeroed in on sea ice coverage in the Arctic Ocean for each of the past ten years.

"We have eight sections of the shield in place. It's about the size of Mexico now and we are beginning to see results. During each of the past three years, summer sea ice has not retreated as far as it did in earlier years. We will make the shield larger and the sea will make more ice. Reversing the warming temperatures of the Arctic and Antarctic oceans is our primary goal, and it's working. With two stellar platforms operating full-time we are enlarging the shield at a faster rate than ever.

"I don't need to tell you that the CO_2 content in the atmosphere is nowhere near leveling off, let alone decreasing. Our atmosphere is a complicated necessity, always responding to the planet's input. What we gain by controlling one factor is lost by an increased interference from another.

"You and I watched the transition from gas powered cars to electric ones. We also saw the mining industry respond to the increased demand for materials needed to make batteries and electronic components for those vehicles. Our power plants no longer belch smoke from coal fires, that's good. But you and I don't want to know how far and deep they go to harvest the precious elements they use to harness nuclear energy.

"Such trade-offs are necessary in order for the billions of people on this planet to breathe. The scientists have foreseen these industrial consequences. We have always known that society's earth-based solutions to air quality and all related issues would not arrive in time. We began building the shield to buy us time.

"Chief Joseph, Lacey and the others began this endeavor with one goal: to save our species, and it's looking good. Even without stabilizing the CO_2 output, we have cooled the planet. It is a joyous moment to share the benefit of Urgent's actions.

"The increase in sea ice will result in a cooling of the oceans. Our warmer air was predominately due to warmer oceans. We have begun reversing the detrimental temperature trends we have experienced for decades. If we maintain these trends Dad, mankind has a good chance."

Edward examined his son and took a deep breath:

"Now I would like you to bring me up to date on your next flight – the sparrow launch next month."

URGENT LAUNCH

Long range plans for a unique launch vehicle had finally come together - and not a moment too soon. The first passenger on a sparrow was getting more frail by the day. Pope's grandfather had first honors.

"Dad," said Pope, "the trip in the sparrow will be as comfortable as we can make it. The Chief is able to enter the capsule without help, so the flight looks like a go."

Urgent leaders, as per their attorneys, had agreed on a set of physical and mental capabilities of the occupant. Chief Joseph was still able to stroll a few steps without his cane or walker.

The engineers knew any launch vehicle containing a living cargo must accelerate gradually. A slow take-off allowed the occupant to survive the process. The daily space vehicle launch from the canyon edge was like a shot from a rifle. No breathing creature could survive that much instant force. That was why a unique launch craft had been built for these special flights.

Engineering had created a vessel that was as user-friendly as possible: they named it the LISA-V. The Light Silent Ascent Vehicle was specifically designed to carry the sparrow on its back, climb to the edge of the dense atmosphere and, after a short burst of speed, let it go. Its pressure chambers would provide another burst of acceleration the moment of release. The small surface controls would point the sparrow in the perfect direction to permit the little craft to climb and enter orbit.

"The trajectory," Pope began to explain, "has been plotted to allow three orbits of the planet, with each being a bit higher than the previous.

URGENT LAUNCH

At the end of the third orbit the sparrow will open the cargo hatch and release the Spirit Capsule. Once clear, the capsule automatically activates its small, one thrust booster and heads for deep space.

The Chief will be awake during the entire ascent. Being on the back of the launch vehicle is only a plane ride, I'll make sure of that. The launch burst after separation takes the package up to an acceleration rate of twice that of gravity. The jack rabbit start of a fast car is the equivalent.

"I will have communication until the moment of separation. After that, there is a recording device in the sparrow. Three orbits of the earth is plenty of time to reminisce and leave words of wisdom for friends and family."

Edward did not mention that the occupant of the Spirit Capsule was asked to finish the message in two orbits. Different people would lose consciousness at different times in the oxygen deprived environment. Monitors on board the Spirit Capsule would send vital signs to PlatCom, confirming the presence of life. No living entity was to be released into deep space.

"Hello Chief," started Pope. "Are you feeling comfortable up there?"

"Master Pope," as he always called him, "I am looking down at the top of your head. If I raise my head I can see forward but my neck will ache if I hold that position for too long. I'll just stare at my favorite grandson and all the controls in his hands."

Pope wondered if there was more than a literal translation to that statement.

"We are going to start our trip to the runway now," he advised. The plane quietly moved along the taxiway at the airport and onto the main runway. Pope increased speed and left the ground in a smooth manner without even the typical rotation of the aircraft. His intentions were to circle the grounds and that part of Wyoming in an ever-higher series of loops. He knew he was the only thing flying within five hundred miles.

The first pass above the impressive airfield was so near the ground that the Chief could recognize the people below. Standing in front of the long line of airplanes were well-wishers that had flown to Urgent from all across the continent. He recognized the philanthropists and other visitors as they extended a salutation by placing both hands over their heart.

Brian and Myrlene were watching with their arms interlocked. Steven was in his wheelchair, being pushed out of the shadow of the hangar by Henry. The chief knew Marina Whitehorse had died years ago. Across the runway, on the access road he noticed lines of cars, small trucks, and the occasional grouping of horses. Decades of friendships and honest dealings were represented by that mis-matched contingent.

Chief Joseph saw the grassy field adjacent to the mill as they crossed the canyon for the third time. He remembered fifty years ago when that very field had been dusty and filled with residents of Urgent celebrating the completion of the large industrial mill. One early resident had flipped the switch that turned on the steel mill. When he closed his eyes he could see seven-year old Leah.

Opening his eyes, he could see that same field, again full of citizens. He had invited the Nation to celebrate. Every person on the ground had both their arms opened towards the sky as Chief Joseph flew past. Only the gentle sound of a breeze disturbed the silence beneath him. Pope let the electric plane gently drift over the canyon. The Chief said nothing.

South of the mill complex and the gathering of Urgent's somber residents, was the modern WYIST campus. The students had been excused from classes and research, as had the faculty. These folks were gathered in front of the large auditorium building, overlooking the canyon. Hundreds of well-wishers looked skyward as the shiny plane drifted by.

To the north of the mill comlex he looked for the first wind turbine, knowing that its foundation contained Leah's secret meditation retreat. She smiled up at him and held one hand over her heart. The other hand was lovingly held by Lizzy, executing the same salute.

The parking area in front of the Tribal Facilities complex was organized with vehicles parked around the lot perimeter. Within that defined barrier were hundreds of native citizens, all wrapped in their colorful, ceremonial dress. Traditional drums were beating, but the members were not dancing; only holding their arms out to the sky.

Once above the continental divide the pilot spoke to his grandfather, "Chief, we are going to begin our ascent now. There will be changes in pressure in there. Just swallow when you feel your ears tingle." He directed the craft higher.

"If you look forward out the window you will notice the change in the color of the sky. That red look over the sun is from the dirty elements in the air. As we look south we are viewing a warmer climate and those almost-invisible particles tend to show up where it is warmer. Your home in Wyoming is far enough north to have cleaner air. Also, as you know we have been cleaning our air ourselves for years now. Urgent citizens do not breathe that nasty stuff."

He knew that the Chinese, the Europeans and even the Russians were spending massive amounts of money to purify their air. Regardless, they had started so late that tens of thousands of their citizens were dying prematurely from pollution related disease. Those facts were not a topic of conversation on this flight. He looked at the instruments and read that he was about to take a steeper attitude.

"Chief - we are minutes away from your going into orbit. I cannot be with you then. This is the moment that this aircraft was built for, but the moment that is hardest for me. As is the case with all young people, they realize only late in life how valuable their elders are. By then, even though the young behave in the manner required of them, there is never enough said. Any attempt to be the family member the elder would be most proud of, seems to fall short. I can only confirm how much I love, honor and respect you."

"Master Pope. You went into space, yet you ride horses to the pond. You built this airplane, yet you teach children how to catch frogs. You help print metals that come from the center of the earth, yet I have seen you roast marshmallows over a fire you started with sticks. I have always marveled at your ability to honor the old ways while you absorb the new technology.

"Your father is a smart man but even he will admit to being amazed at your abilities. We are both proud of our family legacy and astonished at what you now define as family. It is I who should be honoring you and your vision.

"Good-bye Master Pope."

That was his cue - there was nothing more to say.

Pope put the plane in a steeper climb and increased the speed. He felt it as he was thrust back into the pilot's seat, and knew how much his grandfather could withstand. Being careful not to be too aggressive, he flew past the desired 70,000-foot mark before the custom-made aircraft reached 900 miles-per-hour, at which point he released the sparrow and leveled off.

He could see the small shiny object float for a second, then noticed a shimmer of turbulence appear behind it. In another second it was out of sight.

Pope knew the boost from the sparrow pressure tank would send the small vehicle into an orbit in the stratosphere. It would be an ever-higher orbit due to the speed. This particular layer of atmosphere was not deathly cold. In fact, it warmed up as the craft climbed.

Temperatures would turn dangerous if flying through the mesosphere, the next higher layer of earth's atmosphere. Although that extreme cold would not occur before the third orbit, and would not be felt: oxygen deprivation would have taken its toll. The separation of the Spirit Capsule from the sparrow had also been the separation from the human's oxygen source.

Pope's communication channel with PlatCom had been open the entire flight. The "package away" message was acknowledged with a "roger" from the ground.

URGENT LAUNCH

Giving him a few seconds to compose himself, FJ then added,

"Pope, what's the appropriate Native American phrase at this time?"

"There is no death, only a change of worlds," Pope replied.

"Beautiful launch Pope." Said Sara from the ground, as she hugged FJ even closer.

"Time to head for home." Pope told himself.

He knew this flight was historic. There was a list of people waiting to be allowed to follow Chief Joseph's path. When the names of potential passengers had been discussed there had been hundreds on the list. Pope had been in those conversations with his dad and Willard Graham.

The selection process was confidential, and the parties to that process were known to only a few. The criteria were also not well known. The public did know that nominations could be made anonymously and knew the nominees would be asked if the committee should consider the possibility. It was common for people to admit they were not about to fly to their deaths. Others were fascinated with the idea.

The vetting process took time. A few worthy citizens were not physically able to meet the requirements. Others simply did not live long enough. However future flights of the sparrow with a Spirit Capsule cargo were guaranteed to launch because of the demand.

The LISA-V touched down at the Urgent airport. Pope piloted it into a special hangar to be readied for the next flight. He cleaned up the unique plane, then drove to Tribal Facilities to decompress.

There he could relax with a drink and imagine his grandfather's flight into deep space. He knew the elders were there; he recognized neighborhood transportation. He also recognized that they had left him a parking place at the front door.

No words needed to be spoken to Pope. Yet each person in the crowded meeting room had conveyed condolences to the young grandson. He found himself seated next to his father on an old, over-stuffed sofa that was the prized seat. Pope knew that Chief Edward, as he would now be called, was contemplating his seventy years on this land and reflecting on his father's long life.

As for his own thoughts, Pope was considering the alternatives if he chose not to pilot the next scheduled Spirit Capsule trip – Sean Crockett's flight.

His communication chip vibrated and he replied with a quick "Yeah?"

"Pope, this is FJ at PlatCom. We just downloaded the Chief's recording and he indicated he wanted the entire nation to hear it. Don't you think we should listen to it first?"

"I'll be right there."

"It's beautiful," he had begun. "The TV pictures of earth from high above are only two-dimensional. The real thing is more than breathtaking. Before I get into the orbit and overwhelmed with the view, I want to say thank you. It has been a great honor to be the Chief of our Nation, and a greater honor to be a father, husband, and grandfather. Edward has been given all I am capable of.

URGENT LAUNCH

"He has always been my successor - I'm proud of you son. We owe you more than our collective wisdom can imagine.

"I am named after one of the great chiefs of all time. Chief Joseph has been written about. I am only his shadow. Edward has been named after one of the most honest men I have ever had the pleasure of meeting. I was very young when I met my first white man and I pledged at that time to remember his name. Edward Curtis's service to our people those many years ago, has strengthened and honored our nation.

"Not long after his death, my generation was asked to bring our family out of the past and into some prosperity. With the guidance of other elders and some new friends we have accomplished that. This flight is testament to this progress. This flight is also a sign of the demise of the old ways.

"Your generation is now asked to escort mankind out of the past. On your fingers you can count the number of generations since our land was endless, as was the buffalo. Do we have a future of equal length? If the planet I'm looking at is to survive, our leaders need to continue the course begun on our Nation's land.

"There will be those who do not see the future as we do. They may even threaten to do battle to preserve their old ways. While we may not put on war paint for such events, we need to be prepared to fight. The weapons of our fathers are long gone yet their strategy and teachings can help us in our struggles. The price paid for face-to-face fighting is too great, and our people are too few. With the help of our partners in this future we will fight an invisible fight if need be."

Joseph was taking deeper breaths at this point.

"I have had the opportunity of meeting the men whose fortunes make my flight possible. These are honorable men. The long term planning they shared with me may well enable our species to survive. You will know within a generation or two.

"It seems improbable that man can be driven so blindly in the wrong direction. Even the buffalo will turn or stop before falling off the cliff. You will be witness to whether man has the same survival instincts. If not, you are active participants in the last great hope. Work with and believe these visionary men. Your children, and their children's children must have a small part of the planet to call home.

"Many years ago I stood on the edge of our great canyon with a newfound friend. We spent many hours together trying to second-guess the future, trying to plan and map a new community. I still remember the brains and brawn brought to this project by the younger citizens. Those of Edward's age actually made Urgent; Pope's generation may manage it.

"Today I stand on the edge of our great Mother Earth with some old friends and newfound knowledge. Just as one generation must make way for the next, our old science must be augmented by the new. When Tom Lacey and I were dreaming of the village I doubt either of us truly believed each other. We do now.

"Tom is too young to be here with me today, but I can confirm to him that our early dream has come true, and the next one is not far behind. Consider that I am broadcasting from such a height that my son, standing on the canyon edge, cannot see me. Then consider the technology that allows this mortal being to be launched into space and in one hour, view all the canyons on the planet. I am blessed.

"From up here, our home looks healthy and inviting. It is hard to believe our species is in danger and could be brought to an end by something not even visible from my perch. There is a volcano over there and a hurricane beyond that sea. Where is the culprit?

"If millions of small actions cause the damage, we need millions of larger actions to turn it around and fix it. The true believers on the Wind River land are the folks I am most proud to be associated with. Your energy and actions honor your heritage and what Master Pope calls his people.

"Oh," there was a long pause. "I am again going from day into night. Look at that planet glow. Above, the silhouette of the shield is drifting in front of the moon.

"I think it's time to close my tired eyes."

His voice trailed off . . .

URGENT LAUNCH

GLOSSARY and DEFINITIONS

3D Printer: a machine that extrudes layers of material to produce a desired shape.

ARB: Air Resources Board

Atacama Desert: South America location.

Attribution Science: the effort to scientifically ascertain mechanisms responsible for recent global warming and related climate changes on Earth.

Brasilia: Capitol city of Brazil.

Cape Fanshaw: Alaska location.

CITES: Convention of International Trade in Endangered Species

CoP 21: numbered Conference of Parties re: environmental goals (#21 was in Paris).

COST: Consortium for Overseas Student Teaching

COT (fict.): Carbon Dioxide powered robot.

Cryogenics: physics branch dealing with cold temps.

DARPA: Defense Advanced Research Projects Agency, division of Defense Dept.

Dave: Urgent's super-computer.

DRC: Democratic Republic of Congo

DefBot (fict.): Defensive robot.

Edward Curtis: pioneer photographer specializing in recording Native-America history.

Electrolyzer: device that uses an electric current to provide the energy that splits a water molecule (H_2O) into hydrogen (H) and oxygen (O).

EPA: Environmental Protection Agency

Europol: The European Union Agency for Law Enforcement Cooperation

URGENT LAUNCH

FAA: Federal Aviation Administration
FishHide (fict.): exterior ripple skin for space
  vehicle.
ForCI (fict.): Forestry Consortium International
GEAD (fict.): Global Environment and Atmosphere
  Doctrine
Greifswald: city in Germany.
GPS: Global Positioning System
Haida: Native-America nation.
hfc: hydrofluorocarbons-a greenhouse gas
  component.
ICOS: Integrated Carbon Observation System
IITF: International Institute of Tropical Forestry
IPCC: Inter-governmental Panel on Climate Change
INTERPOL: International Criminal Police
  Organization
ISS: International Space Station
ITER: International Thermonuclear Experimental
  Reactor - fusion experiment.
LISA-V (fict.): Light Silent Ascent Vehicle
Mach 2: two times the speed of sound
  (2 x 760 mph).
Materials Science: interdisciplinary field.
Max Planck Inst. for Plasma Physics: one branch of
  the Max Planck Society for the Advancement of
  Science.
Maximum Dynamic Pressure: the period of
  maximum aerodynamic structural load on a
  rocket.
Mechatronics: multidisciplinary branch of engine-
  ering that works with both elect. and mechanical
  systems.

mph: miles per hour.

NASA: National Aeronautics and Space Administration

NOC (fict.): Nation's Office of Consideration

NRC: Nuclear Regulatory Commission

OCU (fict.): Odd Case Unit

OSU College of Forestry: Oregon State University

owlt: one way light time.

Perovskite Solar Cells: high-efficiency solar panels, big advantage is flexibility.

Photorespiration: a process in plant metabolism where some of the energy produced by photosynthesis is wasted: excess CO_2 is the byproduct.

PlatCom (fict.): Platform Communications complex.

ppm: parts per million.

Pressure solution (fict.): rocket fuel.

SAS (fict.): Steam Assist Start

sop: standard operating procedure.

Sparrow (fict.): daily vehicle launched to grow shield - from SPace ARROW.

Spirit Capsule (fict.): compartment aboard sparrow for human to occupy.

Spruce Bark Beetle: insect responsible for devastating forests of evergreen trees.

Spud Barge: a jack-up barge with on-board pilings that can provide stability.

Stellar platform (fict.): corner anchor of each space shield section during construction.

STOL package: modification to aircraft to allow for short take-off and landing.

Sun-synchronous position: on earth, an object permanently positioned between the sun and earth.

TSA Committee: Transportation Security Administration

Tasman Sea: Southern Hemisphere location.

temptank (fict.): temperature retention tank.

Temuco, Chile: South American location.

Thermochemistry: study of the heat energy which is associated with chemical reactions and/or physical transformations.

Tlingit: Native-America nation.

Tongass National Forest: Alaska location.

Tribal Facilities (fict.): a building for gatherings.

UAS: University of Alaska Southeast

UCS: Union of Concerned Scientists

USFS Office of Tribal Relations: United States Forest Service

Wendelstein 7-X: nuclear research project in Germany.

WBBRG: Western Bark Beetle Research Group

WMO: World Meteorological Organization

World Economic Forum: Davos annual event.

WYIST (fict.): Wyoming Institute of Science and Technology

Wyoming State Bank - fiction

Yukon Territory: Northern Hemisphere location.

URGENT LAUNCH

URGENT LAUNCH

Key Words

A $\bullet$ —

B — $\bullet$ $\bullet$ $\bullet$

C — $\bullet$ — $\bullet$

D — $\bullet$ $\bullet$

E $\bullet$

F $\bullet$ $\bullet$ — $\bullet$

G — — $\bullet$

H $\bullet$ $\bullet$ $\bullet$ $\bullet$

I $\bullet$ $\bullet$

J $\bullet$ — — —

K — $\bullet$ —

L $\bullet$ — $\bullet$ $\bullet$

M — —

N — $\bullet$

O — — —

P $\bullet$ — — $\bullet$

Q — — $\bullet$ —

R $\bullet$ — $\bullet$

S $\bullet$ $\bullet$ $\bullet$

T —

U $\bullet$ $\bullet$ —

V $\bullet$ $\bullet$ $\bullet$ —

W $\bullet$ — —

X — $\bullet$ $\bullet$ —

Y — $\bullet$ — —

Z — — $\bullet$ $\bullet$